THE SPINNING MAN THE SPINNING MAN

G. P. Putnam's Sons

New York

THE SPINNING MAN

THE SPINNING MAN

GEORGE HARRAR

G. P. Putnam's Sons
Publishers Since 1838
a member of
Penguin Putnam Inc.
375 Hudson Street
New York, NY 10014

Library of Congress Cataloging-in-Publication Data

Harrar, George, date.
The spinning man : a novel / by George Harrar.
p.   cm.
ISBN 0-399-14983-X
1. Philosophy teachers—Fiction.   2. Teenage girls—Fiction.
3. Kidnapping—Fiction.   I. Title.
PS3558.A624924 S64   2003   2002074532
813'.54–dc21

Printed in the United States of America
1   3   5   7   9   10   8   6   4   2

This book is printed on acid-free paper. ∞

Book design by Chris Welch

To Linda, my wife and personal editor,
who inspires me with ideas and gently watches
over every word I write.

ACKNOWLEDGMENTS

I'm grateful to my agent, Esmond Harmsworth, of Zachary
Shuster Harmsworth in Boston, who encouraged me to pur-
sue this philosophical mystery; and to my editor at BlueHen,
Fred Ramey, who offered wise suggestions for its improvement.

I'm indebted to Ray Monk for his wonderful biography
Ludwig Wittgenstein: The Duty of Genius, which gives great
insight into the philosopher's public and private lives.

A man can bare himself before others only
out of a particular kind of love. A love
which acknowledges, as it were,
that we are all wicked children.

—*Ludwig Wittgenstein*

CHAPTER 1

The bare wood steps squeaked under Evan Birch's wet shoes. The rain hadn't let up all day, not since he'd arrived on campus for his freshman orientation duties until late afternoon when he finally made it to his office. More than once people said to him, "It's a godsend, isn't it?" Such inconsistencies of human mythology fascinated him: Why was the rain heaven sent but not the summer-long drought?

At the receptionist's desk he reached into the straw basket for a Callard & Bowser candy. What he pulled out was wrapped in an uncharacteristic white plastic. "No butterscotch?"

Carla shook her hair in the way he liked, as if a quiver of delight had just passed through her. "New year, new candy, Professor. Live dangerously."

He popped the piece in his mouth, and a cheap peppermint flavor spread over his tongue. She saw the displeasure on his face and lifted the large gray wastebasket to his mouth. "I guess it's an acquired taste. You'll get used to it."

He spit out the candy. "Well, Carla, my father always said that you can get used to anything if you do it long enough. But why would you want to?"

She licked her lips, and their pale purple color darkened to crimson. He wondered what the name of her lipstick was and how it would taste, like grape or some more subtle flavor. He had tried lipstick once, the morning Ellen left her Indelibly Frosted Peach sitting open on the bathroom sink. The name intrigued him. He felt a little perverse rubbing the rounded pink head on his lips, and the image of himself in the mirror looked startlingly sensual. With just this slight coloring of his appearance, a new strange self seemed to emerge. He wasn't sure he would want to meet the man with bright lips and pale skin staring out of the glass. He was sure that his wife wouldn't. He asked himself, what small urges did she succumb to when she was alone? He feared there might not be any.

The phone rang as always, more loudly than Evan liked. He wished Carla would turn down the volume but had never asked. She walked around the small partition of her work space, took her seat, squared herself to the desk in front of her, reached for a pen from her coffee mug, and answered. "PsychologySociologyAnthropologyPhilosophy—how may I direct your call?"

It impressed him how quickly and precisely she could recite the departments, giving each of the humanities its own slight inflection.

"Professor Birch," she said, "he's sort of head of philosophy now. He's been here the longest of anybody left. Would you like to speak to him?"

Sort of head of the department—Carla had captured the tenuousness of his position precisely. The Pearce College philosophy curriculum was being whittled away, an entirely reasonable response, he had to admit, to the flight of students to the employable fields. Philosophy was at subsistence level with just six majors, all seniors. The rest of the full-time faculty had already sought positions elsewhere. Only he remained, the interim head of a vast department of one, with a few adjunct professors to fill in. At the last faculty meeting the dean had called him "a loyal academic in a trying time." As he acknowledged this tepid compliment with a little wave of his hand, the impulse struck him to quit on the spot. He had to grip the cold arms of his seat to resist standing up and declaring himself done with teaching, and not yet fifty! It would have been a grand act, resigning effective immediately—that day, that moment. He might even claim, like Wittgenstein, that his tenure as a professor had been "a living death." That would make them wonder.

He motioned to Carla that he would take the call in his office.

"Okay, goodbye," she said and hung up.

"Wasn't that for me?"

She pushed her chair back from the desk and stretched her short bare legs out in front of her. "It was *about* you, Professor, not for you."

"What does that mean?"

"He just wanted to know who was head of philosophy, he didn't want to talk to you." Then she gave him a curious expression, her mouth stretched flat to the sides, her cheeks bunched up.

"Are you smiling?"

She wiped her lips with the back of her hand. "No, I'm not smiling."

He turned toward his office and saw a large brown box sitting on the edge of his desk. He looked back at Carla.

"They came," she said.

"*They* came?"

"Your book. The FedEx man delivered them ten minutes ago."

She handed him a letter opener and followed him into his office. He slit open the box and reached through the Styrofoam pellets. When he pulled out the book, the cover shocked him a little. It looked bolder than on the galleys—without a trace of restraint. The title, *Disturbing Minds,* ran across the top in deep red letters. In fainter red, the subtitle said, *Mania, Mayhem, and Melancholy in the Philosophic Life.* Behind the letters appeared the black outline of a head, and then two piercing eyes.

"It's beautiful," Carla said over his shoulder.

"You really think so?"

"I love those eyes."

He flipped the book over and read the jacket quotes:

"A work of immense pleasure, ambitious in scope and illuminating in its analysis."—Dr. Kenneth Lamm, The University of Queensland.

"In unraveling the common thread of peculiarity, if not madness, among history's greatest philosophers, *Disturbing Minds* validates William James's dictum that the value of an idea should be judged independently of its origin."—Prof. Maxwell Sherman, Wiggins Chair of Modern Philosophy, UCLA.

"Are you thrilled?" Carla asked.

"I am . . ."—*relieved* occurred to him as the fitting description of his feeling about a book that had taken three years to research, two years to write, and one year to see into print. But Carla was looking at him so hopefully that he said, "I *am* thrilled—ecstatic actually."

"I'd be shouting out the windows if I had something published."

He opened to the title page, scribbled a few words, and handed the book to Carla. "You get the first copy. It would have taken me another year to finish without your xeroxing and fact-checking."

"That's really nice, Professor, but shouldn't you give this to your wife?"

"She gets the second copy."

Carla hefted the book in her hands. "It's heavy."

Heavy—that was certainly the single indisputable characteristic of his work. Critics could debate its depth of research or scholarly biases but certainly not its weight.

"Yes, my book is heavy and expensive, probably too much of both."

"I'm not sure when I'll get to this. I'm not much of a reader, you know."

"That's okay, use it as a doorstop if you want. Books can serve many purposes."

She shook her head and poked him in the shoulder. "If I had a coffee table," she said, "this would be the only thing on it."

CHAPTER 2

He didn't know what to make of the phone call. He asked the man to start over and expected him to break out laughing, unable to carry the gag any further.

"As I said, I'm the editor of *Humoresque,* an independent journal exploring the nature of humor. Your publisher sent us a review copy of your book, and I was struck by the quote: 'I would have liked to have composed a philosophic work that consisted solely of jokes. Sadly, I have no sense of humor.' Did Wittgenstein really say that?"

"The quotation is attributed to him, yes."

"I wonder if you would consider writing a piece for us on the function of humor in philosophy?"

"I'm not sure there is a function of humor in philosophy. It's not a particularly humorous field."

"That's my point," the editor said. "Why can't philosophy be funny?"

Evan did not have a ready answer. He had included Wittgenstein's statement solely to illustrate the duality of character, the vast gulf between what the philosopher wished to be and what he thought he was. Otherwise, Evan had not reflected deeply about the remark nor considered at all what a philosophic work consisting solely of jokes might be like. He supposed that if Wittgenstein were the writer, it would be full of fractured tautologies.

"You wouldn't have to answer that question specifically," the editor said. "I'm just looking for a thousand words on philosophy and humor. You could quote from your book and throw in a few jokes at the same time."

"Well, let's see. . . . Wittgenstein overheard a French politician boast that French was the best language to speak because the words come in the order in which you think them."

The editor did not respond, and Evan felt ridiculous for offering such an in-joke. He didn't even think it was funny himself.

"Obviously you have to understand something about his philosophy to appreciate the humor. I wouldn't use that in an article."

"Of course not," the editor said, "though I'm sure it's very amusing."

The rain slackened as he drove home. The sky was lightening a bit over the hills, and the air seemed to be drawing up moisture from the surrounding fields. Fog swaddled the legs of the cows, making them appear to float on clouds. He liked this illusion, a heavy thing seeming weightless.

He was trying to think of something more appropriate to the readers of *Humoresque* than his anecdote about the French politician. The story of the Russian poet visiting London came to mind. He stopped a man on the street, "Please, what is time?" The Englishman responded, "That's a big question. Why ask me?"

That was about as funny as philosophy ever got, it seemed to Evan. Of course, there was Lord Russell, an unremittingly caustic observer of religion—quite entertaining if one didn't happen to be religious. But beyond a few such examples, philosophers were a sober bunch. Evan supposed the discipline had been set on its somber course by Plato, who feared laughter would incite violence and disrupt the social order of his republic. Socrates concurred (if one trusted Plato's accounting of his opinions) that laughter should be sparingly used.

Evan turned the wiper control to spray the windshield, but nothing came out. He couldn't remember the last time he'd filled the well with cleaning fluid. It may have been years. He hunched forward and cocked his head right to see through the one clear spot on the glass, about the width of a hand. He felt silly contorting himself like this.

Of course, it wasn't just philosophy that reeked of solemnity. In religion, where was humor? Medieval Christians were obsessed with the apparent fact that Christ never laughed. Was His demeanor intended to be the model for man or simply the appropriate bearing for one who deemed himself the Son of God? No one asked this question anymore.

And what about God—what joke could man tell that would make Him laugh? It seemed to Evan that one might consume a lifetime figuring that out. He was not interested in the challenge himself, and besides, he didn't have a lifetime left to devote to it. But he could conceive of the perfect title—*The Joke That Made God Laugh.* Three hundred blank pages, and somewhere in the middle, the joke—a parable of some kind, with an O. Henry twist.

Evan turned off the winding road into the foothills of Pheasant Run. He couldn't remember passing the deserted Army barracks, the old brick library, or Silva's Bakery where he often stopped to pick up Portuguese sweet bread. In fact, he couldn't really say he had passed these landmarks. It surprised him that he could drive so far and not be aware of the time and space he had passed through. He promised himself to pay better attention.

His sons were identicals, two blond, sea-eyed boys with long brown eyelashes and slightly crooked smiles. They looked like they had been cloned rather than born.

He thought of them as miracles. He couldn't imagine seeing just one face like theirs, hearing one voice calling him, having one hand grabbing for his. He felt sorry, sometimes, for fathers of single children.

When he came through the family room door they jumped up from their game and kissed him on opposite cheeks, Adam on the right as always, Zed on the left. He loved how easily they showed their affection, even at ten years old. He couldn't remember hugging his own dad, and he didn't know why that was. Had the fault been in himself or his father?

"Were you bored without us, Dad?"

"Bored to death," he said. "How about you—no fun at all without me?"

"A. fell out of a tree," Zed said.

"Not all the way," Adam said. "I landed on some branches. Z. lost his rocket watch because he took it off to go in the creek and then forgot it when we heard the bear."

"You lost your new watch?"

"Dad, there was a *bear*."

"A bear at Grandmom's?"

"We didn't really see one, but we heard him."

"It kind of roared," Adam said, "like a bear."

"Well, sounds exciting. But you'll have to pay for the watch in chores, Zed."

"I know. Mom already said."

Zed elbowed his brother in the side. "Oh yeah," Adam said, "we brought you something. It's not like a gift or any-thing—I mean, it is a gift, but we didn't buy it." He reached into his jeans pocket and pulled out a small package, wrapped in newspaper and sealed with several layers of black tape.

"What's the occasion?"

"You used to bring us stuff when you went away, so we did for you."

He peeled away the tape, a single piece about a foot long.

"It's a trilobite," Zed said. "It's millions of years old."

Evan ran his finger over the hard ridges of the fossil. "This is great. Where'd you get it?"

"We found it at the creek," Zed said.

"There are probably hundreds of them," Adam said, "but we had to leave."

"Because of the bear?"

"There wasn't really a bear. We were just pretending to scare Mom."

Evan put his arms around his sons and kissed them on the top of their heads, first Adam, the older by nine minutes, then

Zed. "I think I'll take this to my office, keep it on my desk for everyone to see. What do you think?"

"Sure, Dad, whatever."

The boys dropped to the floor again on either side of their latest creation, a board game marked out on a square of plywood. He watched them for a few minutes, how they handed each other the dice and moved the markers for each other. It wasn't so long ago that their games dissolved into shouting and wrestling within minutes. They appeared older to him physically, too. He saw a slight thickening in their arms reaching across the board and in their legs jutting out to the sides. Was this how children grew, in spurts that you didn't notice until they were gone from sight for a few days? For so many years they hadn't seemed to grow at all, just stretch out a bit.

They had changed in small ways, of course—the darkening hair, the lengthening fingers, the widening feet—but always at the same rate. He waited for the slight imperfections to surface, the odd mole or freckle or skin discoloration. Nothing did. Except for the inch-long birthmark on Zed's hip, they were as indistinguishable as pups in a litter.

He remembered taking them as seven-year-olds to Twins Day in Twinsburg, Ohio, and he wasn't surprised that they won the "Most Identical Boys" prize. When they posed with the "Most Identical Men," he stayed at the rear of the crowd, feeling like a singleton in a bifurcated world. After the picture the four of them started walking away together, toward the parking lot. He called to the boys. For a moment he feared they might keep on going, dissolve into some other dimension inhabited only by twins, but they came running back to him.

"Dad?"

"Yep?"

"You want to play or something?"

"No, I was never very good with high finance."

"That's okay, this is Anti-Monopoly. You try to miss all the places that give you money. You lose if you're rich."

"Well then, I might be good at it. But I don't think you should be aiming for poverty."

"It's just a game, Dad," Adam said as he rolled the dice. "I bet we could make a million bucks selling it."

Evan climbed the few stairs leading to the hallway. When he opened the door, Ellen was waiting for him. He dropped his briefcase and surrounded her with his arms. He smelled perfume on her neck, a strong vanilla scent he didn't recognize. He assumed she had just put it on for him. He imagined her hearing the garage door rising and hurrying to find her purse, then splashing the new perfume on her neck where he would surely kiss her. He suddenly missed her, as if she were about to leave rather than had just returned.

"I hate it when you go away," he said. "I never feel right." He would have liked to be more precise, but what he hated was exactly the shapeless, odorless, soundless sense of not feeling right when she was away. His mind always conjured up ways he might lose her—car accidents, plane crashes, lightning, flash floods, the unexplainable collapse of buildings. There were so many dangers in this life. Sometimes he woke up in the middle of the night picturing her in some other bed, alone, her lips slightly parted, drawing air in and out with barely a sound. It would take so little to smother such a fragile breath.

She slipped her cold left hand in his jacket pocket. "We were only gone two nights, Evan."

"It seemed a lot longer."

She kissed him quickly, her lips just grazing his, her way of teasing him, and pulled her hand from his pocket along with a matchbook. The cover said, "Swing at The Sanders Ballroom," the words arching over a tiny top hat. "Go dancing without me?"

"No, I guess I haven't worn this jacket in a while." He felt inside his pocket—there was nothing else. "How were the boys with your mother, they behave?"

"They had her undivided attention. She took them biking during the day and camped out at night with them to teach them the stars." Ellen pulled off a match and struck it against the box. She held the fire in front of her face for a moment, then blew it out. They both inhaled the sulfuric air between them. He couldn't explain why, but something in that smell reminded him of *Disturbing Minds*.

"Close your eyes," he said and reached into his briefcase for the book. "Now open them."

"Evan, it looks wonderful."

"Not too flashy?"

She ran her fingers over the large red letters, as if they had some thickness to them. "It's perfect. Those eyes alone will make people pick it up. You might have a best-seller."

He wasn't sure if she was kidding or had lost her mind for a moment. She kept staring at the eyes. He said, "Do you know how many philosophy professors there are in this country?"

"I have no idea."

"Just a few thousand. Society requires philosophers only to teach philosophy classes. Otherwise, who really needs one?"

She sniffed the book cover. "The President."

"What?"

"He must get into an existential panic once in a while. I can imagine him calling a philosopher for advice on how to run the country. Suppose he called you, Evan, what would you tell him?"

She was putting him on the spot—to be witty or profound on demand. She often challenged him like this, and he didn't mind.

"There's an old Zen saying, 'Rule a large country as you would cook a small fish.'"

"Hmm, very inscrutable," Ellen said. "Could be interpreted any way a president wants. That's good."

She lit another match and let it burn to her fingertips before dropping it to the tile floor.

CHAPTER 3

*A*ll *my possessions for a moment of time."*

Evan scrawled the dying words of Queen Elizabeth on his notepad. It intrigued him that one of history's most powerful people would think of her wealth in terms of time—and not a year, month, week, hour, or even a minute. Just a moment, she wished for, but that was still more than all her riches could buy.

He was not looking forward to teaching the new interdisciplinary seminar entitled "The Necessity of Time." The course had been assigned to him just a week before when the original professor, a physicist, fell ill. So far Evan had prepared little more than his opening remark: "Time was invented to keep everything from happening all at once." It was a philosophically trivial observation, but he figured it was good for a laugh. The students would grant him that much the first class. They might even consider him an eccentric character, dressed in jeans, sneakers, and T-shirt. Perhaps he'd wear the one he'd bought in Athens two summers before, with Aristotle's nine categories listed on the front—Quantity, Quality, Relation, Position, Place, State, Action, Affection, and Time. It pleased him to think there was some uniformity in the world, that every imaginable thing could be described by this simple taxonomy.

Time is like a river that flows past you, and you can't see its beginning or end. This idea—the flow of events past a stationary "I"—was among the oldest conceptions of time. It was a simplistic image, yet he would use it because students always liked one thing expressed in terms of another. He never understood the lure of the metaphor, though. Why not try to comprehend the essence of the thing itself?

That wasn't to say that he didn't admire the beauty of language. He might surprise them one day with poetry, perhaps Cavafy's "Waiting for the Barbarians" or Yeats's "The Second Coming." How did either relate to The Necessity of Time? Not directly, he would have to admit. But there was a certain freedom to watching one's job wither away. He could teach however he liked.

Does God exist in time or out of it? The question made little difference to him, since he didn't believe in any higher power governing the universe. If such a power existed, it certainly didn't seem to be doing much governing beyond imposing a few basic rules of math and physics. Otherwise, Evan observed, the world was chaos.

Sometimes, for his sons' sake, he wished he could believe in an active, kindly God. One day they came home from church describing in great detail the horrors that nonbelievers would suffer for all eternity. He told them not to worry, God would not send him to hell—a presumptuous statement, he would grant. Even as he said these reassuring words he realized they were useless. No one believed you when you told them not to worry, especially children.

Of course, denying his descent toward hell implied a longing for its lofty opposite, heaven, a place that was actually so dull and useless that nobody in the history of human existence had ever imagined how a single day there might be spent. Why did people see only two dichotomous possibilities, anyhow? Why not something between heaven and hell? Not limbo or purgatory, either, but a few grades of lesser grace, and lesser condemnation. The afterlife needed some options.

Can the arrow of time be reversed? A future possibility becomes a present experience which turns into a past memory—wasn't that a reversal of time, at least in a person's psychological perception of it? As for one's individual reality, he could see no point in reversing time. Instead of moving forward toward death, one would be moving backward toward birth, an equally precipitous change of existence, with equally unforeseeable consequences. The afterlife had two ends to it, depending on time's arrow.

Know that life can leave you at any moment. Then how will you live today? His students would never accept the wisdom of this statement. They felt immortal, as he once did. At what age had that wonderfully naive feeling left him?

When he came into the bedroom, Ellen was sitting at her dressing table in her white robe, brushing her hair with short, sharp strokes. She looked like a beautiful actress in an old movie who doesn't realize a mysterious man has just entered her room. He stopped at the bed to see how long it would take her to sense him. A minute went by.

"Why are you standing there, Evan?"

"No reason." He pulled out a handful of coins from his pants pocket and dropped them noisily into the drawer of his night table.

"Finished preparing your lecture?"

"Not finished, but done enough."

She switched hands with her brush. "I called the Institute for my schedule. They want me to work Tuesday to Thursday through the fall. You might have to be home for the boys some afternoons if they don't have an activity."

He went to the rear window, gazed out into the blackness for a few seconds, then pulled down the shade. "Looks like you worried for nothing all summer about not being hired back."

"It's because of Tyco. They said she forgot how to count, but I think she just won't do it for anyone but me. I should ask for a raise."

He sat on the bed and nudged off his shoes. "Descartes thought monkeys might be able to speak but didn't to avoid taking orders from humans."

"Tyco's a chimp, remember? Chimps don't have vocal cords like ours. Neither do monkeys."

"I guess Descartes didn't know that."

Down the hall there was a shout, the slam of a door, and some muffled cries. Ellen didn't turn her head, didn't stop brushing, didn't show any evidence that she had heard. It seemed to him that she had an animal-like sense of which noises needed her attention, and which did not. The value of such an ability was obvious—the minimizing of false arousals. But why wouldn't frequent arousals prime the alarm system, rather than deaden it? He assumed behaviorists had studied this question and concluded one way or the other.

"I didn't tell you about our cab ride from the airport," she said. "The driver was from Tanzania and used to work for Jane Goodall in Gombe. He said something I thought you might use in one of your classes."

"What's that?"

"He said that fear is the foundation on which rests all of the misery of mankind."

This assertion seemed curiously precise to Evan, which made him wonder if these were the cabdriver's exact words or Ellen's embellished rendition of them. He could conceive of many other equally plausible foundations for mankind's misery—hope, certainly; ego, desire, insecurity. Fear he considered the naturally healthy reaction to reality.

"So, when are we having this philosophical fellow over for dinner?"

She turned halfway around. "What?"

"The cabdriver. You got his name and number, didn't you?"

"Actually, I gave him *my* name."

"Close enough." He pulled off his watch and set it upright on the nightstand, next to the alarm clock. "Maybe we should have a barbeque sometime for all of the people you've met on airplanes, in cabs, on the street corner. It would be an international block party."

"At least I don't have boring encounters with people."

As he did? Was that what she was implying? "Nobody said promiscuity isn't interesting."

"Promiscuity?"

He had used a loaded word to make his point, yet he thought it was the right word if he could explain himself, which he obviously had to do. "You talk to everyone," he said, "and give your card to anyone. That's being kind of promiscuous in your relationships, isn't it?"

The hand wielding the brush stopped mid-stroke. "That's an offensive way to put it."

He moved behind her and ran his hands through her hair. The thin strands excited his fingers. "I'm sorry, I shouldn't have said that."

"But you still mean it?"

"I mean that sometimes it seems like you're collecting people. I worry that you don't filter out the dangerous ones."

She resumed her brushing. "Despite what you think, I'm very careful, with myself and the boys."

"But you'd never offend anyone. You could be alone in an elevator and the weirdest-looking guy in the world could walk on—you wouldn't get off for fear of offending him. Anything could happen."

She pulled the long brown hair from the bristles and then placed the brush in the dresser drawer with four others of different sizes and colors. He wondered what determined which one she would use on any given night. Did she have a method?

"You paint such wonderful scenarios for me," she said. "Maybe I should forget going back to work and just stay home to take care of you and the boys."

"Sorry again. I'll shut up." He unbuttoned his shirt and hung it on the clothes post. "Almost done?"

"Almost."

He watched her squirt Jergens lotion on her hands and rub it on her cheeks in widening circles, the last of her bedtime rituals. But then she leaned toward the mirror and started flexing her face, stretching the skin over her cheekbones in bizarre contortions. Her mouth jutted out to one side, then the other. She looked like someone with a recently paralyzed face practicing how to laugh again.

"What are you doing?"

Her eyes widened into moonlike circles. Her lips drew back, baring her teeth. "I read about these exercises in the airline magazine on the way home. They're supposed to tighten your face muscles in five minutes a night."

"Every night?"

"Every night."

"That's something to look forward to for the next fifty years."

He pulled back the spread to the bed, and an image from an old TV show flashed through his mind—a snake crawling from underneath a pillow, then lunging at the neck of the sleeper. He couldn't remember exactly when this sight had been burned into his adolescent memory. Was he the twins' age yet or a little younger? For a long time thereafter he checked his bed each night before climbing in. Even after getting married he picked up his pillow now and then and swept his hand over the sheets.

"Why do you do that?"

He turned around. She was staring at him in the reflection of the dressing table mirror. He understood from the tense of her question that she had seen him do this before.

"I was just smoothing the sheets," he said. "Why, what did you think?"

She turned up one hand, a motion she often made when she sensed something vaguely wrong but couldn't say what.

When she came to bed a few minutes later he wrapped himself about her, pressing the full length of his body against hers. It was the position in which they always started the night, his front to her back, his arm over her hip.

"I'm sorry I made fun of you and your cabdriver," he said. "I didn't mean to."

She twisted under the covers to face him. "I don't want to be afraid of people," she said in a soft voice that he could feel on his face.

"I don't want you to be afraid, just cautious." He leaned forward and kissed her neck to show that it was out of love that he worried about her, not jealousy or resentment. The vanilla scent was still so potent on her skin he thought he might become drunk with it.

CHAPTER 4

As he sat on the stage of the Arts Auditorium looking out over four hundred freshmen and their parents, Evan was thinking about decapitation. He recalled a joke making the rounds at the World Congress of Philosophy a couple of years before, and it seemed to him a candidate for making God laugh. A heretic priest being placed in the guillotine asked to be turned faceup so that he could see God at the moment of his death. The king agreed. The executioner let loose the blade, and it stopped a few inches from the waiting neck. The king declared that a miracle had taken place and spared the priest. A commoner was next; he said he wanted to face God as well. The executioner let fall the blade, and again it stopped a few inches short. The commoner was spared, too.

A philosopher came next. He didn't believe in God but figured Pascal's Wager applied—he had nothing to lose and perhaps much to gain by facing heavenward. As the executioner readied the blade, the philosopher cried out, "Wait, I think I see the problem!"

The professors on either side of Evan turned toward him with various expressions of surprise. Apparently he had spoken the punch line out loud.

"As you see," Dean Santos said from the dais, "our last faculty speaker is eager to address you. So without further introduction, I call on Professor Evan Birch, an esteemed member of our philosophy department."

Esteemed? Evan wasn't sure he wanted to be esteemed by anyone at this point in his life. Appreciated, certainly; admired and respected. But *esteemed*—along with its treacly cousin, *beloved*—sounded more fitting for a professor emeritus tottering from one building to another.

Evan stood up and reached into his back pocket for his prepared remarks. But the paper slipped through his fingers to the floor, which he took as an omen. He would wing it.

He leaned down to the microphone. "Any budding Nietzscheans out there?"

Someone in the rear laughed. Evan waved in that direction.

"How about any rationalists or logical positivists?" The crowd was silent. "There must be a few existentialists." A half-dozen hands raised.

He poured himself a tall glass of water from the chrome pitcher even though he wasn't thirsty. He sipped the water and then set the glass on the front edge of the podium. It would make people nervous. They would watch.

Where was he heading with his questions? He wasn't sure.

"Philosophers used to wield great influence over society,

beginning with Socrates and Plato. Today we identify with football teams, TV stars, and rock groups, not philosophers. I don't know, maybe that's okay. Beliefs can constrict thinking when they're held too tightly."

There wasn't a sound in the hall except for the squeak of a seat, perhaps someone leaving. His face burned in the hot white light. He suspected he was being too didactic. A few people coughed. A few more seats squeaked. Time was passing. He was dying out there, like an old stand-up comic who needed new material. He should have stayed with his speech, but it was too late now. He would offer an historical anecdote.

"When the great French thinker René Descartes died, the masses turned out along the roadsides for a glimpse of his corpse being transported across the country. Some folks cut off pieces of him, like fingers or ears, to keep as a remembrance. When his body finally went into the ground, it was considerably reduced in size."

Evan paused here to let the image sink in of a man so revered that people would hack up his body into keepsakes. He couldn't imagine the same fate for any philosopher today. There were some benefits to living in a belief-less age.

"According to another story, Descartes stopped in a cafe one day and ordered coffee. The waitress asked if he wanted a muffin, too. He replied, 'I think not'—then poof, he disappeared!"

Behind him on the stage, the dean groaned. After a few seconds, several people murmured their understanding. The professor raised his hands as if to quiet a riot of laughter. He liked the incongruity of this gesture.

"Those of you starting college this week, ask yourself, what is the purpose of your time spent here—to be educated or merely trained? I suggest that at a liberal arts school such as Pearce you may begin the quest to 'know thyself,' which is the prerequisite for all other learning. But I should warn you, self-knowledge may not equal self-esteem. As Goethe said, 'I do not know myself, and heaven forbid that I did.'"

Evan could see now what he was doing—leaving an entire audience of bulky parents and their skinny teenage children shaking their heads. But perhaps some of the young minds would be intrigued by the obvious absurdities in his remarks. That was all he wanted, the few students who were ready to follow a thought down whatever dark and twisted path it might lead them.

It was time for him to conclude in the way that he had prepared.

"Wittgenstein, one of the most penetrating intellects of the twentieth century, described philosophy as a sickness of the mind. I agree, in part. But philosophy can also be a healing art, creating meaning out of apparent chaos. In the next few days you will be choosing your courses. I invite you to sign up for philosophy and explore your mind."

Explore your mind—it sounded like the tag line to an Army recruitment commercial. That was embarrassing. But the words had been said. They couldn't be retracted.

He sipped some more water and then stepped away from the podium. Dean Santos patted him on the shoulder as they passed, and Evan couldn't tell if it was a touch of commendation or commiseration. The polite applause died out before he resumed his seat.

Evan stared at the blank notepad resting on his lap. It was becoming painfully obvious that, like Wittgenstein, he had sadly little sense of humor to share with the world. He should not have agreed to write an article on humor in philosophy just for the little publicity it would bring to *Disturbing Minds*. Besides, how did he even know *Humoresque* was an appropriate publication for an academic to appear in?

"You're back early."

Evan looked up as Ellen came into his study with *How Proust Can Change Your Life* swinging in her hand.

"I skipped out as soon as the convocation was over. I wanted to get some writing done before dinner. Where were you, anyway? The boys didn't know."

"I told them I was going up to the field. They're supposed to remember that kind of thing."

"They remembered you left at three. That was an hour and a half ago."

"I met the woman who moved into that grotesquely huge new house on the hill, and we got to talking."

"Is she grotesque?"

"She's Indian. Her family just moved here from Calcutta, and she's thrilled to have so much room." Ellen sat on the edge of his desk, and he closed the flap of his notepad. "Did your speech go okay?"

"Well, the dean called me *esteemed,* which made me feel eighty years old. Then I dropped my notes on the floor and decided to just speak off the cuff, so I'm pretty sure I confused just about everyone."

"Was that your goal?"

"Confusion's never my goal. But sometimes it's on the path to the goal." He nodded at the book. "Is Proust changing your life?"

"Not yet, but I'm only on page forty-three. I think I'll read *Remembrance of Things Past* next."

"You better be careful. People have spent their whole lives reading Proust and gone crazy doing it."

She pushed up the sleeves of her white linen blouse, and they immediately fell down again. He wondered how many times a day she did this.

"What do you think of Matt and Margaret?"

He didn't recognize the combination.

"Matt McKenzie and Margaret Hope," she said.

"They're together?" He pictured the two in bed, and it was a frightening image—the ex–rugby player Matt flopping on top of the flute-playing Margaret. "When did this happen?"

"It hasn't yet."

So the union was just another figment of her marital imagination, which rarely became reality. In fact, as far as he knew, she had a perfect record of not bringing people together. "You realize he's six-foot-six, weighs maybe two hundred and fifty pounds? She barely comes up to my waist."

"She's not that short. We're almost eye-to-eye."

"Well, I think this is the worst match you've ever come up with. I suggest you reconsider meddling."

"*Helping,*" she said, "they've both asked me to help them find somebody."

"Just don't involve me, okay?"

"I never involve you."

He could count three occasions off the top of his head where she had lured him into abetting some chance meeting or used him as an unwitting messenger to a male acquaintance. But he didn't see any need to bring up her past deviousness. He would change the subject.

"The McKees still coming to dinner?" He tried to muster some enthusiasm in his voice and knew he had failed.

He could pretend a lot of things, but enthusiasm was not one of them.

"Why wouldn't they be?"

Sickness, accidents, crises with children, car problems, leaky roofs, deaths in the family—there were a dozen good possibilities. "No reason, I guess."

"You don't sound like you're looking forward to seeing them."

Of course he didn't look forward to spending an evening with the endlessly bickering McKees. He thought he had made that clear after the last dinner party. "They argue over everything," he said. "They'll be in the door five minutes and Bob will make some little noise. Sheryl will tell him to excuse himself and from then on they'll be at each other's throats the whole night."

"We argue. All couples argue."

He took her hand and kissed it lightly. "We spar verbally sometimes—it's just a game to us. We don't mean it."

She brushed her hand across his cheek. "When you smile you look just like the boys."

He turned his face into her hand and kissed her palm. "It's my main genetic contribution to them—that and their double-jointed fingers."

"You could have passed on worse traits than a sexy smile," she said.

"The boys have sexy smiles?"

"They will. And the girls will be chasing them, just as they did you."

He remembered running through the hall in fifth grade, three girls at his heels. He wasn't sure now or then why he had felt the need to flee. They only wanted to kiss him. The scene had ended badly—his running into a door being opened by the science teacher. Evan recalled a bloody nose, a lump on his forehead, a reprimand from the teacher, and the laughter of the girls. He didn't think he had ever told Ellen this story. Had she just assumed he was pursued?

He stood up. "Okay, we better get moving on dinner. What can I do to help?"

She pulled out the page marker from the book. "I need you to go to Stonehill Farm for vegetables. Here's the list. And I told the boys they had to go with you. They've been on the computer all day."

He walked into the hallway and called up the stairs. "Adam, Zed, let's go!"

They didn't answer. They didn't come. That was unusual.

"Try Castor and Pollux," she said.

"What?"

"Castor and Pollux, the twin stars. I can't remember which is which."

"How long is this going to last?"

"I told them just till school starts tomorrow."

"Castor! Pollux!" he called with as much seriousness as he could muster, "present yourselves."

Zed arrived a few steps in front of his brother, which was surprising. He was wearing a crimson T-shirt that said "Harvard Sucks" on the front. Evan had never seen this shirt before and figured it was the kind of present Ellen's mother would give.

"Why do we have to go for vegetables, Mom?"

"Because you've been inside all day. Consider this a trip into the real world."

"The real world's boring. I wish it would disappear."

"And what would take its place?" Evan said.

Zed bit into his lower lip, his way of stalling when asked a difficult question. "They could put a little chip in your brain, and there'd be like different channels you could choose just by thinking of the number. Then that's the world you'd see in your head. Like channel one could be snowboarding and channel two skateboarding and channel three video games and . . ."

"Okay, I get the idea. How about tuning in to the going-to-buy-vegetables channel?"

Zed twisted his mouth into a fake smile. Evan wondered at what age children learned to do that, and was there an evolutionary reward for fake smiling?

"Come on," Adam said, as he grabbed Evan's arm and tried to pull him toward the garage door, "let's get this over with."

"You used to beg to go places with me," he said. "The farm stand, the hardware store, the cleaners'—you didn't care. Everything was an adventure to you."

"We were like five years old, Dad," Adam said.

Zed nodded. "Yeah, we got a life since then."

It was true, they had gotten a life of sorts, a fact Evan was a little sorry to admit.

He walked down the row of vegetables with Ellen's list in hand. Her instructions were precise, with key words underlined—a dozen tender stalks of asparagus, four organically grown tomatoes, three not-too-ripe avocados. He picked out these items with the care implicit in her notes. He was sure she would be pleased. When he turned to hand the plastic bags to the boys, they were gone. He rose on his toes to scan the market and saw two dark red shirts pushing through the rear door toward a mound of pumpkins in the field. It surprised him to see pumpkins so early in the season. They had to be from out of state.

As he turned back he bumped into a small elderly woman holding an odd-shaped squash.

"I'm sorry," he said, "I didn't see you."

"I'm invisible," she said. "Nobody sees me."

He laughed at what he supposed was a joke. The woman held up her squash. "This looks like Idaho, don't you think?"

He did see a vague likeness. "Yes, you're right."

"Nobody will buy a squash that looks like Idaho. I'm going to take it."

She shuffled away from him with no further comment. He wondered if this squash fit into her collection of vegetables of the fifty states. Or was she expecting Stonehill to give her a discount for buying deformed produce? He watched the woman open the screen door for a young couple coming in. Then she walked out, cradling the squash in her arm. She did not, as far as he could tell, pay for it.

"Can we buy this?"

He looked around, and there were the boys balancing a large pumpkin between them. "Be careful you don't drop that," he said.

"Thanks for telling us, Dad. We thought we were *supposed* to drop it."

"Don't be rude to me, Adam."

"Sorry. So can we buy it?"

"*We* as in you two buy it out of your allowance, or *we* as in I buy it?"

"*We* as in you buy it for us for coming with you," Zed said. "It would be a nice thing for you to do."

The pumpkin was more squat than round, with a hacked-off stub for a handle. It was spotted brown on one side and more green than orange on the other. Evan had never seen a worse-looking pumpkin. "Is there some reason you picked this particular one?"

"It's the ugliest we could find," Adam said, "unless you want to give us more time to look."

"This one is ugly enough," he said and pointed the way to the cashier.

On the ride home, the boys sat in the back, their arms leaning on the huge fruit between them. He considered pointing out that buying a pumpkin was not likely to be as satisfying in any virtual world, but how did he know that? Perhaps the experience would carry the same vicarious pleasure as reading.

He took the highway home. The McKees would be arriving in an hour, and he imagined Ellen leaning against a wall somewhere in the house trying to finish *How Proust Can Change Your Life*. She would need help with dinner. He always found it odd to see her reading standing up, especially when she did knee bends or leg lifts simultaneously. It unsettled him sometimes how focused she could be.

He flipped on his turn signal to change lanes. In the rearview mirror he saw a police car about twenty yards behind, so he turned off his signal and eased back on the accelerator. He glanced at his speedometer—the indicator arrow was falling from sixty to fifty-five. It was still light enough at six o'clock not to need the headlights, but he turned them on anyway.

He drove for a mile or so like that, the car trailing at the same distance. When he slowed to forty-five miles per hour, so did the police. Evan hit the cruise control button and gripped the steering wheel with both hands.

The blue light started flashing. He edged toward the inside of the lane, allowing plenty of passing room. But the squad car came up behind him. He pulled off the road onto the soft shoulder. The police followed, and a sudden uncertainty swept over him. What did they think he had done?

"Hey, Dad, were you speeding?"

"No, I was only going five miles over the limit. They always give you at least five miles." Then he remembered that woman from Texas—wasn't she arrested because her children weren't wearing seat belts? He glanced over the backseat. "Both your belts on?"

"Yep."

He looked in the mirror. The trooper appeared to be talking on his radio. Evan considered getting out and asking what the problem was, but he assumed that the police preferred to initiate the interaction. Authority figures were like that. So he sat.

"Maybe your speedometer's broken, Dad, and you were really going ten miles too fast. They don't give you ten miles, do they?"

In the mirror, he watched a short, stocky policeman get out of his car and come toward them. He bent over at the window, his hand on his gun, and looked in the car.

"Something wrong, Officer?"

"License and registration, please."

Evan opened the glove compartment and found the registration card. Then he pulled out his license from his wallet.

The officer shined his light on the cards. "Who's in the back?"

"My sons," Evan said and then felt an odd need to explain them. "They're twins."

"Would you hand me the key to your car, Mr. Birch?"

"The key?"

"That's right. Take the key out of the ignition and hand it to me."

He pulled out the key and laid it in the palm of the officer's hand. The trooper returned to his squad car.

"Wow, Dad, you must be in big trouble."

"He's just checking something. Maybe my brake light's out or the registration's expired."

On the highway, cars were slowing down, and Evan thought that this was how traffic jams were often made, from curiosity. Several people waved as they passed. One man gave the thumbs-up sign. Another slashed his hand across his neck and laughed.

"May I have a Life Saver, please?" Adam asked.

The exaggerated politeness irritated Evan a little. He opened the well between the front seats and fumbled inside for the candy bag. His hand felt sunglasses, a plastic fork, a packet of tissues, a cell phone, a small flashlight, an empty film container, and several pens. No Life Savers. "We must have eaten them, Adam."

"*You* must have eaten them."

"Maybe we'll be on 'Cops,'" Zed said. "He's probably got a camera hidden on his hood."

A car door shut. In the mirror, the trooper returned. His body language hadn't changed—he still seemed tense, or maybe it was just the customary state of readiness. His right hand remained on the handle of his gun. Evan suspected that some new regulation required this caution.

"Mr. Birch?"

"Yes?"

"Please step out of the car."

"What's going on, Dad?"

"He just wants to talk to me," Evan said as he got out. "Anything wrong, Officer?"

"Please turn around and place your hands on top of the car."

He heard the words clearly, but he couldn't help but say, "What?"

The policeman touched Evan's shoulder. "Turn around and place your hands on top of the car."

He had taught the boys to obey police— "*Always* do what the officer says." Of course he would do the same.

The trooper tapped his legs. "Spread them."

The order was incomprehensible. How could an ordinary citizen be ordered out of his car and told to "spread them"?

He spread his legs. The officer patted down his chest, around his waist, and then down each leg.

When the search was finished Evan twisted his head around. "Would you mind telling me what this is all about?"

"I'm going to have to ask you to come to the station."

"The station? What for?"

"There are some things to talk over."

"But my wife is expecting me home any minute. We're having guests for dinner. And I have my boys in the car."

"You can call your wife from the station and tell her you're delayed."

Evan turned his shoulders around as much as he could while keeping his hands on the car roof. "Look, I'm trying to be reasonable here, but you can't just pull someone over and search them and take them to the station without explaining what's going on."

"Detective Malloy will answer your questions at the station."

"But that's the point—I don't want to go to the station for an explanation. I want you to tell me."

"You're refusing to go in?"

The option to refuse hadn't occurred to Evan. Perhaps there was some constitutional right not to cooperate. Didn't the police need a reason to stop a person in the first place?

"Okay, yes, I'm refusing. What I *will* do is call my wife and tell her I'll be dropping the boys off, then I'll go to the station to clear up this matter. How's that?" He reached into the car to get his cell phone.

"Hold it," the trooper said.

"I'm just getting . . ."

He felt the man's hands grip his arms and jerk them around his back. In a second, handcuffs clicked around his wrists. The quickness of the maneuver amazed him. There had been no time to resist, and he figured that was good. Resisting was not an appropriate impulse to follow in this situation.

Adam stuck his head out of the back window. "Dad?"

Evan turned toward him to hide the handcuffs. "It's okay. Just sit down for a minute till I get this straightened out."

"Walk with me to the squad car, Mr. Birch."

He moved around the rear of the Jetta, guided by the trooper's hand on his arm. Passing cars steered into the outside lane. He turned his face away from them and thought about all of the suspects on the TV news with their jackets pulled over their heads.

Evan stopped. "Look, Officer . . . Antonelli," he said, reading the name tag, "I want to know what's going on. You can't handcuff me just for trying to make a phone call. My kids are in the backseat, for God's sake, and I'm not leaving them. You can't force me to do that."

The trooper reached into his pocket and brought out a small card. "Mr. Birch, you're under arrest for suspicion of kidnapping."

"What?"

"You have the right to remain silent . . ."

"This is crazy."

"Anything you say may be used against you . . ."

"You must have me confused with someone else."

"You have a right to stop answering my questions at any time . . ."

"Kidnap who?"

"You have a right to a lawyer . . ."

"Don't I have a right for you to answer my questions?"

"Do you understand each of these rights that I have explained to you?"

"I don't understand anything that's going on."

The trooper nudged him toward the passenger side of the squad car.

"My sons—you can't just leave them out here."

"We'll wait for another officer to arrive to pick them up. As soon as you get in the car, I'll go talk to them."

"*I* need to talk to them. They're only ten years old. Don't you have children?"

"Yes, I am a father, Mr. Birch, of a teenage girl as a matter of fact. That's why I'm asking you not to give me any more trouble. Just get in the squad car."

What trouble had he given? Questioning being handcuffed and arrested? Anyone would do that. He looked back at the Jetta. The boys' heads were sticking out of either side window. He started to raise his hand to wave to them, then realized he couldn't. "Everything's going to be fine," he shouted. "Just do what the officer says. I'll call Mom from the station."

Everything's going to be fine—how could he say that? When it came to the future, he had always thought that bad things were much more likely to happen than good.

CHAPTER 5

n the small, windowless interrogation room, Detective Robert Malloy rocked back on the legs of his chair, his hands behind his head. The sergeant, Jill Killian, leaned against the wall and picked at her fingernails. Evan rubbed his wrists to smooth out the indentations in his skin and tried to interpret their casual poses—were they meant to put him at ease or off guard?

"Sorry about the handcuffs," the detective said, and Evan noticed that his eyelids weren't closing exactly in synch with each other. He wondered what the world would look like one odd blink at a time. "The trooper got a little overzealous," Malloy continued. "We asked him to bring you in for a few questions, and when you resisted—"

Evan leaned forward. "I didn't resist, I refused. There's a big difference in the words."

"Okay, you refused, and then you reached into your car. The trooper did as he's trained to at that point."

"I was reaching for my cell phone to call my wife. I told him that."

"People say things all the time. We still have to take every precaution."

What precaution did they take not to handcuff an innocent man in front of his sons? It was a question Evan thought he would ask at some point.

Sergeant Killian raised her right boot onto one of the folding chairs. She hadn't said a word yet, not even hello, though she may have nodded slightly when the detective introduced her.

"We're conducting an investigation into the disappearance of Joyce Bonner, a sixteen-year-old girl from Eastfield," Malloy said. "Are you aware of the case?"

"I heard something on the radio about it. She was a cheerleader, wasn't she?"

"That's right. We've received a number of phone calls offering information, and one tip said a man in a gray Jetta was watching the girl from the parking lot of the state park where she was working on the afternoon she disappeared."

Evan made some dismissive noise that came out as a squeak. He cleared his throat. "There must be hundreds of gray Jettas in this area."

"It is a fairly common make. But the informant also said that the car's license plate started with EZ and then a number, two or three."

EZ-2134—he repeated the Jetta's license plate to himself. "Okay, so there's a coincidence about my license plate—"

"And the make and color of the car," the sergeant added.

He shifted his gaze to the woman. Her holster bulged on her right hip, giving her a lopsided appearance. She was still picking at her fingernails. "Yes, the make and color, too. But obviously that doesn't mean I had anything to do with the girl's kidnapping."

"We didn't say she was kidnapped," the detective said.

Evan heard the slight emphasis on *we*, implying that he had come up with the description of the crime on his own. It pleased him to correct them. "You better tell Officer Antonelli then, because that's why he said he was arresting me—suspicion of kidnapping."

Malloy waved his hand a little, as if it were an unimportant matter.

"There is one other coincidence," the sergeant said. "The gray Jetta observed in the parking lot of the state park had a Pearce College sticker on the back window. Your gray Jetta has a Pearce College sticker on the back window, correct?"

Evan disliked questions where the answer was already known. They served no purpose. He also disliked people who repeated whole sections of sentences. "I believe you know that's correct," he said. "So you have three coincidences that relate to me—the make of car, the partial license plate, and the sticker." He listed these things in an offhand way, but he began to wonder himself about their significance. How many other cars might share the same attributes?

"Coincidences are a lot of what we follow up on," the detective said. "Most of them lead to nothing, but you understand why we have to pursue every one, don't you?"

"Pursue how?"

"We just need some more information. Can you tell us your whereabouts ten days ago, the 23rd of August, at three P.M.?"

"August 23rd, three P.M.—that was during orientation for freshmen. So I guess I was at the college."

"You guess?"

"I'd have to check my schedule to make sure. I keep it on my computer in my office. That would say where I was."

"Actually," the sergeant said, "it would show where you were *supposed* to be, correct? I know I'm not always where the schedule says I am. Sometimes we're called away or do things spontaneously."

The mixture of pronouns intrigued Evan. *You, I, we*— apparently he was free to evoke whatever form of himself he wished in response. "Yes, I suppose we do things spontaneously sometimes. But you asked me a question, and I'm giving you my best answer without checking my schedule to jog my memory."

"Have you ever met Joyce Bonner?" the detective asked.

"I don't think so."

"You could have?"

"I mean that I don't remember meeting a girl with that name, but I see a lot of young people at the college. And sometimes I speak at events on campus that local high-school students come to. So it's conceivable I've met her. What I am sure of is that I don't know I have."

Detective Malloy exhaled on his hands as if they were cold, an odd thing for a man to do in such a hot room, it seemed to Evan.

"You may have met her and not known it?"

He nodded.

"Would you mind speaking your answer?"

Evan scanned the room. "Am I being taped?"

"It's just better if we both hear your answer."

"Okay, I said yes, that's what I meant."

The detective laced his fingers together at the knuckles, like at the beginning of the children's rhyme, "Here's the church, here's the steeple . . ."

"So, Mr. Birch, how long have you lived in town?"

Evan noted the change in questioning, from the specifics of a car sighting to the generality of his background. Was his whole life being investigated? He sat back in the chair, crossed his arms, and extended his legs. He wanted to appear comfortable to them. He thought he might actually feel more comfortable, too, simply by pretending to be. Behavior could influence feeling, he was sure.

"Not quite twelve years. My wife and I moved here when I was offered a position in the philosophy department at Pearce."

"Philosophy," the detective said, "'I think, therefore I am'— that kind of thing?"

"Yes, I teach Descartes in my introductory course, along with the other Rationalists, like Spinoza and Leibniz." He glanced from the detective to the sergeant and was surprised to see their apparent interest in the philosophers he was naming. So he continued the rundown. "I spend some time on the English, of course—Bacon, Hobbes, Locke, Hume, Mill. Sometimes we make it all the way to Russell."

"How would you describe what you do?"

"You mean teaching?"

"I mean philosophy. What does a philosopher do?"

Evan laughed at the oxymoronic question. Nothing—that was the joke, wasn't it? Of all professions on earth, was there any that produced a less tangible product than philosophy? "Philosophers contemplate the world in an organized way, trying to make sense of it. You might consider the process of philosophy as the logical clarification of thoughts. But I have to say I'm more of a teacher than a practicing philosopher." He felt foolish explaining himself like this, especially to the police. But was that a kind of prejudice, an unwarranted judgment that they wouldn't understand if he truly described philosophy? And where would he start—at the nature of existence, the foundation of ethical behavior, or some dusty corner of the philosophic life? "Is all of this relevant in some way?"

"You never know what's relevant till you hear it," the detective said. "One thing can lead to another, and that thing to another . . ."

Evan nodded to acknowledge his familiarity with perpetual causation and to cut off the next ". . . and that thing to another."

"Ever go to the state park, Professor?"

"Sometimes."

"You live in Pheasant Run, right?"

Pleasant Run? Had he heard right? The idea of a subdivision being named Pleasant Run struck him as funny.

"You're laughing?"

He thought of Freud's explanation of laughter—a release of pent-up nervous energy. Certainly that was why he had just laughed, but why bring Freud into this? "No, I just misheard you, and yes, I live in Pheasant Run."

"That's a nice neighborhood. I used to shoot in those hills years ago. Best pheasant hunting around. You get a lot of your college people living up there now, don't you?"

"Yes, it's convenient to the highway for commuting."

"Convenient to the state park, too?"

Of course the park was convenient. That was one reason they had chosen to live in Pheasant Run. The boys would have a small bit of wildness nearby. Could some premeditation be seen in this decision? Was the detective using *convenience* as a substitute for *opportunity?*

"It's a few minutes away, if you don't go through town."

"When was the last time you went to the park?"

Evan tried to think. Sometimes he stopped at the lake on his way home and jotted down notes for his lectures. Was the last time two days ago? Two weeks? He was not very good at keeping straight the trivial events of his life. A philosophy professor could certainly claim that his mind was occupied by loftier thoughts than mere time and place, but wasn't complex reality built out of just these things, the atomic facts of life? He didn't like using absentmindedness as an excuse, anyway. Being absent of mind was not—

"Professor?"

"Yes, I'm thinking." What if in trying to be absolutely clear he misspoke or remembered wrong? His words could be held against him. They were establishing a record here that he might have trouble explaining later. It was stupid of him not to have realized that earlier. "Maybe I should call a lawyer," he said, "if you're going to go on much longer. This is all kind of overwhelming."

The detective let out a disgusted little sigh. "It's a straightforward question, isn't it? When was the last time you went to the park? There's nothing tricky about that."

Sometimes he intended to stop in the park but took the bypass instead. Other times he'd be heading home and decide to divert into the park for a ten-minute respite from the world. The sight of water always relaxed him. And when he was relaxed he thought best. Would it be better to offer that he might have been at the park August 23, since that would explain the sighting of his car? Or should he maintain he hadn't been there for weeks to avoid being connected at all to the girl's disappearance?

"I really can't say."

"How about giving us an approximate date?"

Obviously the detective wasn't going to give up on this line of questioning. Evan thought hard.

"Well, approximately . . ." August 23rd—yes, the last day of camp for the boys. He remembered being early to pick them up and so stopping at the lake first. But how could he admit that after just saying he couldn't remember at all? It would appear that he had been hiding something, or lying. And then he would be questioned about what he had seen and what he had done. It might take hours. Equivocation seemed like the safest path, which surprised him. By Wittgenstein's dictum, the essential work of language was to assert or deny facts, not circumvent them. Wittgenstein, Evan assumed, had never been grilled by the police.

"Like I said, Detective, I'm really not sure."

"Well, when you did go to the lake, was it generally to the area where the boat rental is?"

"Yes, to there and the smaller lot on the other side."

"In any of your visits to the lake this summer, do you remember seeing a blond girl, about sixteen years old, working at the information booth?"

"No, I can't say as I do."

"You mean you don't remember seeing her?"

He had begun to notice from the pattern of follow-up questions that police, like philosophers, were accustomed to an unusual kind of exactness. He decided he would try to satisfy it. "That's right. I don't remember seeing any blond girl, let alone a sixteen-year-old one, working at the information booth. I don't remember anyone working at the booth, girl or boy. I don't remember any blond girl—any girl at all, in fact—working or not working at the information booth. I've never actually gone to the information booth, never sent anyone else to the information booth, barely even thought of the information booth until now, when you asked me about it."

Neither officer reacted. They seemed to accept his convoluted answer as if it were a normal conversational response. Wittgenstein was right—the police were playing their own peculiar language game, one he would need to adapt to.

The sergeant flipped back to an earlier page in her notebook. "When Detective Malloy asked you if you had heard about Joyce Bonner's disappearance, you said, 'She was a cheerleader, wasn't she?' Do you remember saying that?"

"Yes."

"She *was* a cheerleader?"

"I was speaking offhand. I suppose she still is a cheerleader, except she's missing and I presume she's not off cheerleading somewhere."

The expression on the sergeant's face darkened, as if oil had secreted from her pores. "I assure you, Mr. Birch, this is not a situation to joke about."

He did not like being reprimanded. He did not like every word being used against him and each nuance of tone being analyzed. In fact, he did not like this sergeant with the sloping shoulders trying to peer into his soul through the lens of language. The attempt affronted him, and he didn't consider it the least bit condescending to feel that way. "I wasn't joking," he said, "I was explaining. If you're going to try to trip me up you have to expect I might get a little sarcastic."

There was a knock at the door. The detective excused himself. Evan looked at the hairline cracks in the walls and the air vent in the ceiling, anywhere but at the sergeant, who was looking at him. A strange question came to mind—was the vent wide enough for a body of his size to squeeze through?

The detective ducked into the room. "You're free to go."

"Go? I thought I was arrested."

Malloy shook his head. "Like I said, the trooper was over-zealous. We never formally booked you."

Overzealous—it was a handy word for the police, a catch-all to explain away every wrong they committed. Evan wondered what the similarly exculpatory word would be for his own profession—*thoughtless,* perhaps?

He got up to leave. As he passed the sergeant, she said something he couldn't hear. When he asked her what, she said, "Nothing."

CHAPTER 6

E llen canceled dinner with the McKees, which Evan considered the one positive side effect of his encounter with
the police. He heard her on the phone telling them that
"something's come up—no, nothing serious. We'll reschedule
soon." He wondered why she couldn't say to their old quar-
relsome friends, "The strangest thing just happened—the police pulled Evan over on the highway and questioned him
about the disappearance of that girl in Eastfield. Can you
imagine anything more outrageous?"

When she hung up she saw him standing in the kitchen
doorway. He supposed he had adopted a questioning posture.

"I don't see any reason to tell anyone about this," she said,
"do you?"

"Actually, yes. I think people should know they can be out driving someday with their kids and arrested for no reason."

Ellen opened the cabinet over the stove, stretched up on her toes to look in, then closed the door. "I wouldn't say 'no reason,' Evan. A teenage girl is missing, and they had a tip about a suspicious car like yours where she was last seen."

"You think a tip should be enough to arrest someone and traumatize his kids?"

She wrote something on her pad. From upside down it looked to him like "ol oil."

He thought that maybe he hadn't adequately conveyed to her how much of a shock the arrest had been, to him and the twins. He would try again. "When the trooper led me to the squad car, the boys were hanging out the windows calling to me. It was as if they were in a burning building and I was abandoning them. That's how I felt. I'm supposed to be the symbol of stability in their lives, and then they see it's all fake. Their father can be dragged off from them at any moment."

Ellen shoved a stack of magazines out of the way and leaned over the marble island. "What about a mother, what's she supposed to be the symbol of?"

He didn't understand. Her tone seemed good-natured, but her question pointed. "I guess it would be just as devastating for them to see this happen to you," he said. "We both try to project stability to them. We want them to feel secure."

"Maybe that's wrong. Maybe this is a good lesson about the world—they can't count on anything."

"They're only ten, Ellen. Couldn't they learn that lesson a little later?"

"We don't get to choose the timing of lessons," she said. "We're only in control of how we react to them."

"And you think I'm overreacting?"

She shrugged and wrote something else on the pad. He couldn't decipher the word at all.

She suggested it might help for him to go over everything again. Help how? he wondered. What he really needed was for the police to go over everything and admit to a mistake.

But she was at least right that he should get his own story straight in his mind. He might have to retell it. So he sat on one of the new chrome stools as she continued around the kitchen making up the shopping list. The bars on the back pressed against his spine, and rather than complain to her again about buying them he just leaned forward a little. "Like I said, we were driving on Rte. 4 and a policeman pulled me over. I thought I had a brake light out or something. He asked for my registration and license, and then he told me to give him the key. I did everything he asked, didn't argue at all, and believe me, I wanted to tell him to take his fucking hands off me."

"That wouldn't have been a good idea," Ellen said as she opened the refrigerator. She stooped down to investigate the row of salad dressing bottles, pulling each one out to see how much was left inside.

"It didn't make any difference. I was polite as can be and he still handcuffed me."

She closed the refrigerator and headed for the pantry. "Behind your back?"

That seemed to him like the kind of detail one would ask about when she wasn't really paying attention. He couldn't say that to her, of course, because she would just recite his last five sentences to prove she had been listening. She could probably name the five kinds of salad dressing left in the refrigerator, too. She had that sort of mind.

So he continued. "Yes, behind my back. Then the trooper took me to the station and put me in their interrogation room, I guess it was. After a few minutes two other cops came in and started questioning me about . . . Her name starts with a J."

"Joyce?"

"Yes, that's it. How did you know?"

"I must have heard it on the news."

"Well, they said she disappeared from the park in Eastfield on August 23rd. And someone called in a tip about a suspicious car like the Jetta parked near the information booth where she worked."

"Wasn't that the day you picked up the boys at camp?"

"Yes."

Ellen sat on the chrome chair opposite him. "So that's your alibi."

Alibi—there was a word he didn't like associated with him. What was next, *probable cause, prime suspect, motive?* This was the police language he would have to master.

"The thing is," he said, "I was early going for them, and I think I stopped at the lake on the way."

"You *think* you stopped?"

"I'm pretty sure I did, but you know I'm not great at remembering things like that."

"Okay, let's say you were there, that would explain why somebody saw your car."

"It would, except I didn't tell them that."

She cocked her head a little, a quizzical expression he rarely saw on her.

"I wasn't sure at first, so I kept saying I didn't know the last time I went to the park. When I definitely remembered I felt guilty admitting it. Besides, I wanted to get out of there as quickly as possible."

"But if someone can identify you as being at the park, they'll find out you lied, and then they'll have one more reason to suspect you."

He nodded that it was so. "It's easy to see that now. But when you're being questioned in a stifling little room about kidnapping a teenage girl, it gets confusing. The questions keep coming at you, and you hear what they're asking, but you're trying to figure out how they're using the words, what they're really trying to get you to say. It's not a straightforward conversation."

Ellen sat back in her stool, up against the bars. "If you got confused, imagine how it is for thousands of other people arrested each day who aren't as educated."

He picked up a fork lying on the table and ran his palm over the tines. The sensation was surprisingly pleasant. He didn't feel like he had much spare sympathy to spend on those thousands of others in a similar predicament, educated or otherwise. He couldn't imagine any of them were worrying about him at that moment.

She traced a circle on the marble, her index finger going around and around the same path. "This doesn't make sense. A person called the police about seeing a gray Jetta like yours at the park right before the girl's disappearance. I can understand that if you were there. But why would they remember your license plate? The girl wasn't reported missing at that point. He didn't actually see an abduction. So there was no reason for somebody to pay attention to your car."

Evan jabbed the fork into his palm a little. There was still more pleasure than pain. He wondered how much force he would need to apply to cross the threshold.

"You see what I'm saying?"

Of course he did. There was no reason in the world for

someone to connect him to the disappearance of a sixteen-year-old girl. What was the chance that he'd happen to turn up at the location of a crime and be remembered? He assumed the odds were astronomical.

She poured them drinks, and they went over what happened again and again until it occurred to him that this was becoming the most analyzed event of his life, and he was sick of it. He finished his glass of wine and stood up. "I can't talk about this anymore. There are purely random events in the world that don't make sense, and this may be one of them."

She reached across the island to stroke his arm. Her touch was feathery against his skin. "I love you," she said.

"What do you mean by that?"

She pulled back her hand. "Just that I love you, that's all."

"You sound a little fatalistic, like I'm heading off to prison for twenty years."

"I don't mean it that way. I just mean that I love you no matter what happens."

"Nothing happened, and nothing's going to happen." The cadence of his words reminded him of the line from Wallace Stevens's "Blackbird" poem, "It was snowing, and it was going to snow." He had always marveled at how this little bit of poetry could fill up the vastness of time. Perhaps that was the poem he would read to his "Necessity of Time" class.

Ellen opened the pantry door and pulled out a large Staples bag. "Why don't you take the boys their school things, get back to normal?"

"And say what to them?"

"You told them the police made a mistake. Leave it at that. The more we make of it the more they will."

That seemed to him like one of those generalizations that sounded perfectly fine in theory, but where was the supporting evidence? It was equally possible that the boys might always feel some terror lurking just below the surface if they didn't talk about it. He felt sure that seeing a father handcuffed and arrested could leave scars, and he didn't even know where to look for them.

He carried the bag of supplies upstairs, slung over his shoulder. The door to the boys' room was open a crack, and when he knocked, it opened wider. "Can I come in?"

"Yeah."

"Mom said to give you your stuff for tomorrow." He poured the contents of the bag on the bed, and the twins grabbed their notebooks, calendars, calculators, pencils, and pens. Zed sat cross-legged on the floor and began marking his possessions. Adam stuffed his things into his bookbag, hung it on the door hook, and went back to the computer. Both of them said thanks.

He was used to more responsiveness from them. It was as if they had found out some secret bad thing about him and didn't know what to do with the knowledge. He would have to work to make them forget.

"So what did you do with your pumpkin?" He glanced around the room.

Zed pointed to the closet.

"You're not putting it out?"

"Maybe later," Zed said.

"Like when it's Halloween," Adam said.

Evan walked behind Adam and looked over his shoulder. On the computer screen an odd-looking cartoon character with big eyes and tufted hair was getting off a train with a blond, big-eyed girl.

"What are you playing?"

"It's not a game, it's an animated series. You just watch it."

"I see. What series is it?"

"Zombie College, the first episode."

"Zombie College?"

"It's really Arkford University, but everybody calls it Zombie College because living kids and dead ones both go there."

"*Un*dead ones," Zed said.

"Yeah, undead kids."

Evan pointed at the cartoon boy. "Who's that?"

"It's Scott, he's the main character. He got into MIT because he's like a genius, but he went to Zombie College since that's where Zelda was going. She's his girlfriend. But then she told him she wanted to see other guys. That's pretty cold, isn't it."

"Yes, pretty cold."

This was the usual time of his visits to their room, just before leaving, when he would offer some parental advice or news. How would they react if he broke the routine, said something downright subversive—"You don't really have to study so hard this year. School isn't *that* important." He'd always wanted to say something like that to them. He would get their attention, no doubt.

This wasn't the night to shock them, though. "You two are going to have to cut back on your computer time now that school's starting," he said.

"We know," they answered in unison. "An hour a day during the week, two hours on the weekend. Mom already told us."

"I suppose she also told you nine o'clock's your bedtime tonight?"

"Yes."

"And you have to get up at six to make the bus?"

"Yes."

"Well, as usual, your mom's covered all the bases." As he turned to leave, the red ink on the black bookbag caught his eye—"Personal Property . . . of Adam Birch."

"Zed?"

Both boys looked up. He pointed at the twin on the floor writing on the cover of his notebook.

"Why are you writing 'Property of Adam Birch' on your stuff?"

"Because I *am* Adam Birch."

Evan leaned over and took hold of his son's right ear. What he saw surprised him—a jagged half-inch scar curling around the lobe.

The boy twisted out of his grasp. "That hurts."

"When did you get this?"

"It's my ear, Dad, I've had it forever."

"You know what I mean—the scar."

Zed shrugged. Or was it really Adam, the one who had snagged his ear on a thorn of roses last year?

"You don't remember how you got it?"

"I fell skateboarding, okay?"

"When was that?"

"I don't know. I fall all the time."

He stared at the boy. The boy stared back.

"Pull your waistband down."

"What?"

He reached for the top of the shorts and tugged them down an inch.

"Dad, cut it out."

"I want to see your birthmark."

The boy squirmed across the floor. "That's a private area."

"It's just your hip. There's nothing private about that."

"No, Mom! Dad's getting weird."

When he heard her coming down the hall he thought about pulling his hands away from his son's body. But this was his own flesh and blood. He had a right to touch it in an innocent way as much as his own body.

"What's going on?"

He turned toward the door as Ellen came in, a basket of laundry in her arms. When he looked back, both boys were sitting on the bed with their arms around each other's shoulders.

"Dad wants us to pull our shorts down, Mom."

He looked at Ellen. He didn't see alarm on her face, but something like that, perhaps the tracks of alarm after it had passed.

"The boys are trying to confuse me about which is which, so I asked Zed to show me his birthmark." Evan felt a shiver run through him. How had he gotten to the point of explaining himself to his wife?

She handed the laundry basket to the closer of the twins. "Take this down to the washing machine, Zed, and anything else you two want clean for school tomorrow. I'll be starting a load of dark in a few minutes."

The boy took the clothes from her and left without a word. Evan eyed the remaining twin on the bed—Adam, he was sure. "You're not fooling me, you know."

"Right, Dad."

As they left the room Evan said to her, "I haven't been this confused telling them apart since they were babies."

"They were just trying to trick you, dear. The books said they would go through this stage."

"Then how come you aren't confused?"

"I see the differences in them," she said, "you see their sameness."

He heard a bit of arrogance in her voice—she saw differences, he saw sameness. It was the prime work of philosophy to discriminate as finely as possible between like objects or concepts. He wished he were better at it.

CHAPTER 7

Of the twelve students registered for "The Necessity of Time," only seven showed up for the first class. Evan didn't know what to think. Apparently students were dropping his course now without even coming once to hear him lecture. Had he somehow acquired a reputation for being boring?

"Good afternoon," he said, "this is INDS3—'The Necessity of Time,' and I am . . ."

"Shit," said a young man in the back row. He picked up his books, jumped off the third level of tiers, and exited the room.

Evan waited. He almost expected a collective sigh of "Shit," followed by a wholesale rush to the door. Then he could lecture on time to an empty room. Wouldn't that be a fitting climax to his teaching career?

No one moved. The half-dozen students were staring at him with unusual attention. He had used the power of silence before to focus a class at dramatic points in his lectures, but he had never dared go this long. After all, these kids were paying $798 per credit hour to learn. Some of them had no doubt calculated the cost of each minute. They expected words, not a professor sitting at his desk with a stare as blank as the blackboard behind him.

Of course, if he never spoke at all, he might go down as one of the teaching legends at Pearce. At reunions decades later students would claim that they had been in that class—what was it called, "The Need for More Time"?—when the professor stopped in mid-sentence and didn't say another word. Dozens of students would remember being there.

"Whereof one cannot speak," Evan said, "thereof one must be silent." He turned and wrote the aphorism on the blackboard, then a dash, then "Wittgenstein." How would the students interpret these words, as a warning to keep silent unless they knew what they were talking about? That wasn't a bad message to convey, but of course, he didn't want to stifle all spontaneous responses.

"I'm Professor Birch of the philosophy department. The turnout this afternoon is somewhat less than expected—" So? The sentence demanded a so. "So I propose we move the class outside for a more informal atmosphere on this beautiful day."

A couple of students moaned about the suggestion, perhaps simply at the effort required to lift themselves out of the chairs they had sunk into. He waved them to follow as he walked from the classroom, past Carla sipping her morning

Sprite through a straw, down the narrow back steps and out onto the Arts Quad. He pointed them toward Freedom Oak, a name that always mystified him since it didn't appear in the college's formal history handed out to all faculty. What event could inspire a name but no other memory?

When the students reached the tree they sprawled out around it, as if it were to be the object of their attention. One girl—a biker, he assumed, because of the rubber bands around the ankles of her jeans—stopped a few steps to the side. She reached over her shoulder into her knapsack and pulled out a large can of Off! Then she pushed up her sleeves and sprayed her arms. He veered around her as she applied the repellent up and down in layers, as if adding a new skin. It occurred to him that she might have some fatal allergy to insect bites, and if so, would he be liable if she got bitten? The girl lifted the can to her face, closed her eyes, and pressed down the nozzle. She sprayed her cheeks and her forehead and the top of her head and her neck. He couldn't believe what he was seeing. Did she think her eyes were all that she needed to worry about? What about breathing the fumes? She paused, wiped her lips with the back of her free hand, then sprayed again over her face and neck and head.

"Miss?"

The girl stuffed the can back into her knapsack and opened her eyes. "Yes?"

"Do you think that's a good idea?"

She looked around at the other students on the grass as if she had missed some proposition of philosophy that he had just expounded. "Sorry, I didn't know you had started the lecture already."

He thought it obvious that he hadn't. He was still holding his briefcase, standing outside the ring of students lying on the ground talking among themselves. Had the Off! fogged her brain already? "I meant, is it a good idea to spray repellent on your face?"

She blinked rapidly, like a person waking up in an unfamiliar place. "It's the only way to keep the bugs off. I hate bugs more than anything."

"It would seem a Pyrrhic victory over the bugs, Miss . . ."

"Shepard, Anna Shepard."

"If you keep the bugs away, Ms. Shepard, but make yourself sick in the process, that's called a Pyrrhic victory."

"I know, from Pyrrhus the general. He suffered big losses when he defeated the Romans."

"Yes, that's right."

"Well, I've been spraying myself like this all my life, Professor, and I haven't gotten sick yet."

He acknowledged her reasoning with a slight nod. She was obviously working from a different set of assumptions about the world, and nothing he could say at that moment would be meaningful to her. He stepped over a pair of khaki-clad legs and motioned to the students on the far side of the tree to form around him on this side of it. He leaned against the oak as they slouched into a rough semicircle. The tree, he noticed, had been pruned of its lower branches, and it felt to him like standing beneath a large green tent.

He opened his notebook and saw the first line he had prepared, "Time was invented to keep everything from happening all at once." This observation seemed unbearably stupid to him, not just trivial. He couldn't bring himself to utter it, even for a laugh. He scanned his page of notes for something more inspirational to begin with and saw a bit of poetry he had jotted down. " 'For a moment of night we have a glimpse of ourselves and of our world islanded in its stream of stars—

pilgrims of mortality, voyaging between horizons across the eternal seas of space and time.'"

He looked up from his notebook but kept his gaze over the heads of the students, so as not to cue them to respond. "That was by Henry Beston, from his work, *The Outermost House,* written in 1928. I suggest that it's worthwhile for each of us to contemplate 'the eternal seas of space and time' in which we exist. And that is what we will do in this seminar, from a philosophic perspective. The class could have been titled 'The Necessity of Time *and Space,*' because the two are so bound up with each other that to consider one is to consider both."

Time and space—August 23rd, 3 P.M., and Eastfield State Park. What stream of stars had collided there, what pilgrim of mortality had begun its voyage on the eternal seas? He appreciated the beauty of the images, but he doubted beauty had much to do with what happened that day to Joyce . . . Joyce Bonner—that was her name.

A small breeze riffled the leaves and cooled his face. What next? He had been planning to pull Gerard Whitrow's *The Nature of Time* from his briefcase to make the argument that a concept of time was fundamentally unnecessary. That time was neither an illusion nor a creation of man's imagination, but rather, an observable, testable part of the universe that required no labor of the human mind to make real. It was his acknowledgment of the origin of this seminar in physics.

He heard noise overhead and looked up at two squirrels chasing each other around the tree trunk. Was there any sense in which they realized that they, too, existed in time? Did they ever think, summer is ending, we better start putting away acorns for winter? Did Tyco the chimp realize she was getting older? Or was it the particular curse of mankind to be aware of the clock?

Evan lowered his eyes to the students on the ground in front of him, an arc of three boys and two girls, with Anna Shepard sitting by herself a few yards back. She had segregated herself, perhaps realizing that the other students, along with the insects, would be repelled by the smell of her.

He couldn't bear the sheer weight of *The Nature of Time*. He just wasn't in the mood. He had Queen Elizabeth's dying words to relate and the image of time flowing, but he wanted something more fitting for this first strange day as The Accused Man, and he thought of paradoxes. They were a favorite tool of his to disrupt the normal pathways of thinking, and he could recount them from memory. "There's a fire in the grass," he said, paraphrasing Moore's Paradox, "and I don't believe there is." The students looked quickly behind themselves, saw nothing, and looked back at him.

"Paradox," Evan said, "is a fundamental attribute of any discussion of time and space. Einstein theorized the relativity of time, how dependent it is on the observer. If one of my twin sons takes a trip into space, he would age differently from his twin left on earth, according to Einstein. Which would be the younger, though, if time is relative between the two? Is there any conceivable way they both could be younger than each other?"

Ms. Shepard—Anna—was blinking furiously now. Her body shuddered for a moment, and he thought of Edna O'Brien's observation that involuntary shudders were what reminded people they were alive. Is that what Anna was feeling—thrillingly, twitchingly alive? Perhaps the spray served a dual purpose.

"In the fifth century B.C., the Greek philosopher Zeno devised several intriguing puzzles. His Progressive Dichotomy Paradox proposes that before a person can cross a room, he must walk halfway, and before going halfway, he must cover one-quarter of the distance and so on to an infinite number of decreasing distances. Therefore the man, or woman, could never take the first step. Zeno demonstrated, in a way, that motion is impossible."

Anna was rocking from side to side now, as if to some weird lullaby running through her head. He thought she might pass out, keel over into the thick grass, and then what would he do? Bend over her in a sloppy attempt at resuscitation? Was that advisable given recent events? And what if he were misconstruing the situation? What if she had merely fainted and woke to find his mouth closed around hers? He could almost taste the Off!

"Anna," he said, "is something wrong?"

She sneezed, and her eyes snapped open. "Paradoxes are just word tricks," she said. "They don't teach you anything. I don't like them."

"Well, I'm glad you feel comfortable sharing your opinion of my lecture material." He considered adding, "Perhaps the other students here *are* interested in paradoxes," but what if they shouted out, "No, Professor, we hate them, too"? He wouldn't chance it. "I'll only be spending a few more minutes on them," he said. "Feel free not to listen, if paradoxes disturb you."

"Oh, I'm not disturbed," Anna said. "I just don't want to think about them."

"You're disturbed all right," a boy called out, prompting laughter from the others.

It was always the boys who offered the insulting comments, Evan noticed. He had thought many times that it might be nice to teach at an all-girls college. Not one, however, with too many Anna Shepards in it.

"Paradoxes expose the limits of language to reflect the world," he said, and he hoped that he didn't appear to be defending his use of them. That was a dangerous game to play with students. "We know by experience that people walk across rooms. It's only in our language where uncertainty arises. Think about the words you speak or write, both in this class and outside of it. You may say you *have* a dollar in your pocket and *have* a pain in your neck. But do you possess these things in the same way? You may share your dollar with a friend; you can't share your pain. If you say *I eat* and *I am*, do the meanings of the verbs reflect on you in the same way?" He paused here, even though he didn't expect anyone to venture an answer. This was, after all, the first class. "Wittgenstein said that as long as there are verbs like *to be* and adjectives like *true* and *false* and *identical*—as long as people talk of time passing and space extending—we will run up against the seeming mysteries of the world and, I quote, 'stare at something which no explanation seems able to remove.'"

Evan stretched his left arm out a little so that he could check his watch without appearing to do so. Thirty minutes remained. That amused him because whenever he checked the time during class, there always seemed to be thirty minutes remaining.

CHAPTER 8

At dinner, the twins related their first day at school in their usual manner, alternating sentences, sometimes even words. It surprised Evan that they hadn't yet tired of sharing experiences and retelling them. It seemed that whatever happened to one of them happened to both. He wondered if, in some strange metaphysical way, what one experienced did affect the other as well—spooky action at a distance, as the physicists called it. He thought there must be some way to test this.

The boys raised their chicken legs to their mouths at the same time. Adam took a big bite. When Zed saw this he dropped his chicken on his plate and said, "What do Attila the Hun and Winnie-the-Pooh have in common?"

Adam wiped his lips and started to answer. Before he could, Zed clamped his hand over his brother's mouth. Evan thought it might be time to seat them on opposite sides of the table.

"The answer better be clean," Ellen said.

"It is, Mom."

"We give up," Evan said. "What do Attila the Hun and Winnie-the-Pooh have in common?"

"Their middle name!"

They all laughed, even Adam, who must have heard the joke before. Evan tried to understand why it was funny. Certainly the unexpectedness of the answer was part of the reason, and perhaps the embarrassment of being had. The listener struggles to find some deep connection between two widely different things and then learns that the solution is the simplest one possible. But why would embarrassment turn into laughter? He thought of Freud again—laughter as release of pent-up nervous energy.

It was Evan's turn now to lead the conversation, and for the first time that he could remember, he didn't have anything to say. The day's classes had been singularly uninspiring. He had almost bored himself in his "Philosophy of Religion" class explaining William James's pragmatic view of religious experience. Even when he stated that James's test of any visionary or psychological experience was what one learned from it in the long run, none of the students asked if that included mind-expanding drugs. What kind of generation was this?

Zed sneezed, and Evan thought of Anna.

"One strange thing did happen today," he said. "I took my seminar class outside, and a student, a rather bright girl, it seems, sprayed her entire face with Off! " He held up his fist and squeezed down with his thumb. "She sprayed around her nose, her eyes, her ears—it was incredible. She must have done it for half a minute. I'm surprised she didn't open her mouth and spray her tongue."

"She must be allergic to bee stings," Ellen said.

"No, I asked her at the end of class. She just hates insects."

Ellen nodded in a peculiarly understanding way.

"This makes sense to you?"

She cut off a chunk of her chicken and stuck it into her mouth with her fork still in her left hand, European style. He glanced at the boys—they had moved on to their chicken breasts and were eating them the same way.

"I can see how someone might do that," she said.

He cut off a piece of chicken, switched hands with his fork and knife, and ate it. "How could anyone spray Off! right on her face? It's crazy."

"Obviously it isn't crazy to her, and you said she's a bright girl."

"Okay, she isn't crazy for dousing her face with ethyl alcohol, butane, and DEET."

"Why are you getting so angry?" Ellen put another bite in her mouth.

"I'm not angry. I just don't see how you can say a person doing that isn't totally crazy."

"So we disagree, that's all."

That wasn't all. How could he be married to a person who could conceive of spraying her face with Off!? It was a serious question. He and Ellen differed in their reactions to many things, but this view of hers astounded him. He imagined their going to the park for a family picnic and seeing her spraying her face with insect repellent, then calling over the boys and covering them with a mist of DEET. It would be grounds for having her committed.

She reached into her bag beside her chair and pulled out a thin paperback. "I picked this up to read at lunch. It's about the Children's Crusade in the thirteenth century."

From Off! to the Crusades—such was the typical progression of topics at the dinner table. Tonight he was glad for the quick switch of time and place.

"Two Christian boys in Europe decided to take Jerusalem back from the Moslems, so they started the Children's Crusade. They set off from Germany and gathered thousands of other children along the way. The fantastic part of this story to me is that their mothers and fathers let them go."

"You won't even let us ride our bikes to the park by ourselves," Adam said.

"That's right. The park can be dangerous."

"How far's Jerusalem?" Zed asked.

"It must have been at least a thousand miles. They had to go through Switzerland and Italy to the Mediterranean. It took them months."

"Didn't they have horses?"

"The knights rode horses in the regular crusades, but the children walked the whole way."

"Where'd they sleep?"

"Anywhere they could find—in the woods, along a riverbank, under trees."

"Like camping out," Adam said, "only without a tent."

"Without food, too," she said. "They had to scrounge in the woods or beg for bread and cheese. They made it all the way to the sea, but their plan for getting across didn't work out."

"Wait, don't tell us. They were going to cut down trees and make canoes to row across?"

"No, the Mediterranean is too wide to row across. Actually, they weren't going to do anything themselves."

"They thought it would part for them, right?" Zed said.

She nodded. "They prayed all day for God to part the water, but I guess He had other things on His mind that day."

"So they gave up and went home?"

"No, these children wouldn't give up. They found a boat captain who said he would ferry them across. But once they got out to sea he tied them up below deck and steered to Egypt. He sold the children into slavery."

"They couldn't make me be a slave," Adam said as he folded his arms. "I just wouldn't work."

"They'd torture you until you did," Zed said. "They'd hang you from your thumbs—or your toes. Which is worse, Dad?"

It was their habit to consult him on such bizarre questions, and he always felt compelled to sound authoritative even when he was just making up the answer as he went. He wondered why that was a fatherly role and not a motherly one. "If you were hung from your toes you'd be upside down and all the blood would rush to your head, so that would be worse."

Zed nodded in agreement. Adam shook his head. "I'd rather be hanging from my toes because when the guards left I could sit up and untie my feet."

"You couldn't do that," Zed said.

"Bet I could."

"How much?"

Evan waved his hand between them to get their attention. "There's not going to be any betting on tortures, understand?"

"What's the worst torture you can think of, Mom?"

She speared a cherry tomato with the fork in her left hand.

"In the Middle Ages there was a diabolical punishment called the Little Ease. I've always thought that would be horrible."

"The what?"

"The Little Ease. They put you in a dungeon so small you couldn't stand up or lie down. You could only crouch, with your back bent over."

Zed slipped out of his seat into a duck-walking position. "This isn't so bad. I could do it for hours."

"Try doing it for days," she said. "No, just imagine doing it for days or weeks. It would drive you crazy."

"Little Ease," Evan said, "that's certainly putting a sunny face on it."

"What's your worst torture, Dad?"

He considered the usual possibilities: being blinded with hot irons, driven crazy by drops of water, eaten by rats. That last torture he remembered from 1984, where everyone faced his own worst fear. Had he just encountered his—being accused of a repugnant crime? Surely there were worse things to endure.

"Dad?"

"I don't remember where I heard of this," he said, "but it's called a white room. It's an all-white padded room—no window, no door handle, nothing but the pads, and no color at all. It's also sound-vacuumed so that the person inside can't even hear himself speaking. He's put in naked, and there's nothing for him to see, nothing to hear—no stimulation at all. It's just him."

The boys shrugged.

"Sounds relaxing," Ellen said.

He assumed she was kidding. In a white room, how could language survive without any objects or action or relationships to describe? The mind couldn't subsist long solely on memories.

"I think having your tongue cut out would be the worst," Adam said.

Zed stood up, and his knees crackled. "The worst would be having your tongue cut out and being deaf and blind—you couldn't talk or hear or see or anything."

"The person could still communicate through braille," Ellen said.

"Okay, their hands are cut off, too."

"They could read braille with their nose."

"Nobody can do that, Mom."

"You'd be surprised what you can learn to do if you have to." She pushed her plate away from her. At least a quarter of her chicken, tomatoes, and broccoli remained uneaten. He had suggested to her before that wasting food was setting a bad example for the boys, but she always said that teaching them to eat when they were full made no sense.

Adam pushed his half-full plate away from him. Zed did, too, and then lowered his nose to the table. "The place mat says, 'You may leave the table and go play video games.'"

She laughed and waved them away.

He woke at the sound of ringing, twisted out of the covers, and found himself standing on the cold bare floor next to the bed. The room was quiet—sound-vacuumed, it seemed.

"What?" she said, raising her head slightly. "What's wrong?"

He wasn't sure. He thought he had heard ringing, or had he been dreaming? He waited for the ring again, but there was silence. He sat down on the bed for a moment, then lay back on top of the covers. "Didn't you hear the phone?"

She grunted what he took to be "no," then reached over and patted his leg.

He closed his eyes, but he was wide awake. He thought of Anna Shepard. It was possible that spraying her face with Off! was her only eccentricity, but he doubted it. He could imagine a hundred peculiar habits. Did she sleep standing up? Did she submerge herself each night in a therapeutic bath? Did she eat all of one thing—all protein, for instance, or all carbohydrates?

The phone rang. He sat up and swung his legs off the bed. He waited through the interval of silence, and the ring came again. "That *is* the phone," he said as he got out of bed. "You hear it, don't you?"

"Of course I hear it," Ellen said. "I hope it's not about your mother."

"Why about *my* mother? Why not your mother?" He hurried into the hallway and grabbed the receiver before the answering machine picked up. "Hello?"

No one answered.

"Hello?" he said more loudly.

He heard a rasping sound, like something rubbing across the speaker. "Do you realize what time it is?" he asked as calmly as possible. Without his watch on, he didn't know himself. But certainly it was too late for a phone call.

No one answered. Evan began to count and reached twelve before the person hung up. He hung up also.

He felt himself shaking a little as he stood in the hall, dressed only in his light sweatpants, and he couldn't tell if it was from the slight chill or slight fear. Car lights passed by on the street out front, but there was no sound of an engine. He reached for the window shade and snapped it closed.

He started back to the bedroom and then thought of the boys. He decided to check on them, something he hadn't done in the middle of the night for more than a year. He stepped softly down to the opposite end of the hall. He turned the knob and pushed their door in enough to allow the light to il-luminate the beds. They looked empty. He opened the door wider and squinted—even the blankets were gone from Adam's top bunk. He stepped inside the room to see Zed's bed more clearly, and something moved at his feet. He jumped at the odd sensation and landed on a body. There was a scream, then another. He yelled himself. A pillow whacked his face and he stumbled backward. Another one hit his stomach.

"Help—Dad! Mom!"

He fell back against the bureau. "Boys—it's me."

Light flooded the room. "Dad!" Adam said from the door-way, his hand on the switch. "What are you doing in here?"

"I was just checking on you. Why aren't you in your beds?"

"We were sleeping on the floor," Adam said.

"Why on the floor?"

"Because the kids in the Children's Crusade didn't have beds," Zed said.

"That was the thirteenth century. This is the twenty-first. Now get back in your bunks."

"How come you're so mad?"

He couldn't tell them what it was like for a parent to see a child's bed empty in the middle of the night. There was no rea-son his fears should become theirs. He thought of Joyce Bon-ner's father nudging open the door of his daughter's room, half-expecting the miracle of her return to a pleasant sleep.

"I'm not really angry," he said. "I was just surprised when I didn't see you in bed, and then I stepped on one of you."

"That was me," Zed said. "You practically squashed my face with your big feet."

"Do we really have to get in bed?"

"Yes."

"How about just tonight we sleep on the floor? You won't be coming in our room again, right?"

"Okay, tonight you can stay on the floor, but that's it." He didn't know why he was being so firm about this. It just seemed like one of those obvious Parental Truths—kids should sleep in their beds. But the hard floor was probably better for them anyway. It certainly wouldn't do them any harm. And besides, he disliked being the purveyor of Parental Truths.

"I take it back," he said. "You guys can sleep on the floor every night if you want to."

The boys jumped under their comforters and bunched up their pillows under their heads. "That's okay, Dad, the bunk's more comfortable."

He turned out the light. Cool air blew in through the window, and he thought of lying down between his sons, wrapping himself in their comforters, and listening all night to their peaceful breathing.

"Love you," one of them said in the darkness.

"Yeah, me too."

"I love you both," he said and gently closed the door behind him.

CHAPTER 9

A t the end of the first partial week of classes, Evan was walking across the windy Arts Quad thinking of Willard Van Orman Quine. The famed Harvard logician had typed all of his books on a 1927 Remington typewriter, which he modified by replacing various punctuation characters with mathematical symbols. When asked how he could do without the question mark, he replied, "I deal with certainties."

Evan imagined how he would modify his own 1960s-era Remington, which he still used sometimes for first drafts of articles and speeches. When did he ever use the equal sign, the brackets, or greater and lesser? He could change them all to question marks and probably still grind the thin metal arms flat in a matter of years. Question marks, it seemed to him, were indispensable not just to language but to teaching as well. What tool was more useful than a well-crafted question, especially directed at oneself?

As he entered the Humanities Faculty reception area, he leaned over the partition and saw Carla sitting with her arms folded, staring at the phone. He said hello and she said hello, but without looking up. "Anything wrong?"

She kept staring at the phone. "I'm trying to make it ring."

"How are you doing that?"

"I'm willing it to. People always say I have a very strong will, so I'm trying to do something with it."

"I would think you'd be willing the thing *not* to ring."

Carla shifted her head from one hand to the other, her eyes fixed on the phone. "I put in my vacation request last week to Personnel, and they said they'd let me know by the end of today."

"When do you want to go?"

"December 12th. My boyfriend's taking me to Hawaii. He already bought the tickets, so I'd have to quit in order to go, if I don't get the week off."

"Personnel is pretty good about accommodating requests, Carla. I'm sure yours will go through fine."

"From your lips to God's ears, Professor."

The image of God with ears struck him as funny, but he didn't show his amusement. Carla took her religion seriously. "God's not really in the habit of taking my advice," he said, "particularly about vacations."

"You never know. You may be just the person He's been waiting to hear from."

God with scales, toting up the weight of human opinion on

one side or the other. What in Carla's faith would make her envision His decision-making like that?

"Well, rather than bothering God about this, wouldn't you like me to call Personnel and put in a good word for you?"

The phone rang. She crossed the fingers of her left hand and answered with her right. "PsychologySociologyAnthropologyPhilosophy." She scowled and uncrossed her fingers. "Hold and I'll connect you with Professor Raines." She looked up at Evan. "No, that's okay. I'm dealing with it."

He turned toward his office and saw a young man swiveling in the visitor's chair, his feet lifted a few inches off the ground. The boy's eyes were closed and his head thrown back, like a little kid on an amusement ride.

"Who's that?"

"He said he had an appointment with you," Carla whispered and then tugged on her left ear. Evan tried to remember, was this some kind of signal that they had once agreed upon? "I figured it was all right to let him wait in there, since he had an appointment, and you were a little late."

"He didn't have an appointment."

Evan squeezed into his office past the swinging legs and let his briefcase fall to the floor. The young man's eyes popped open, and he dropped his feet to stop himself from spinning. Then he pushed a sheet of paper across the desk. "I need you to sign this."

Evan did not like such abrupt requests, particularly from someone who had lied to get into his office. Yet he seemed harmless, with an oval face, soft cheeks, and a small bit of hair growing on his chin, like a patch of grass left inexplicably uncut on a lawn. He was wearing thick metal studs in each ear, and Evan imagined him leaning over an anvil as a friend pounded through his flesh with an awl.

"Are you a student of mine?"

"Yeah, Philosophy 101."

Evan nodded at the paper. "And that is?"

"A drop form."

The first "Intro to Philosophy" class had ended barely an hour ago. He pictured the boy sprinting across campus to the registrar's office to get the required paperwork, then dashing over here. You had to admire the effort.

"Why would you want to drop out so soon?"

"Philosophy sucks," the boy said. "No offense."

The tacked-on apology irritated Evan more than the insult itself. He picked up his paperweight—an oblong plastic container of blue liquid—and shook it. Tiny blue bubbles bobbed from side to side. "You could have simply said you don't appreciate philosophy or it's not especially interesting to you. Why choose words that will certainly offend me, a philosophy professor, and then try to cancel them out with 'no offense'?"

The boy didn't answer immediately, and Evan was encouraged that he might be thinking.

"Okay, I don't find philosophy very useful," he said. "How's that?"

Evan swung about in his chair and stacked his day's texts and lecture notes on the shelf. "Philosophy is the rational investigation of the principles and truths of being, knowledge, and conduct," he said, with his back purposely to his visitor. "In other words, it's thinking about everything you do in life." He swiveled around again. "You don't believe that might be worthwhile to you?"

The young man shook his head. "Philosophy is like masturbation is to sex."

Evan was familiar with this mangled quotation. Each semester at least one student, invariably male, managed to insert some version of it into the class conversation. "I assume you mean 'Philosophy is to the real world as masturbation is to sex.' Marx said that. He was wrong about a lot of things, including philosophy."

"Yeah, well, it still sucks."

Evan was beginning to wish he had just signed the form and not asked questions. He reached for the paper and scribbled his name at the bottom. The capital E and B were legible enough, but the rest of the letters rippled together, like a child's drawing of a wave. It surprised him that his signature had disintegrated so much. He remembered learning to write, hunched over his school desk filling pages with perfect capital Os. He had been very good at keeping his pencil between the blue lines. His father had actually praised him for it.

The boy grabbed the paper and headed for the door.

"Tell me," Evan said, "why did you choose to take philosophy in the first place? Nobody forced you to sit through three hours of thinking each week."

The boy folded the paper a couple of times and stuffed it into the back pocket of his jeans. "I need another humanities course to graduate, and my advisor said you were hurting for students, so I figured, how boring could it be?"

"Apparently very boring," Evan said.

"Yeah, it was," the boy said. "No offense."

CHAPTER 10

He had a half-dozen calls waiting for him to return, but he decided to make just two before heading home. First he called the correspondent for *The New England Journal of Philosophic Inquiry* to do a phone interview about *Disturbing Minds*. The questions—about Rousseau's madness, James's peculiar family, and Wittgenstein's repressed sexuality—were so expected that he began to wonder if he had written an entirely predictable book.

As he picked up the receiver to call Dean Santos, who had left his usual "respond at your earliest convenience" message, Evan saw the shadow of a man pass the reception area, turn around, and stop. Carla had left a few minutes before, which meant no one was monitoring access to the Humanities.

He had often thought that the college should institute some kind of security for after 5 P.M., when the receptionists went home.

He stood up at his desk and called out, "May I help you?"

The stranger moved out of sight. In a few seconds he reappeared in the doorway.

"Hello, Professor, remember me?"

Of course Evan remembered the diminutive detective with the unsynchronized eyes. Who could forget his interrogator of less than a week before? He wondered whether Malloy would come out so late in the day to deliver an apology or news that someone else had been arrested.

"Yes, I remember. What can I do for you?"

"We've had some new information come to us, and I wanted to discuss it with you."

"What kind of information?"

"It concerns your whereabouts on August 23, about three P.M."

Evan tried not to blink, or look away, or smile, or show concern. But was not reacting an even more telling kind of reaction in this particular situation? And should he acknowledge right away that he had been at the park that day? He considered how to phrase it—*"It's interesting you should bring that up again because my wife and I were talking it over, and I think I probably was there around the time you were asking about."*

Malloy scratched his head, leaving a wad of hair sticking out above his ear. It gave him a homeless sort of look. "Our informant has made a positive identification . . ."

The detective paused here, and it seemed to Evan that he was waiting for some prompting. "Is that so?"

"Yes, our informant has stated quite definitely that the person at the scene of the crime in the gray Jetta with the license plate starting with EZ and the Pearce College sticker on the back windshield was, ah, you."

Out of that whole sentence, Evan latched onto one key word. "You're calling it a *crime* now?"

"We believe a crime was committed, yes."

"You're not certain?"

"It's difficult to be certain about anything in life, I've learned that. I mean, it's not even sure that the sun will come up tomorrow, right? Just because it always has doesn't mean it always will."

Evan was beginning to think that the detective might be smarter than he let on. Could he have read Hume's theory of constant correlation at some point in his life, or had he just stumbled on the concept?

Malloy smoothed down the hair over his ear, which confirmed to Evan how small changes could make a person look entirely different. Disguising oneself would not be so hard, he thought. "You say the man identified me, Detective, but how could he do that? I wasn't in any lineup."

"We presented your picture along with a number of others, and our informant identified you as the occupant of the car in the parking lot at Eastfield State Park August 23, around three P.M."

"You have my picture?"

Malloy nodded.

"What did you do, take it without telling me? Is that even legal?"

"We didn't take it, no. The dean's office obliged us with a recent photo."

"Wait, you mean you went to Dean Santos and told him I'm a suspect in a kidnapping?"

"We didn't tell them anything over there, except that we needed a picture of you."

"Oh, well, that's much better. You left it up to their imagination as to what terrible thing I might have done that causes the police to come looking for a picture of me." Evan snatched the pink memo note from his desk and waved it in front of Malloy. "And this is the result."

"I'm sorry you're upset. But there was no other way to get a positive ID on you and your car at the park that day."

"Why did you have to prove that? I said I may have been there. In fact, I'm pretty sure I was because I had to get my boys at camp that day and I was early, so I stopped there."

The detective took out a small black notebook. "You're admitting now that you were at the park on the day and time of the disappearance of Joyce Bonner?"

"It's not *admitting*—I'm . . . *allowing* that I was probably there, which I wasn't sure about before."

"What time was that?"

"A little before three, I guess. I was going to pick up my boys and I had some time to kill, so I sat by the lake."

The detective wrote something on his pad. "Are you also allowing now that you talked to Joyce Bonner?"

"No, I'm not allowing anything else except that I was there. I didn't speak to anybody. I didn't even get out of my car."

"You're certain of that?"

He pictured himself pulling into the park, turning toward the lake, and stopping in the lot near the canoe rental. He saw himself adjust the seat backward so that he could stretch his legs out as he gazed at the choppy surface of the lake. Then he took out a paper to jot down ideas as inspiration came to him.

He tried to remember if he had seen anyone—perhaps even another suspect. But Evan remembered no one.

"You're certain you didn't get out of the car?" the detective asked again.

"Yes."

"Well, we're going to have to discuss that a little bit, because our informant saw you opening your car door and getting in, which means that you had gotten out of it at some point. That's pretty logical. Is our informant mistaken?"

Evan sat up straighter in his chair. Who was this genderless person who had observed him, noted him, and reported him? Didn't he have the right to confront an accuser in person?

"Yes, your informant is mis—" The word stopped on his tongue as he remembered getting out of his car for a few seconds to stretch his legs. He had walked to the trash barrel, perhaps ten yards away, and thrown out a few pages of unusable notes he had been making for his speech to the incoming freshman class.

"He's what, Professor?"

Again Evan faced the choice—change his story or maintain it. This time he decided to go with a clear, unequivocal assertion. "He's right, I did get out of my car for a minute . . . to stretch."

The detective reached into his jacket pocket and pulled out a plastic bag with papers inside. "And to throw these away?"

Evan reached for the bag, but the detective pulled it back. "No touching, please."

Evan leaned closer and saw his notes. He could make out a few words—*mania, mayhem, the noise of the rain*—and parts of words, written in red ink. "Yes, see, I was writing down some ideas for a short talk I had to give. I was going to refer to my book coming out, but I decided that wasn't appropriate, so I tossed the papers."

The detective saw *Disturbing Minds* on the desk and picked it up.

"You mean this?"

"Yes."

"*Mania, Mayhem, and Melancholy in the Philosophic Life*—I guess there's a lot of that going on then?"

"A lot of what?"

Malloy pointed at the words—*mania, mayhem, melancholy*.

"Among some well-known philosophers, yes—Rousseau, Nietzsche, Russell, Wittgenstein, of course. But there are quite a few perfectly boring philosophers I could name, too, like—"

"Those eyes," the detective said, "are they yours?"

Evan took another look at the book cover. The eyes were the color of dark, wet sand. They seemed to be looking, even staring, but there was no sense of an object to the gaze, at least nothing of this world. He saw no resemblance to his own.

"No, they're not mine. They're Wittgenstein's eyes, from a picture of him as a young man."

"And the outline of the head—that him, too?"

"Yes, that's him, too."

The detective turned to scan the office. "It rained that day, didn't it?"

Evan tried to think, what could rain have to do with this case? "I don't remember. I doubt it, though, we had the drought for most of the summer."

"Yes, but that day, there was a brief shower mid-afternoon. They closed the information booth early."

"If you say so."

"It's not if I say so, Professor. Rain is rain." He held the plastic bag to eye level. "These words—*the noise of the rain*—were they part of your speech?"

"No, I mean, none of this got into my speech. And the speech I did write I didn't even use."

"Was the rain beating down on your windshield?"

"I told you, I don't remember it raining at all. That phrase is part of a sentence—'Even if his dream were actually connected with the noise of the rain . . .'"

"A dream of yours?"

"No, those were Wittgenstein's last words—his last written words, I mean."

"Wittgenstein again, eh?"

Evan nodded.

"Maybe I should try reading your book sometime. Or is it only for other professors like yourself?"

"It's not an academic treatise, if that's what you mean. Anyone could read it."

"Well, I'm anyone."

Evan did not know how to interpret the remark—was the detective being ironic, self-deprecating, or what?

"I'll let you get back to work now," Malloy said. "I can see you're busy." He extended his hand and Evan took it. They shook for just slightly longer than he felt two men should.

As soon as the detective left, Evan dialed the dean's office. How would he explain the police's request for a photograph? He thought he might say, "*Just a little case of misidentification I'm trying to clear up. There's nothing—*"

The message system answered, and Evan hit 1 to reach the dean's mailbox.

"Hello, Dean Santos, this is Evan Birch. I received your message late in the day. I trust everything is fine with you and that the matter you wanted to discuss with me can wait till Monday. If not, please call me at home this weekend."

Evan hung up. He heard steps in the reception area again and went to the door. A man and a young woman were walking down the hallway toward the sociology department. From behind, he couldn't recognize either of them. He thought she might be a student. As soon as they turned out of sight, the young woman laughed, and the sound of her echoed throughout the Humanities.

CHAPTER 11

For the first time in months he steered into the circular driveway in front of his house instead of parking in the garage. Perhaps it was the unexpected visit from the detective that had thrown off his routine, but the idea of entering through the front door suddenly appealed to him. The color of it was Mediterranean blue—Ellen's choice—and it seemed like a portal now into some island hideaway. He wondered why he didn't come in this way more often.

It was just past 6 P.M. as he got out of the Jetta, and the low sun reminded him of the light when he was pulled over on the highway. It occurred to him that rarely was life consistent—bad things didn't necessarily happen during storms or darkness.

People died on sunny days as often as rainy ones. At least he assumed it was so.

He turned his key in the lock, but the heavy door wouldn't open. He shoved his shoulder against it. Why had they spent extra for oak? It seemed unlikely they would ever need protection from a battering ram.

The door finally gave in to his weight, and he stepped inside. "Donuts!" he called out as he stooped to pick up the mail. He scanned the bills and circulars and felt something wrapped in plastic—a thick, glossy magazine called *Ethical Times*. He flipped the magazine over and checked the label: PROF E. BIRCH.

The hall floor creaked, and Ellen emerged from the basement carrying a large wooden fish. "You came in the front?"

"Bold of me, wasn't it, to come in my own front door?"

She took the donuts from him, opened the bag, and breathed in the sweet aroma. "Jelly," she said, "my favorite. What did you do wrong?"

"Huh?"

"I'm kidding. I just wondered what the occasion was. You never stop for donuts."

He wasn't sure why he had pulled into College Donuts before leaving campus, just as he couldn't explain the impulse to come in the front door. Not all behaviors had conscious thoughts behind them. Some behaviors were just behaviors— describable certainly, but untraceable to rational decision- making. Perhaps some omniscient viewer of the world could untangle all the strands of impulses and influences leading to an individual act, but Evan didn't see himself in any such position even in his own life—perhaps especially in his own life. Besides, she was just asking about donuts.

"I guess I just felt like it," he said.

She closed the bag. "I'll keep them for after dinner, surprise the boys."

He held up the magazine. "This wasn't your idea of a joke was it, ordering this in my name?"

"*Ethical Times*. Not me. Maybe one of your philosophy friends sent it to you."

He read the article titles out loud—"Telling the Truth, Even When It Hurts!" "10 Steps to a More Ethical You!" "Getting in Touch with Your Inner Angel!" The rampant use of the exclamation point surely indicated vacuousness. There was a mark of punctuation he could live without on his Remington.

"It might be one of those takeoff magazines," she said, "like a *Harvard Lampoon* parody."

Evan ripped open the plastic and turned to the first editorial page. The staff box said, "Published Monthly by The Society for a New American Ethics, Wichita, Kansas." *New American Ethics*—that struck him as a curious juxtaposition of words, but hardly hilarious.

"Throw it away if you don't want it," Ellen said. She opened the bag again, took out a donut, turned it over as if to confirm that it was indeed a donut, and bit into it. Dark jelly oozed over her fingers.

He noted how quickly her intention to keep the donuts for dessert had melted away but decided not to call attention to it. She had so few small indulgences, and she did not like them commented on.

"If my name's on their mailing list, throwing this away won't stop it from coming again next month." He picked up the portable phone from the hall table and held the magazine at arm's length to see the number for the subscriptions department. Ellen licked her fingers and headed for the kitchen, the fish under one arm. He dialed, and a live voice answered on the first ring.

"Thank you for calling Ethical Publications. Are you in-quiring about an existing subscription?"

"No—I mean yes, apparently, that's why I'm calling."

"Name please."

"Birch—B-I-R-C-H—Evan."

After a moment the woman said, "I don't show any Birch Evan on our subscriber lists."

"It's Evan Birch—Evan's the first name."

"Hold a moment . . . Okay, I have a Prof E. Birch, ten Paris Drive."

"Yes, that's *Prof.* as in Professor."

"How may I help you?"

"I'm getting your ethics magazine and I don't know why."

"Which magazine is that?"

"How many do you have?"

"There are eleven in our ethics group."

Eleven magazines on ethics? Who in America was reading such things? He couldn't imagine. "I'm calling about *Ethical Times,*" he said.

"Hold a moment . . . Okay, this shows you have a gift sub-scription."

"A gift from whom?"

"Hold a moment . . . Okay, your gift is from Anonymous."

"Who's Anonymous?"

"I'm sorry, sir, 'Anonymous' means the person didn't leave a name."

"An anonymous person can order magazines through you and send them to someone else?"

"Certainly, sir, it's called a gift. If you would prefer some-thing else, we could switch your subscription to *Better World* or *Choices Monthly* or—"

"No, I don't want to replace it. I want to know why I'm getting it. You must have Anonymous's address."

"I'm sure it's in our billing computer, but we can't give out that information. You might try our Ethical Hotline. They're very helpful with all sorts of problems."

"I don't have a problem."

"I'm glad to hear that, sir. Good day."

When Evan hung up he had the distinct feeling of being out-witted by an order taker at *Ethical Times*. He thought about his comment to her—"I don't have a problem." Of course he did. What was being investigated for kidnapping a teenage girl if not a problem? He considered what the Ethical Hotline would advise him. Probably to tell the truth at all times to all questions and take the consequences, which he would so richly deserve. Ethics routinely was stripped down in the popular mind to "always tell the truth." But he didn't have much faith that in this strange situation, the truth would save him.

He didn't tell Ellen of the detective's visit. He hadn't planned on withholding the information. But as she was deveining shrimp for dinner she asked how his day had been, and he found himself saying "uneventful." He wished he had used a more accurate word, such as "unproductive," which still avoided mentioning Malloy's reappearance.

He did not like deceiving her. He might have corrected him-self right away, but she began relating Tyco's latest achieve-ment, which had something to do with looking in a mirror, and he began analyzing the detective. Malloy seemed to be a man utterly without context, and thus, unreadable. He had left that afternoon as enigmatically as he had arrived. Would he show up again? Should Evan consider himself still a suspect? Or had admitting his presence at the park sufficiently explained things? He didn't have any idea, and the reason he didn't was because of the baffling manner of Detective Robert Malloy.

"So what do you think?" she said as she scraped the mound of shrimp into a frying pan with garlic, onions, and celery. "If Tyco had the vocal cords to speak, could she understand herself?"

"I don't know."

She stirred the frying pan.

"I know you don't know, but what do you *think*?"

"I think I don't know."

"Okay then, what would your favorite philosopher say?"

Her question surprised him. "Who's that?"

"Wittgenstein, of course. He's on your cover."

"He had one of the most interesting minds of the twentieth century. That doesn't make him my favorite." Evan leaned over the frying pan and inhaled the fragrance of garlic. "Actually, there was a poll taken of philosophers a few years ago about who they considered the all-time greatest. Wittgenstein came in fifth."

"Philosophers can be ranked?"

"You wouldn't think so, would you?"

Ellen poured more oil into the frying pan and then added pea pods. "All I know about Wittgenstein is that he focused on language and thought. Was that only related to humans?"

"Mostly to humans. But he did say that if a lion could speak, we wouldn't understand him."

Ellen stirred the pan, and the pea pods turned a brilliant emerald. "Maybe we couldn't understand Tyco, but I think she would be perfectly capable of understanding herself."

"Yes," Evan said, "I suppose you're right."

CHAPTER 12

On the first cool day of September, he stood in his living room trying to remember why he had just come there. He saw the marble chessboard, the pot of pink asters, the row of wooden elephants on the mantel. Nothing prompted his memory. It annoyed him to think that his brain—three pounds of gray matter, tens of billions of neurons, just forty-nine years into existence—could forget why he was where he was.

He turned to go back to his study as Ellen entered the room, a Sam Adams in her hand. She never drank beer. She rarely drank in the afternoon at all. Why today? He was going to ask her when she said, "Have you seen *The Art of Happiness?*"

He gestured toward the stack of books on the large chest.

"Should be where it always is." He reached past her shoulder and turned over the top book. The serene, bemused face of the Dalai Lama peered out at him.

"I've been thinking about this story all day," she said as she opened the book to the middle. "It's the perfect example of human perversity."

"You've been thinking about perversity all day?"

She flipped a few pages. "Not all day. I was watching the boys at soccer this morning, and there was one big kid on the other team who kept running into everybody on purpose. He'd knock someone over and then grin, even if he was called for a foul. So I started thinking about the lengths people go to to hurt each other, and that reminded me of this story of a Chinese teacher in Tibet. He knew his Buddhist students revered all life, so one day he assigned them to bring in something they'd killed. Then he graded them." Ellen consulted the page. "One point for a fly or worm, two points for a mouse, five for a cat." She looked up at Evan. "I can't think of a more perverse thing a person could do."

"How much for killing the teacher—a hundred?"

She closed the book and set it back on the pile, faceup. "That's the Western reaction. It wouldn't enter the minds of the Tibetans."

"It's strange," he said as he gazed at the Dalai Lama's beatific smile.

"I think it's just being consistent."

"No, I mean it's strange that the book was facedown. It's never facedown."

She took a quick swig from the bottle, and he observed the exact movement of her arm, no wasted motion.

"I bought it for you last Christmas, remember? You read it on New Year's Day while I was watching football with the boys. That's when you decided to read a book a day. Since then the face of the Dalai Lama has been staring up at me every time I come into the living room."

She yawned, and he saw one bottom tooth turned sideways, out of line with the others, a small imperfection he wasn't sure he had noticed before.

"I guess it's a little strange," she said, "but not worth obsessing about."

It seemed natural to him that a philosophy professor—anyone, in fact—would be intrigued by the exceptions to the normal pattern of life, as this was, even if a small example. That was curiosity, not obsession. "You keep the book faceup—for good karma's sake, right? I doubt it flipped itself over." He turned away and saw the music cabinet door sticking straight out. "Why's this open?"

She picked up the *Times* from the chair. "Maybe it popped out on its own."

He closed the door, and it clicked securely. He jumped up and down a little. He rapped the side of the cabinet with the palm of his hand.

"All right," she said, "it didn't just pop open."

He raised the plastic covering to the turntable and lifted off the album. The title surprised him—"Funny Girl—A New Musical." "You were playing Barbra Streisand?"

She fell back on the sofa. "Not likely."

"Then how did it get on the turntable? Adam and Zed know they're not to use this."

She opened the newspaper. "Somebody visiting could have put that on months ago and we wouldn't have noticed. I can't even remember the last time we played an album."

"Three weeks ago," he said. "We took the boys to E.O. Wilson's lecture on the little creatures that rule the world. On the way home 'Tommy' was on the radio, and I told them how I played pinball when I was their age. Then I put the album on for them while we were making burritos. You were taking a shower." He wondered at his specific recollection of these unremarkable activities. Why were some trivial events so memorable and others not?

"So three weeks ago you used the record player. What do you think happened since then, we've had visitors from the spirit world who have been reading the Dalai Lama and playing 'Funny Girl' while we were out? Does that make sense?"

"It wouldn't have to be spirits."

She held up the newspaper. "Look at this." In the picture a bony, malnourished child was squatting in a road. Even from halfway across the room her flesh seemed transparent to him, as if layers of skin had been worn away. "You can see the girl's in terrible pain," Ellen said, "but she isn't crying. It makes me think there's a point in human suffering where the body can't even spare tears."

This was a familiar habit of hers—juxtaposing some universal theme like suffering to his more mundane concern. He thought she was missing his larger point. "It could have been a person in the house," he said.

Ellen turned the page on the malnourished child. "You mean you think somebody came in while we were gone one day in order to read the Dalai Lama and play 'Funny Girl'?"

"Could you please stop saying reading the Dalai Lama and playing 'Funny Girl'? It doesn't make any difference that insignificant things were disturbed in the house, it's that anything was." He picked up the business section from the coffee table in front of her. "If I know I left this paper on this table when I went out and came back and found it on the sofa, I'd wonder about that, wouldn't you?"

"No, I'd assume I'd left it on the sofa, just where I found it when I came back."

"All right, I grant that you're above thinking about this kind of thing, but obviously I'm not. Are the boys still downstairs?"

"Oh come on, Evan, don't bother them about this."

"Bother them? They're ten years old. What can they be doing that I shouldn't bother them?"

He called them from the hallway, and in a few seconds they came running up from the family room. Adam appeared first, holding a soldering iron. Zed was right behind him, a roll of solder in his hand. Evan resisted the impulse to ask what they were doing. "Did either of you pick up the Dalai Lama book recently?"

"The *dolly* book?"

He took *The Art of Happiness* from the top of the pile and held it up for them. "This book, by the Dalai Lama."

"No, Dad."

"Nope."

Normally he could tell their honest no from their guilty no by the slight hesitancy in their voices. They were reluctant liars. This time he wasn't sure. "It's okay if you did. I just want to know if you happened to pick it up recently."

They looked at each other and shook their heads. "Can we go now?"

He put the book on the shelf, faceup, then saw the record album. "One more thing, were either of you playing 'Funny Girl' by any chance?"

"What's that?"

He showed them the album cover. "'Funny Girl'—by Barbra Streisand."

"No way. She looks weird. And you told us to keep our grubby hands off, remember?"

"Okay, the inquisition is over," Ellen said, "you're free to go."

They dashed down the hallway, shoving each other as they went. When he gave up trying to stop them from running in the house, he discovered he liked seeing their bursts of energy—sliding down the hall in their socks, grabbing the doorjambs to anchor themselves, then taking the steps by twos and threes. He couldn't remember the last time he felt like running to do something.

"Satisfied?" Ellen said.

He sat on the sofa next to her and leaned his body into hers. "No, the mystery has not been solved."

She drummed on his knee with her fingers. "If it would make you feel better you could always take a Polaroid of the living room before we go out and then check it when we come back to see if anything has moved."

"Has *been* moved," he said.

"Right, if anything has *been* moved. Of course, you'll have to take pictures of the bedroom and kitchen, too. How about the inside of the refrigerator? Maybe our visitor likes to eat while he's here. You'll need to make sure no food has been surreptitiously consumed."

He smiled at the ridiculousness of his position and kissed her on the cheek. He also wondered where the Polaroid camera had gotten to.

Later, after he had surveyed all the rooms from the garage to the attic and not found anything else out of place, he saw Ellen in the hallway leaning against the door to the linen closet. She was reading *Hamlet*. He thought he should make conversation to show that his attention was not entirely focused on solving the mysteries of the house. As always, he had her reading to talk about. "So, what part are you in?"

" 'O God, I could be bounded in a nutshell, and count myself a king of infinite space.' " She closed the book on her finger. "I'm kind of stuck on that line. I've read it about twenty times. I can't imagine a more perfect bit of writing."

"If it's perfect, none could be better."

"It makes me wonder why there aren't any Shakespeares anymore. Why no Mozarts or Beethovens or Michelangelos?"

"We're not a civilization of artistic genius," Evan said as he leaned against the wall next to her. "Creativity has been smoothed out into the masses. Any system that develops long enough will tend to eliminate the spikes of performance on either end."

"So everybody ends up together in the middle," she said. "Maybe that's better than having a few geniuses." She opened *Hamlet* again. " 'What a piece of work is man, how noble in reason, how infinite in faculties, in form and moving how express and admirable, in action how like an angel, in apprehension how like a god: the beauty of the world, the paragon of animals; and yet, to me, what is this quintessence of dust?' "

Evan considered the question personally: What was his quintessence? He had always thought stability was his trademark characteristic, or at least, so people said. Of course, they often confused outward behavior with inner personality. He swiped his hand on the ridge above the linen closet door, and a thin powder darkened the tips of his fingers. "So this is what we were and what we become. Not exactly a comforting thought."

"Actually, I think it is comforting. When you know where you're headed, there's no reason to struggle for some different outcome. Nobody comes out ahead or behind in the end."

"But in between people do come out ahead or behind."

She nodded, then just stood there, without any apparent intention to say anything else. She seemed to be staring at the floor.

"What are you thinking?"

"Nothing in particular."

"After nineteen years, I can tell when you're thinking."

"That's not so hard. I'm always thinking."

"I mean something specific. You look down and to the right a little, as if there's something on the floor by your foot."

Ellen lifted her head. "You've been a bit unsettled lately, and I was thinking that, with what happened, you're going through first-world fear."

"First-world fear as in *not real* fear?"

"It's real to you."

"But not as important as third-world fear?"

Ellen shrugged. "Third-world fear is about survival. A person living in the first world has the luxury of worrying about other things—like inconvenience, suspicion . . . books and records out of place in the house."

It didn't feel to him like a luxury to be a suspect in a kidnapping. If he could claim to be an expert about anything, he figured it should be his own life. But at that particular moment, that life was utter mystery to him. And he thought it would be so no matter which world he lived in.

CHAPTER 13

Evan picked up the nearest utensil, a knife, and with it pinned a tea bag under the hot water in his mug. Ellen set a plate of wheat toast on the kitchen table and checked her watch.

"Seven minutes," she said.

"Do you want me to call them?"

"I already did three times. They have to take some responsibility for making the bus."

He scooped the tea bag out of his mug and stirred. The water turned dark, and he inhaled the vanilla-hazelnut fragrance. If he had never heard of vanilla and hazelnut, how would he describe the aroma? He didn't think he knew the words that would capture the subtle smell. Perhaps they didn't exist.

Perhaps humans didn't have the capacity to parse out the component elements of such simple things. Vanilla smelled like vanilla, hazelnut like hazelnut. These statements were the purest of tautologies, but what purpose did their certainty serve? He could see in them only what Wittgenstein did— their "self-returning emptiness." Evan sipped his tea, and it tasted good.

The boys came rushing into the kitchen and dropped their bookbags on the floor. They were wearing shorts and T-shirts, despite the chill of the morning. Adam's shirt had Aristotle on the front, his head leaning on his hand in a thinker's position. Zed's shirt said "Harvard Sucks."

Evan pointed with his spoon at Zed. "Should he really be wearing that to school?"

Ellen peeled a banana, broke it in two, and gave a half to each twin. "It's not in the best of taste, but you can't argue with the sentiment."

"You sure you're allowed to wear that, Zed?"

The boy stuffed the banana into his mouth. "I've worn it before, Dad."

"And the teachers didn't say anything?"

Zed drank his orange juice in one long swallow, and when he was done his lips were yellow. " 'Suck' isn't a swear."

"Yes it is," Adam said, "it means—"

Evan tapped his arm. "We know what it means."

"I was just—"

Evan tapped him again. "No definitions."

Zed took his glass to the sink. "The teachers never see it anyway. I keep my jacket on all day."

"Why do you do that?"

Zed looked over his shoulder as if amazed at the question. "To cover up the shirt, Dad."

For the first time that he could remember, he wasn't eager to go to work. He assumed that being accused of a crime had much to do with the lassitude that had suddenly overtaken him. But he also suspected he was becoming uneasy with teaching itself. Standing in front of several classrooms of students each day required a certain sense of authority that he felt ebbing in himself lately. Sometimes he felt like a fraud, a teacher who prodded his students to think deeply about their own existences but did very little of it himself.

He was driving to the college the back way, through the center of town, instead of bypassing it on the highway. He glanced into backyards and onto porches. He peered through shop windows. He stared inside passing cars. Everywhere he saw people moving, going somewhere to do some thing, and the immense weight of humanity suddenly overwhelmed him. So many people—more than six billion of them—all with their special desires and ambitions bumping up against each other. The world would surely be better off, he thought, with one fewer person trying to get ahead.

If one isn't striving to get ahead, then what is one striving for? Ellen would ask him this question, and he didn't know how to respond. He wondered if this was the stage of his life when he could frankly admit that he had no answers. For instance, he couldn't say why being mistakenly arrested had so disturbed his equanimity. Where had his sense of self gone? Why couldn't he see the familiar patterns of his life anymore? How could he not even tell one son from the other?

A more immediate question came to him. Why had he chosen the labyrinthine route through town this morning, which meant crawling through traffic sandwiched between SUVs the

GEORGE HARRAR

size of buses? He hated not being able to see over them or around them or through them. He felt small. Driving an SUV was one of the most clear-cut acts of selfishness in the modern world, an indignity to the environment as well as to fellow drivers. Yet millions of otherwise community-minded people did it every day. It baffled him how they could retain their civic self-image. How would *Ethical Times* explain it?

As he approached the intersection at Five Corners the light turned yellow, and he stopped quickly. From behind someone honked. Evan looked over his shoulder, and a man in a small red car was shaking his fist. He turned to the front again and saw a woman walking with a child in a jacket several sizes too big. Every few steps the girl lost her footing, and the woman yanked her standing again.

He watched them until the light went green, and then he turned right to follow them, even though it was not his route. The woman was dragging the limp girl behind her now, like something dead. He could imagine the child's arm popping out of its socket.

His foot eased off the accelerator. The car coasted a little. The woman and girl, linked by their hands, grew smaller in his side-view mirror. They would fade away soon, be gone from his consciousness. Yet still the woman would be dragging the girl. He would not be able to get that image out of his head all day, long after the dragging had in reality stopped.

Evan turned the wheel sharply, swerving the car into a grassy patch by the side of the road. He jumped out as the two turned up an alleyway.

"Excuse me," he called in a voice just loud enough for them to hear. He wondered whether he really wanted them to, or was he making a purposely futile effort?

Evan trotted after them. "Hello?" he called more loudly.

108

The child twisted her body to see him, and her feet slipped out from under her again. The woman jerked the girl upright, and for a moment he saw her blotchy little face. It showed no expression at all. That scared him—why wasn't she crying? Couldn't her body spare the tears?

"Stop!" he yelled.

The woman looked around. "What do you want?"

He wasn't sure. Was he just relieving his own distress at seeing the child treated badly—like Thomas Hobbes giving money to a beggar—or did he truly care about the girl? Evan couldn't decide which was his motivation, but either way, he would act the same.

He pointed at the child. "If you keep pulling her like that, you could dislocate her arm."

The girl plopped down on the sidewalk and scooped up some dirt in her hand. The woman swatted her arm, knocking the dirt back to the ground. "Mind your own business," she said.

"It is my business. You can't abuse a child just because she's yours."

"Not mine," the woman said with a bitterness that surprised him. "I wouldn't have one like this." Then she leaned over and lifted the bulky body to her hip. "Now go away," she said, shooing him with her free hand, "leave me alone."

He watched as she lugged the little girl to the corner and turned out of sight. What then? Did she drop the squirming weight to the ground and drag it again?

Evan returned to his car, climbed inside, and clutched his hands together to keep them from shaking. He couldn't believe what he had just done. It amazed him that he had jumped out of his car and admonished a perfect stranger—why were strangers always *perfect,* anyway?—about how to handle a child. He had intruded into their lives as if he knew all of their history, all of their circumstances, and could determine what was right. What had possessed him? There was another question for which he had no answer.

Walking across the expansive Arts Quad to his first class, Evan heard his name called in the resounding baritone of Dean Santos. Evan turned around and was surprised to see that the dean was so far away, almost at the library. Several students passed by, and as always they lowered their heads or coughed, anything not to make eye contact with a professor and thus be compelled to utter an awkward hello. Evan felt like grabbing one of them by the arm and engaging him with some odd question or comment. But forced conversation, he supposed, could be viewed as harassment of a certain kind. Besides, he feared he would encounter not just shock on the faces of the students, but boredom as well.

"Professor Birch," the dean said as he approached with a large mongrel dog running ahead of him, "I tried to reach you."

Evan felt compelled to pet the mutt. At the same time he diverted its prying nose. "Yes, I know, I returned your call late Friday, but you had left." Of course, today was Wednesday. He could have tried the dean again on Monday or Tuesday. "I've been meaning to get back to you," Evan said.

"Well, I'll just come out with it. I had a visitor in my office last week."

"I think I heard about that."

"Then you can imagine my embarrassment when he pulled your book from his briefcase and asked me what I thought of it. What was I to say?"

Evan was confused. The dean was chasing him down to

talk about *Disturbing Minds?* What about the police and his photograph? "Well, Dean, of course I wouldn't presume to know what you think about my book."

"How can I think anything? I didn't even know it was out. We have a long-standing policy in this school that professors make sure the dean receives a copy of any publication as soon as it appears. I'm surprised you weren't aware of that."

"I'm sorry, Dean Santos. Of course I asked my publisher to send you a copy. You were at the top of the list. There must have been some mix-up. I'll correct things today."

"Please do," the dean said. "The title intrigues me." Then off he walked, with the dog at his side.

The class size for "The Necessity of Time" was diminished this Wednesday by one—Anna Shepard. Evan was thankful in a way, because now he could end the class with another paradox.

"A king in ancient times made a law that anyone who came to his city must state his business, and if he lied about it, that person would be hanged. A sophist arrived in this city and when asked his business said, 'I've come to be hanged under the king's law.' What then was the sophist doing, telling the truth or lying? Should he be hanged?"

None of the five students called out an opinion. No hand raised. No one even shifted in his seat. All eyes were open, though, which Evan took as a compliment, given that he had already been talking for almost an hour.

"The question isn't academic. One might assume that if humans can postulate an antimony, or paradox, that humans should be able to solve it. But we possess minds of finite ability, and we can't always reach a satisfying conclusion, particularly when we're exploring questions of time, space, or logic. When reason fails us, we may use instinct or faith or belief—all subjective faculties—to determine our view."

A figure passed outside the glass door, lingered for a moment, then moved on. Evan moved on, too. "The cosmological argument reasons the existence of God from the existence of the cosmos. The universe exists, and unless it self-created, then something created it. Some people call the proposed creator God. But believing in God as Creator doesn't settle philosophic debate, because if God exists, does He do so in time or outside of it? Is He subject to the logical contradictions, or paradoxes, that—"

The four o'clock bell rang. Evan knew by experience that his class would stop listening immediately, so he had become accustomed to stopping his lectures mid-sentence. In fact, he had never had a student come up afterward, bursting with curiosity about how a barely begun thought would have ended. He had long ago decided he would award such an inquirer an A on the spot.

The students suddenly became animated, talking and joking among themselves as they left the room. It was as if they had been freed, not from hell exactly, but certainly from purgatory. He admitted to himself a feeling he had never expressed before—he was glad to see them go.

"Hello, Professor."

Evan turned. In the doorway stood Robert Malloy. The detective walked slowly into the room, as if there for some idle purpose. He passed the desk and moved toward the window. "I never realized how nice a campus you have here. My daughter will be thinking about college next year and I'd like her to take a look, but I think she wants to get as far away as possible." Malloy laughed when he said this, as if it was funny that a child would want to flee home at the first opportunity.

Evan snapped shut his briefcase. "Some want to stay close, others can't get away fast enough. I guess it depends on the family."

"That's true." Malloy tightened the knot of his tie close to his neck. Evan felt uncomfortable just looking at him. "You're probably wanting to know why I dropped over."

"That's a reasonable assumption."

"I'm sorry it's not for a more pleasant occasion." He pulled a piece of paper from his jacket pocket and held it out.

Evan took the paper and saw the county seal on top. "What occasion is it?"

"That's a court order empowering us to impound your car for the purposes of our investigation into the disappearance of Joyce Bonner."

"Impound my car?"

"Yes."

"Take my car away from me?"

"That's what impounding is, yes."

"You can't do that."

"I'm afraid we can," the detective said.

"You're *afraid* you can?"

"It's just a manner of speaking."

"What gives you the right to impound my car?"

Malloy pointed at the paper in Evan's hand. "That does."

"Then what gives you the right to get this?" Evan held up the paper.

"You were at the park the day and time Joyce Bonner disappeared, and you weren't forthcoming with us about that."

"I told you everything I remembered at the time."

Malloy nodded—a confusing gesture, it seemed to Evan. What was he assenting to? "Memories *are* tricky things," the detective said. "That's why we look for facts."

"And you expect to find them in my Jetta?"

"I don't deal much in expectations. I just follow the evidence and see what turns up."

"What about your informant? He must have been at the park, too. How come you're not impounding his car?"

"We don't think that's necessary."

"Why not? I'd like to know."

"Our informant uses a wheelchair, Professor. He can't get out of his car on his own."

Evan nodded. What else could he do? But he was still upset, and justifiably so, he thought. "What am I supposed to do while you search my car, fly to work?"

"I'm sorry the law doesn't provide for compensation in this situation. You'll have to call your insurance company. Maybe they'll pay for a rental."

"You think my insurance company is going to pay for me to rent a car because the police impounded mine in a kidnapping investigation?"

"It's worth a try," the detective said. Then he just stood there. The conversation was apparently over. It took Evan a few seconds to realize what he was waiting for—the keys to the Jetta. Evan scanned the court paper and saw nothing ordering him to relinquish them.

"So, can I have the keys then?"

"No."

Malloy squinted. "You understand that Judge Shea has directed us to take possession of your car?"

Evan handed back the paper. "Show me where it says I have to give you the keys."

The detective nodded, another inappropriate gesture it seemed to Evan. He wondered how a man could survive in the police business constantly sending off the wrong social signals.

"If that's the way you want it, we'll tow," Malloy said. "But it's harder on the car, if that matters to you."

"That Jetta has been backed into, thrown up on, submerged in a flash flood, and pelted by snowballs. A towing would be the least of its trials." Evan picked up his briefcase. "And don't bother asking me in which of the five lots I parked this morning, either."

The detective stared for a moment, then smiled a little. "Suit yourself, Professor."

Suit himself? He didn't think that was possible in this situation, but he would certainly try.

CHAPTER 14

He asked Carla for a lift home. She was happy to go out of her way for him, she said. She didn't ask why he needed a ride, and he didn't offer the reason.

She dropped him at his door and said what a wonderful color it was—"ocean blue" she called it. It embarrassed him to realize that he had never invited her to the house.

He leaned in the side window. "That reminds me, did you hear from Personnel about your vacation?"

Carla grinned. "It's all been cleared. In three months and two days, I'll be swimming in the Pacific."

"That's great. I was thinking, how about you and your boyfriend come over for dinner when you get back and you can show us your pictures? I've never been to Hawaii."

"Really?"

"Sure, Ellen and I have been talking for months about having you over."

"No, I mean, you've never been to Hawaii?"

"That's true. The opportunity hasn't presented itself."

"I thought you'd done everything, Professor."

"There are a lot of places I haven't been and things I haven't done, Carla, but I'll get to them. I've got time."

He entered the house just as Ellen was crossing the hallway, headed for the kitchen.

"Coming in the front again?"

He nodded and shrugged. He didn't feel like explaining yet.

"I stopped at the organic market over by the Institute," she said. "You can help me unpack."

He was pleased to be enlisted in a chore right away and followed her into the kitchen. He unloaded the bags, sorting the items for the freezer and refrigerator.

"I'm going to shop there more often," Ellen said as she shoved things back on the shelves to make room. "It's worth the extra cost. The fruit is displayed like a work of art. You feel you're ruining it to take something."

"Sounds counterproductive to sales."

"No, I asked the man working on the pineapples. They're doing great." Ellen took a limp stalk of celery from the hydrator and threw it in the sink. "Oh, and he said he knows some great places to stay in the Dominican Republic. He can get us a deal."

"We're going to the Dominican Republic?"

"We talked about it, remember?"

"We talk about going a lot of places." Evan tossed a yellowish round vegetable about the size of a baseball in the air a few times and felt its weight against his hand. It occurred to him that he had no idea what he was holding. He felt stupid for having to ask. "What is this?"

"A turnip."

"I thought they were long, like carrots."

"That's parsnips."

"Oh." He picked up a plastic bag stuffed with something green. "A new kind of lettuce?"

"It's kale," she said. "I read about it in a magazine—it's a miracle vegetable in terms of vitamin C."

"We're having turnips and kale for dinner?"

"Why not? There are thousands of foods on the shelves, and we buy the same thirty or forty things each week. It's time to expand our horizons."

"I don't think a horizon can be expanded. It is what it is."

"Well, we're going to try. You realize the Indonesians have seventeen different varieties of durian?"

"No, I didn't realize that. What is durian, exactly?"

"It's a fruit. The man at the store said it smells like a skunk and looks like a hedgehog."

"That's a great pitch for it."

"But it tastes divine. That's what he says."

Evan peeked in the remaining bag. "You bought some of that, too?"

"I asked them to order it. We could try a new food every day of our lives and not run out."

Evan pulled out the last things—mushrooms and tomatoes—and was glad to see he could identify them.

"Leave those on the counter," Ellen said, as she stood up. "I'm making quesadillas for dinner."

He stepped back from her. A little distance always helped

in these delicate situations of breaking bad news. He considered going to his study and not telling her about the car until morning. She would have so many questions, and he had so few answers. The world worked best, it seemed to him, when there was a rough balance between the two. Unfortunately, he didn't think he could wait till that equilibrium occurred. He would have to blurt it out.

"The detective came to the college today," he said. "They towed the Jetta."

She looked up at him in puzzlement, as if he had left out some crucial bit of information, and he supposed that he had. "Who towed the Jetta?"

"The police."

Ellen straightened up and closed the refrigerator. Then she took the three large grapefruit from the counter and placed them in the wooden bowl on the island. As far as he knew, nobody in the house particularly liked grapefruit. But he had to admit they looked like a work of art.

"The police took your car?"

"Yes."

"Then they're still investigating you?"

"Seems so."

"You said this was over with, Evan."

He was sure he hadn't made any such definitive statement, except perhaps to the boys. And why was she faulting him rather than the police for the continued investigation?

"They must not have any real suspects," he said, "so they're checking me out since I'm the only one they know was there. Me and the disabled guy."

"What?"

"Their informant, the one who took down my license plate number, he uses a wheelchair. That's why they ruled him out."

Evan picked up the squeeze jar of honey but didn't know where it should go. He didn't think they had used honey in years. He set the jar on the counter. "Man Who Doesn't Know Where Honey Goes Suspected in Kidnapping." It was a silly thought, but it didn't make any more sense to him to say "Devoted Father, Loving Husband Questioned in Girl's Disappearance."

"Sometimes," he said, "I wake up thinking that this can't be happening to me."

Ellen took the honey from the counter and put it in the pantry. "I know it's hard, Evan, but it's not just happening to you."

"Sure, it affects you and the boys, too."

She turned back to the bowl on the marble island and adjusted each of the grapefruits so that their faint red spots were hidden. "What I mean is that the tragedy happened to the girl and her family. We should be thankful it's not Zed or Adam missing."

She often reversed the boys' names like this, and it never failed to bother him a little. It also irritated him that she was always putting his life in perspective. Why couldn't she just sympathize or get angry on his behalf? Perspective, it seemed to Evan, often got in the way of justifiable emotion.

"Given the number of tragic things that could happen to us, yes, we're very lucky. On the other hand, I'd like to feel a little sorry for myself for being wrongly accused." He took the coffee bag from the counter and handed it to her. "It feels terrible to be suspected of a crime. And I don't even know why it's happening—it's a wholly irrational experience."

Ellen opened the coffee and inhaled. "Well." She paused here, as if needing to concentrate on rolling the top of the bag back up. He didn't want to wait.

"Well what?"

"Maybe this happened because you always expected it to."

"What?"

"Look, Evan, you've worried about something bad happening to one of us since the boys were born. Now it has."

"Of course I worry. Every father does."

"You worry differently. You keep turning around in your mind all the bad things that could happen. It's like an obsession. You drive out the good thoughts."

"That's interesting. How do you know what goes on in my mind?"

She shook her head a little, as if it were a trivial feat to read his inner thoughts and fears. That aggravated him, too. Then something else occurred to him. "Wait a minute, are you saying I brought this on myself?"

She adjusted the grapefruits again. How many times was she going to do that?

"Not consciously, no."

"Then in what unconscious way, exactly, did I engineer my own false arrest?"

"It's not that. I just think we get the life we expect."

He had heard this "murderee" concept before, and it surprised him that Ellen would express an idea with so many obvious fallacies. Just for starters there was the problem of causation: What would be the possible mechanism for affecting future events?

"*We get the life we expect,*" he repeated. "That's very pseudo-philosophical of you."

"Characterize it how you like, I think it's true."

"If my thoughts are so powerful, I suppose I can redirect them at the stock market then, right? Or my book sales. Better yet, I guess all I have to do is *expect* that this police investigation into my life will cease, and it will be over to-morrow."

Ellen didn't respond. It was a familiar move of hers in an argument—simply stop talking. Sometimes she left the room. This time she opened the box of wine on the tabletop, took out a bottle, and scratched at the price tag with her fingernail. He wondered if they were drinking organic wine now.

He wasn't done with her or her crazy suggestion. He leaned over the counter, purposely close to her. "So when did you come up with this penetrating analysis of my situation?"

She peeled the price tag off her fingertip, then took out another bottle. "When you called from the police station and said you were arrested, it struck me that I wasn't that surprised."

"You weren't surprised that the police picked me up for kidnapping a sixteen-year-old girl?"

"The specific charge, yes. But I think your life has always been pointing toward something like this. If it wasn't kidnapping, it would have been something else that went wrong next week or next year."

He stood up, turned around, and found himself exactly where he had been—facing Ellen, and utterly bewildered. "Where do you get these ideas?"

"Lower your voice, the boys will hear."

"This is my regular I-can't-believe-what-you're-saying voice."

"Call it what you want, I don't like it."

"I don't like being told I'm somehow responsible for my own false arrest." He sat on the edge of the stool, and a thought came to him so quickly he didn't have time to stop it on his lips. "Or don't you believe my arrest was false?"

She picked at another price tag. He watched her fingernail

dig under the edge, then pry up the tag with short, precise flicks. He heard the click of the kitchen clock, and each second she didn't answer further confirmed her doubt to him. "You know the answer to that," she said.

"I'm not sure I do."

"You should be sure."

"I'm full of doubts lately, so humor me, okay? Do you believe my arrest was false?"

She took out another bottle of wine, set it in front of her, then got up and left the kitchen. He heard her climbing the stairs and walking into their bedroom overhead. In a minute or so she returned with a newspaper in her hand. She held it out to him.

He unfolded the paper and saw a picture of Joyce Bonner in her cheerleading uniform under the headline "Foul Play Suspected in Girl's Disappearance."

He didn't know what to make of it. "If this is like where Perry Mason springs the secret evidence on everyone, you're going to have to explain it to me."

"I was hanging up your green sports jacket last week, and this fell out."

"So?"

"It's a story about Joyce Bonner dated August 25th—two days after her disappearance."

"And?"

"You said you didn't know anything about the disappearance. You couldn't even remember the girl's name. But you had a story about her in your jacket a few days before the police stopped you."

"Oh, Jesus, Ellen. I have to prove myself to you, too?"

"I'm just showing you what I found. It brings up questions."

"How about this question: Did you ever think that I didn't actually have a story of Joyce Bonner in my pocket, what I had was a section of the newspaper that happened to have her story in it? There's a big difference."

Ellen didn't answer. She started scratching at another price tag.

"Would you stop doing that?"

She looked up. "What?"

He turned his hands out in obviousness. "Could there possibly be a less meaningful thing to do in life than taking the price tags off wine bottles?"

She kept picking at the stubborn tag. "So much to be annoyed about, and so little time."

"Sarcasm—from you?"

"It's just an observation."

"So your observation is that I'm always looking around for something to be annoyed about, and here comes this little matter of my being arrested and having my car impounded, which I blow all out of proportion?"

She said nothing.

"Well, you're right. I am annoyed. You're telling me that I'm responsible for my own arrest at the same time as you're picking price tags from wine bottles. The incongruity of it kind of provokes me, but I guess I'm just an irritable kind of guy."

She scraped off the remaining bit of yellow sticker from a merlot, then reached into the box again. It was empty.

Later, as he sat in his office easy chair reading *The Jew of Linz,* she came up behind him and began massaging his neck, which Evan took to be a kind of apology. She rarely said "I'm sorry," and he wasn't sure if that was because she rarely was sorry or simply couldn't speak the words.

She reached around him and unbuttoned the top of his

shirt, then began kneading his shoulders with her thumbs and forefingers. "Who's the Jew of Linz?"

"Wittgenstein. He went to the same school as Hitler for a while, and apparently that's where he developed his anti-Semitism. Hitler, I mean. He writes in *Mein Kampf* about a particular Jewish kid he had problems with. The author says that it's possible the course of the twentieth century was radically influenced by a quarrel between two schoolboys."

Ellen stopped massaging his neck. Evan left his shirt unbuttoned.

"Wittgenstein caused World War Two? That seems like a big leap to make."

"Of course. But his family did represent everything Hitler hated most. They were part of an economic cartel with the Rothschilds, they converted to Christianity, and they married Aryans."

She didn't say anything. He twisted around to make sure she was still there.

"I want you to call Paul Curry first thing tomorrow."

"Paul the lawyer? He handles divorces—is that what you have in mind?"

Her mouth twisted up into a quick smile to show that she got his joke. "He does criminal law now. And if he's not right he'll turn you over to someone else in his firm."

"You know my opinion of lawyers. They muddy things up until it takes a judge to sort them out."

"Evan, they impounded your car. They'll probably find nothing and that will be the end of it, but—"

"They'll *probably* find nothing?"

"I assume they'll find nothing. I hope they'll find nothing. I expect they'll find nothing. But if they find something, wouldn't it be better to have a lawyer?"

"All right, I'll call him." Evan stood up to give her a hug, his way of acknowledging acceptance of her apology as well as her advice. In the doorway stood one of the twins. It was a recent trick of theirs to suddenly appear, as if materializing out of the air. Evan supposed it was his fault for giving them a book on magic for their birthday.

"Time for me to read to you?"

"I need to ask you something, Dad."

"Okay."

"I mean in private."

"I can see I'm not wanted," Ellen said. "I'll go upstairs."

"You're wanted, Mom, just not for this."

She gave him a kiss on the cheek as she passed him. "I was just kidding."

"So what is it?" Evan asked.

"They can't put a kid in jail unless they absolutely, definitely know he did something, right?"

"Who do you mean by *they?*"

"The police and judge and everybody."

"Well then, yes, that's the way it's supposed to work."

"So like, if somebody says they saw a kid—"

"Wait a second, Adam, you're not worrying about this because of the police pulling me over, are you?"

"I'm Zed."

Evan leaned closer to get a better look and smelled the strong scent of raspberry shampoo. "You're Adam—you can't fool me again."

"Okay, Dad, if you say I'm Adam, I'm Adam, now can you listen?"

"It's not because I say you're Adam."

"Yeah it is. You named me—you and Mom."

"We named you Adam ten years ago—"

"So if I'm Adam it's because you said so. And I'd be Zed if you named me that. Can we get back to my question now?"

Evan nodded.

"This is just a pretend question, so don't get all nervous. If somebody says they saw a kid do something wrong, like an eyewitness saw him steal some money or stuff, and they arrested him and he was on trial, then his identical twin could walk in the court and the eyewitness wouldn't be able to tell which one did it and they'd have to let both of them go, right?"

"That sounds like the evil-twin scenario. The suspect says, 'It wasn't me robbing the store, it was my evil twin.'"

"Yeah, and they wouldn't want to lock up a guy who didn't do it, right?"

"Yes, but—"

"So he'd be free."

"Adam, you're not planning to put this theory of yours to the test, are you?"

The boy looked at him with a sudden grin. "No, Dad, but I told you, I'm Zed."

"Okay, well, whichever name you want to call yourself, are you ready for me to read to you?"

"Sort of, I mean, *I'm* ready."

"What's the matter? I always read to you guys on Wednesday nights."

"I know."

"What, is Pollux busy on the computer?"

"I'm Pollux, he's Castor. I think Castor wants to read by himself."

"Is something wrong?"

The boy shrugged. He picked up the wooden whale from the bookshelf and rubbed his hand over the smooth, curving back. "She thinks you did it, doesn't she?"

"What?"

"Mom. She doesn't believe you."

"Of course she believes me."

The boy pulled apart the four pieces of the whale, then set them back on the shelf in a row. "Maybe you have an evil twin, Dad. That would explain everything."

"I think I'd know if I did."

"Grandpa and Grandmom could have given him away when you were babies because they knew he was evil. They wouldn't have told you that, would they?"

"I suppose not, but I can't ask them now since Dad's dead and Mom is non compos mentis."

"Crazy?"

"Just not all there. Remember when she saw you last time she kept calling you Evan?"

"Yeah, she thought both of us were you when you were a kid, like you were twins. That was weird."

"Yes, very weird. So we're going to have to go with the assumption that I don't have an evil twin and the police just made a mistake."

The boy nodded. "*I* believe you, Dad. I know you wouldn't do anything bad."

Evan put his arm around his son, and it surprised him how solid and strong the boy felt. "Thanks, Adam. It makes me feel good to know that."

"Zed, Dad. I'm Zed."

CHAPTER 15

The second disturbing phone call came at 2:34 in the early morning of Saturday. Evan saw the numbers on the alarm clock as he threw back the covers and jumped to his feet.

"Be careful," Ellen said in a dreamy voice, and he wondered what she meant—be careful of knocking over something in the dark, or was there a greater threat he should be prepared for?

He hurried down the hall and grabbed the phone. He thought he heard a motor running. "Hello?"

In the background someone laughed. The motor kept running.

"Who is this?" Evan said.

"Who is this?" came back to him—his own voice.

"I don't know what kind of game this is," Evan said.

"I don't know what kind . . ."

He hung up and looked at the phone, expecting it to ring again. He waited for a minute and then went back to bed. Ellen was sleeping soundly.

In the morning, he dialed 411 and asked how to report a crank call. The operator said she would connect him to the Call Annoyance Bureau. Then there was silence. He tucked the receiver between his shoulder and chin so that his hands were free to butter his toast. "Anybody there?" he asked. The silence stretched on.

He assumed there would be music if he had been put on hold. Of all organizations, surely the phone company wouldn't leave a customer without some cue that the line was still live. He counted to ten, then decided to count to twenty. A woman answered.

"Thank you for calling the Call Annoyance Bureau. How may I help you?"

The greeting seemed inappropriate to Evan. It was like thanking people for calling to report a crime.

"I want to know if you can trace a call that was made to me in the middle of the night last night."

"That is possible in certain cases."

Evan detected a broad Midwestern accent—Iowa, perhaps, or Nebraska. It was a soothing voice.

"Was this an annoying or harassing call?"

Evan wasn't sure if he was being given a choice or if the call had to satisfy both conditions. "Yes," he said.

"How many annoying or harassing calls have you experienced?"

"Two," he said, which didn't sound impressive enough to him, "two recently. We had some hang-ups a few weeks ago."

"Could you describe the nature of the annoyance or harassment?"

"What do you mean?"

"What exactly was said to you?"

"There was breathing."

"Breathing? That wouldn't constitute annoyance or harassment in and of itself."

"There was a motor running, too, like in a car."

"Was anything said to you?"

"Not really, at least I don't think so. I mean, I heard words, but I think they were my own."

"You heard your own words?"

"I asked 'Who is this?' And a voice said, 'Who is this?'"

"That sounds like a mix-up in the phone lines."

"I don't think it was a mix-up. I think someone's calling on purpose, and I want to know if you can trace the call."

"If you were reporting multiple calls with threats of bodily harm, for example, we could put a trap and trace on your line."

"And then you could tell me who was making the calls?"

"No, we only release trap-and-trace information to the police. It's up to them to decide what to do with it."

Evan imagined Malloy getting the report about two annoying phone calls. No doubt he would find it amusing.

"So you can't do anything?"

"Not at this point," the woman said. "You haven't demonstrated there is an actual threat."

"As opposed to an un-actual one?" Evan said.

"I suppose so."

"Okay, I'll wait till the annoyance and harassment becomes much worse, then call you back."

"Very good," the woman said. "Anything else I can help you with today?"

Evan called Paul Curry after breakfast and was surprised not to get an answering machine. He wanted to get an answering machine, which is why he had agreed to call on Saturday.

"This is the day I catch up on paperwork," the lawyer said. "Nobody calls."

Evan explained his situation, and Curry asked questions for half an hour. At several points the lawyer said, "I wish you'd called me earlier," or, "You shouldn't have talked to the police without counsel."

Evan didn't like the implication that at the first sign of trouble, a person should resort to an attorney, rather than use his own common sense. "It seemed like a simple mistake that I could correct by just answering their questions."

"That's what everybody thinks," Curry said with a little chuckle in his voice that Evan found condescending, "and it rarely works out that way."

Ellen suggested getting away for the afternoon to Singing Sand Beach. He didn't see how a person could escape an accusation. Once accused, always accused. But he didn't want to appear negative, for surely that was another attribute of first-world fear, and so he said, "Sounds like a good idea."

They drove for an hour. The boys played chess in the backseat, with the miniature board and magnetized pieces they had bought outside the Parthenon in Greece. Adam always took black, the Spartan side, and Zed white, the Athenians. They punctuated each move with a shout or growl. The Athenians usually won, which Evan found comforting.

Ellen read the whole time, which made him nauseous. He wondered how that could be. He couldn't be identifying with her discomfort, because she wasn't experiencing any. Apparently he was identifying with what he thought she should be feeling. Somehow his intuition of his likely sickness in her situation had resulted in a visceral sensation of sickness in himself. How would Wittgenstein have explained that?

Evan tried to take his mind off his nausea by thinking of something else, and a headline from the morning newspaper came to mind: "Baboons Take Their Revenge in Saudi Arabia." The story was three or four paragraphs, enough for him to picture the scene: a half-dozen baboons, crouched on a small hillside overlooking a winding, sandy road. At the sound of an engine, the leader of them, a bulky male, rose up a little, his eyes widening, his nostrils flaring. The others turned and watched his shoulders tighten. As the sound passed by, his muscles relaxed, and so did they.

Perhaps they groomed each other or tossed small stones to pass the time. The younger animals may not even have known why they had returned to this place where one of their family had been run over. As evening approached, they probably became hungry and distracted.

The sound came again, the hundredth time that day. The big male rose up, his huge shoulders taut. The others saw something different this time—his hand curling around the large rock at his side. With a grunt unlike any they had ever heard from him he vaulted over the top of the hill. They gripped their own rocks and scrambled after him, sliding down the sand until they were standing behind him in the road, a wall of baboons.

The vehicle sputtered around the curve. The fierce male waited until he could see the driver inside, see his head wrapped in a scarf, see his small dark eyes, see his jagged teeth, and hurled his rock. It cracked into the windshield. The Jeep swerved a bit, then straightened again. It bore down on them, but they'd seen this before and jumped out of the way. As the vehicle passed by, the other baboons threw their rocks, and the man looked at them with an unimaginable fear in his face.

Evan liked this story, whether it had happened exactly as he pictured it or not. He tried to imagine for what other purpose baboons would wait all day. Was revenge unique in its power to motivate their planning, their patience, and their coherence as a group? It was a question he was saving for Ellen when she was done reading.

"Hey, Dad?"

"Yep?"

"How long can you stay underwater without breathing?"

Underwater . . . without breathing. He tried to link the two in his memory. "I remember doing almost a minute in the pool in high school. Of course, that was thirty-some years ago."

"Can I have your watch?"

"What for?"

"We're going to time ourselves holding our breath."

He let the steering wheel go for a moment to unstrap his watch and hand it over the seat. He wasn't sure which of them grabbed it. Sometimes it seemed that they shared one voice, one hand, one intent.

"Are we going over that bridge again, the one with the tower at the top?"

"That's the only way to the island."

He heard the unclicking of a seat belt and glanced over his shoulder. "What are you doing?"

"I saw this on TV. When you go over a bridge you're supposed to unhook your seat belt and unlock the door and roll down the windows. That way if you crash in the water, you can get out."

"We're not going to crash," Ellen said as she turned a page, "so put your seat belt back on."

"The guy on TV was saved because he *didn't* wear his seat belt."

"Put it back on."

Evan felt the Accord drifting right a bit and steered to the middle of the lane. He imagined the sensation of sailing off the bridge at sixty miles per hour and plunging toward the water. What would he do in those few seconds the car was dropping—brace himself against the impact, or give in to the exhilarating weightlessness? And could he hold his breath long enough underwater to get everyone out?

The sign said, "Bridge 3 Miles." He glanced at Ellen. The book was propped against her knees. He pictured the car tumbling through the air, saw himself leaning toward her for a last kiss. Would she tell him to hold on a second as she tried to cram in one more paragraph before hitting the water?

"So," he said, "what are you reading about today?"

"Ties."

"Ties . . . like railroad ties? Or Thais from Thailand?"

"Very funny. Ties like gentlemen wear around their necks. This book says there are exactly eighty-five ways to tie a tie. Physicists figured it out. And only thirteen of them are aesthetically pleasing."

"I don't think physicists should be considered the great arbiters of aesthetics."

Adam blew out a mouthful of air. "What are you guys talking about?"

"Tying a tie in an attractive way," Ellen said. "There are only thirteen ways to do it."

The mid-morning sun was slanting through the trees in short bursts, like pulses from a strobe. Evan found himself blinking in rhythm to the light.

"I'm never going to wear a tie again," Adam said. "You could snag it in a car door and be dragged to death."

"It could get caught in a meat grinder and pull you in," Zed said.

"What do you know about meat grinders?" Ellen asked.

"I saw one in a cartoon."

"Bridge 2 Miles," the sign said. Already Evan could see the top of it, a thin arch of gray steel grazing the sky. From a distance it seemed unimaginable that cars could pass over it.

His foot suddenly pulled back from the pedal. The car decelerated quickly, and a horn blew from behind.

"What's the matter?" Ellen said.

The *matter?* It was such a genteel way of asking, "What the hell are you doing?" He wasn't sure.

"The car feels a little funny," he said. "I'm going to stop to check that everything's all right." He steered onto the narrow soft shoulder. The Accord dipped on the passenger side, then straightened a little farther on as it came to rest. The difference between stillness and movement suddenly seemed enormous to him.

"Are you all right?" Ellen asked.

"Yes, I said the car feels funny."

"I didn't feel anything."

"There was a little shaking in the steering wheel—you wouldn't be able to feel that, would you?" He didn't like the sharpness of his voice, but why did she have to challenge his reason for pulling off the road in front of the boys?

Zed leaned between them from the backseat. "I have to pee, Dad."

Good, Evan thought—the stop now had a purpose, even if after the fact. He pointed across Ellen into the woods. "You can go behind the bushes there. You go, too, Adam."

"I don't have to pee."

"Go with your brother anyway."

"Mom, do I have to watch Zed pee?"

"Zed can go by himself," Ellen said. "It's not that far."

Evan looked over the backseat. "I'm telling you to go together, understand?"

Adam got out of the car and followed Zed into the bushes. Evan noted where they went out of sight, just to the right of a thin white pine tree. He wondered if all parents did this, kept track of the last sighting of their children in case they needed to be searched for. And what about the father of Joyce Bonner—had it occurred to him as he dropped her off in the park three weeks ago that some danger might be hiding in the trees?

"Am I allowed to ask what's going on?" Ellen said.

Evan rolled down his window, and a gust of wind whipped into the car as a van rushed by just a few feet away. He wondered who was in that vehicle, what man or woman could speed on so confidently toward the bridge. He felt strangely connected to them, even if just by the air and dust stirred up in their wake.

"Evan?"

He nodded ahead at the immense structure rising from the

water. "I'm feeling a little nervous . . . about going over the bridge."

Ellen lifted the visor on her side. "You've driven over it dozens of times before."

"I know, but this time it bothers me. The lanes are very narrow, and I have this strange feeling the car might swerve over the side."

There was silence between them. Evan wished she would say, "It would bother anybody," or "I don't like driving over it either," and "They shouldn't build bridges that narrow." She said none of these things. He glanced over and saw her worried look. Apparently she understood what he was really saying, that he felt *he* might steer the car over the side of the bridge. How could she ever feel safe riding with him again?

She opened her pocketbook, took out a tube of lipstick, and rubbed on the color without looking in the mirror. Evan assumed she was pretending to be at ease. "You're just letting the boys' talk of going over the bridge get to you," she said. "You've been under a lot of stress. It's not surprising you're feeling a little panic."

A little panic—Evan didn't think there could be such a thing.

"And you're not used to driving my car. It's wider than the Jetta."

It would have been easy to agree with her. It was understandable that an unfamiliar car might make a driver anxious. But it wasn't the truth.

She reached over and patted his leg. Evan felt the sympathy oozing from her, and he hated it. All sympathy could do was confirm to a person that he was in a pathetic state. He almost preferred her icier manner.

There was the crash of brush outside as the boys came racing back to the car. "How about I drive?" Ellen said and unbuckled her seat belt.

"No, that's okay." He always drove on trips like this. The boys would ask what was going on. Besides, now that he had confessed his fear, he felt a little bit free of it. Maybe all that he needed was this moment off to the side of the road where he could realize that he didn't have to drive over the bridge if he didn't want to. It was his choice.

Evan turned around as the boys quieted down. They had brought back two sticks, each about a foot long. He presumed they would become swords at some point during the day, and he resisted telling them they could poke each other's eyes out with them. If he kept instructing them in the obvious, they might not listen to him when there was something important to warn them about. Besides, how often did you hear of a kid poking his eye out with a stick? Evan couldn't remember a single time.

"Buckle up," he said.

"Did you fix the car, Dad?"

"Everything's fine." Evan started the engine. He waited until there was a long open stretch of road behind him before pulling back into the slow lane.

"How about I put on some music?" Ellen asked.

It was her calming voice, the one she had used with the boys when they were colicky babies.

"No, that's okay."

In a few minutes he reached the circle before the bridge and saw the exit road. He didn't turn.

"You missed it, Dad," Adam said.

"There was a truck behind me that wouldn't let me get

over. I'll go around again." He maneuvered to the outside lane and circled about.

"There it is!" Adam called out.

Evan turned toward the bridge. The four-lane road rose gradually for about fifty yards, bounded on each side by a two-foot-high guardrail. The barrier seemed ridiculously small. It could never block a car swerving wildly out of control.

"The Institute's having its fall open house in two weeks," Ellen said. "We should really go this year. It wouldn't hurt for me to be more visible."

Evan gripped the wheel at ten o'clock and two, his hands in perfect balance with each other. If one started to oversteer, the other could quickly compensate.

"They might want me to introduce the video I made last spring of Tyco and maybe have her count in person, if I can get her back to six."

From the backseat, one of the boys inhaled a big breath. The other one said, "You mean *in chimp,* don't you, Mom?"

"What?"

"They want her to be there *in chimp,* not *in person.*"

The road crested. Thick support beams stretched up to the top of the span. It seemed as if the rest of the earth had dropped away, leaving just this ribbon of road spiraling into the air.

"Look, Dad, there's a guy waterskiing down there."

"Your father's driving," Ellen said. "He can't look."

Evan straightened up in his seat. He opened his mouth, and it surprised him that he yawned. In the rearview mirror he saw cars backing up behind him. Was he driving that slowly? He kept his head straight, focusing on the solid white lines on either side of the car.

"How do you know it's a guy?" Ellen asked.

"What?" Adam asked.

"You said there's a guy waterskiing way down there. How do you know it's not a woman?"

"I don't know. It could be a girl. I meant 'guy' like either one."

The road leveled off. In a few moments they were on solid ground again. He had made it across. Of course, he would have to drive back over this bridge in just a few hours, this time at nightfall.

As they walked down the beach, the soft wet sand pressing up between their toes, she said, "I had an interesting experience when I went to town last week. There was a young man with a sign saying 'Arguments $1—1 Minute.' I paid him two dollars and we argued for two minutes about happiness."

"You argued about happiness?"

The wind gusted, and Ellen put her arms out at her sides to let the sea air blow over her.

"I didn't have anything in mind, so I let him choose the topic. He said happiness is overrated. I agreed with him because I've always felt the Dalai Lama's wrong. Our purpose in life shouldn't be to seek happiness. We don't have a right to it."

"Doesn't sound like you got much of an argument for your money."

Evan slowed as the narrow beach curved right. He wasn't interested in seeking happiness at that particular point in his life. He simply wanted to be not-accused. Getting rid of a bad thing could be just as satisfying as achieving a good thing. He zipped up his windbreaker and looked behind him. The boys were just ragged drops of color in the distant sand.

"Maybe we should head back."

"Let's walk a little more," she said. "They'll spend hours building their castle."

The gray ocean seemed endless. Of course, anything just larger than a person's capacity to see would appear endless. He imagined sailing into the sea centuries ago, not knowing if there was land anywhere ahead or whether the world ended in a cliff. How did the sailors deal with the uncertainty?

A small wave trickled out at their feet. He put his arm around Ellen's shoulder, and it surprised him that her body felt so unfamiliar to him. Maybe it was the slope of the beach, but she felt a little taller, and his arm was arched at an un-comfortable angle.

"I think Tyco has the potential to be the next Nim," she said.

"Nim?"

"The chimp who grew up in a human family. I told you about him. He was considered the smartest animal in the world—smartest non-human animal."

"Why's that?"

"For one thing, he learned about three hundred words in sign language."

"How many does Tyco know?"

"We're teaching her numbers, not signs. Six is a great num-ber for a chimp, and she's only five years old."

Evan bent down and drew in the sand with his finger—1, 2, 3, 4, 5, 6. The progression seemed wonderfully logical, the forms of the numbers perfectly expressing their value. Who had chosen these symbols and for what reason? It was the kind of question the twins would ask him. He could under-stand the number 1, and perhaps 2 and 3. But 4, 5, 6? Where did these shapes come from? Evan retraced 6 to make it more visible, then added 7, 8, 9, and 10 to the list. "Remember we used to have the boys practice their numbers in the sand like this?"

"And they cried when the waves washed away their numbers."

"Adam cried. Zed just wrote the numbers again."

Somewhere down the beach a child yelled. Evan stood up and looked. At the edge of the water a father was swinging his young son by the arms. The boy's legs kicked wildly into the cold September waves. Evan had never thought to do that with Adam and Zed, and they were too big now. He tried to recall the last time he had been physical with them in any sort of game. It seemed like years.

"How old were they when they could count to six?"

"It was before they were two," Ellen said. "I had them count for my mother at their second birthday party."

Evan assumed that was an achievement. The twins had always reached their milestones early. But if a five-year-old chimp could be taught to count, how important could that aptitude be?

Evan dropped the beach towels on the washing machine and turned down the hallway into the living room. He heard Ellen in the kitchen playing the messages on the answering machine. The voices sounded muted, as if they were coming from a faraway radio station. He heard the boys in the cellar hammering away in their workshop. It amazed him how quickly they could come into the house and start up a project. They didn't seem to need any transition time. They did need to be doing something, anything, every moment of their lives. The pleasure of relaxation was still years away for them.

He stepped out of his sandals onto the bare wood floor. His skin felt parched. His face was red and warm. He couldn't say if it was windburned or sunburned.

The trip back had been uneventful. In fact, the darkness made driving over the bridge easier by obscuring the open air on either side of the railing. It took less than a minute to cross, and then he had begun breathing again.

CHAPTER 16

When Evan stopped in his office between classes on Monday afternoon, a phone message from Paul Curry was waiting. "Pls. call ASAP," Carla had scribbled, and then added in parentheses, "sounds important."

Evan called, reached Paul Curry's secretary, who called the lawyer's cell phone, and within a minute the two were connected. It sounded to Evan as if Curry were speaking from a bowling alley.

"I have some bad news," he said. "I reached Detective . . . ?"

"Malloy."

"Yes, Malloy. I talked to him this morning, and it looks like they're going to be holding your car awhile longer."

"Why, Paul? What did he say?"

"Apparently they found hair in the backseat, a few blond curly strands that appear to match hair from a comb on Joyce Bonner's dresser. They're going to run some tests."

Evan imagined dozens of men in white lab coats and women in hair nets looking through microscopes, all working at that moment to convict him of a crime. And whom did he have on his side but one lone lawyer more used to settling divorces than defending alleged kidnappers?

"We'll just have to wait and see what the tests show, Evan."

"Look, Paul, I don't understand this. How could there be hair from that girl in my Jetta? Unless they planted it—they could have done that, right? They had the hair from her brush. Any one of them could have dropped some in my car." His suggestion was logical, but still he felt like some common criminal saying, "I'm being framed!"

"The police have procedures to keep that from happening, but we'll look into it. We might have to challenge the whole chain of supervision over the evidence, if this goes any further. But now I want you to think, is there any way Joyce Bonner could have been in your car?"

"No," he said quickly and then thought that he should be more precise. "I mean, not that I know of."

"What if you didn't know it? Do you ever leave your car open, maybe at the park that day, or any day you were there, could you have gotten out for a walk and left the door unlocked?"

Evan wanted to say yes, but he couldn't deny his whole character. He no doubt locked his car even to walk the ten steps to the trash bin in the parking lot that day. "I never leave the car open, Paul. It's a bit of an obsession of mine."

"Well, did you ever pick up a girl on your way home, like a hitchhiker?"

"I stopped picking up hitchhikers years ago, Paul."

"How about at the college? Do you ever give students a ride?"

"I've made it a policy not to socialize with my students anymore."

"Anymore?"

"I was more open to it when I was younger. I guess I was flattered by the attention. Some students get the wrong idea, though."

"What kind of idea?"

Like being friendly means you're coming on to them—that was what Evan had in mind, but he didn't see the relevancy of his past affairs to the matter at hand. "Let's just say I don't customarily mingle with the students after hours. But wait a second, I did give some high-school girls a ride about a month ago. They were on campus for the Summer Arts Camp. I was an advisor on the academic component."

"How many girls?"

"Three, and a boy, too. I remember because they all squeezed into the back, which I thought kind of funny. None of them wanted to sit next to the old professor. I wondered if I looked that scary."

"Where did you take them?"

"Just across campus. It looked like there might be a thunderstorm, so some of the faculty were pitching in to get the kids to the library from the student center."

"Was there a girl named Joyce?"

"I didn't ask their names, and I didn't deal individually with any of them at the camp. I was just an advisor. I didn't even teach myself."

"But you've seen pictures of her, haven't you?"

"The police showed me one—the same as in the paper."

"Did any of the girls look like her?"

Evan remembered the soft face, the wide eyes, and the slightly jaded expression, a weariness with the world that teenagers often affected.

"Maybe. I don't remember."

"Well, there's something else," Curry said. "They found a stick of lipstick in the backseat—Red Red it's called. She used that color."

Evan heard the past tense, and it scared him. Was Curry implying that Joyce Bonner had been found dead, or just that she certainly would be? Either possibility was frightening.

"One of the girls in the car was putting on lipstick," he said.

"Are you sure? That's a small detail to stick in your mind."

He remembered her leaning between the front seats so that she could use the rearview mirror. He should have told her to sit back so as not to block his view, but he was charmed by the face filling up the small, rectangular mirror. Her lips looked huge.

"Yes, I'm sure."

"Well, you'll have to get me the attendance records from the camp. This would be an incredible coincidence if Joyce Bonner was there."

It didn't seem so to Evan, and he thought he should explain why, in case their possible meeting became important. "Listen, Paul, lives intersect like this all the time. We just don't know it unless something happens to make us pay attention. Then we say, 'Isn't that incredible?' when actually, things like this should be expected."

"You think it's expected that the girl who disappeared at the Eastfield State Park may turn out to be someone you had in your car a few weeks before . . . and you were at the park the day she disappeared?"

"Not *that* specifically. I'm saying that what we think of as coincidences really shouldn't surprise us. Take any event and look backwards, you'll come up with hundreds and thousands of things that had to happen at exactly the right time for that event to take place. Everything seems like coincidence, when you look backwards."

"I'm not sure Malloy is going to buy your logic."

"In logic nothing is accidental."

"What's that?"

"It's just a saying from a philosopher. But look, it would be good if it turns out she was in my car, right, since that would explain the hair and the lipstick?"

"If it turns out the Bonner girl was in your car, Malloy's going to assume you struck up some sort of relationship with her. It ties you to her, and you don't want to be tied to a missing girl, trust me."

"I guess you're right."

"We have attorney-client privilege here, Evan, so I want us to get things clear. You're telling me you didn't have a relationship with her, is that true?"

"True" . . ."false"—Evan had always disliked these words. To state something as true could only have meaning if the falseness of the declaration was an equally plausible possibility. To assert innocence was in effect to admit the potential for guilt. He did not want to do that.

"I don't know this girl and never did," Evan said. "Is that enough for you?"

"Yes," Curry said, "but I'm not the one you have to convince."

Evan was not surprised to look up and see Robert Malloy coming into his office. Perhaps this was the detective's strategy, to dull a person's reactions with familiarity. Evan didn't feel upset or angry, either, which he thought odd, since he had just learned that the police were keeping possession of his car for further testing. Surely a certain justifiable *something* would be warranted—indignation, or even rage. Instead he felt a little bemused.

"Good afternoon, Detective," he said. "Nice to see you again." He stressed the *nice* on purpose, just to show that he was not unnerved by another visit.

"Is this an inconvenient time, Professor?"

"I have a class in fifteen minutes. And my lawyer is upset with me for speaking to you without him present."

Malloy massaged his right elbow. Evan suspected tendinitis. "That's fine, Professor. We can set a time and get everybody down to the station."

Evan sat on the edge of his desk. It made him claustrophobic just to think of undergoing another session in the police interrogation room. "Well, I've already talked too much anyway, right? So I guess a few minutes more won't hurt."

Malloy picked up the trilobite from the desk and felt its ridges. Evan wondered why he didn't make any comment or ask what it was—did he already know? Or was he just not curious? That wouldn't make sense for a detective.

"I stopped by the college bookstore the other day," Malloy said. "Bought myself a copy of your book."

"My publisher will be pleased to hear that, but I hope the department reimburses you."

"Oh, I'll put in for it, yes. That Wittgenstein fellow—am I saying his name right?"

"The W is pronounced like a V—*Vittgenstein.*"

"He lived a colorful life, didn't he?"

"In some ways, yes."

"I can't say I understand his philosophy. Seems like he went to a lot of trouble to muddle up even the simplest things. Like the shopkeeper opening his drawer to get six red apples— wasn't that one of them?"

"Five red apples," Evan said. It intrigued him that the detective would remember the shopkeeper, the drawer, and the apples, yet mistake six for five. Was number the least important element of the story?

"But his private life," Malloy said, "that really wasn't so different than what you see nowadays."

"I suppose not. People have their issues to deal with no matter when they live." *Issues*—Evan couldn't believe he had used this pseudo-psychotherapy word. But he couldn't think of any other neutral way to describe what Wittgenstein had gone through.

Malloy set the trilobite back on the desk exactly where he had found it, even pointing the head in the same direction. "His issues were particularly interesting, though—I mean the secret life he was living."

How could a life be secret? And from whom? Only if you subscribed to the notion that some generalized entity called "society" had the right to know all of a person's behaviors and thoughts and relationships would "secret life" have any meaning. But Evan didn't want to get into this with the detective.

"As I said in the book, it's speculation about any so-called secret life. The executors of his estate deny it quite vehemently."

"The evidence seems pretty substantial, from what you write. He went out to the park to pick up strange men, right?"

"They weren't necessarily strange men, just men who were strangers to him."

"Of course. I didn't mean to judge anybody. On the other hand, they're in the park at night looking for some quick sex. That can be a pretty rough scene."

"I imagine so."

Malloy picked up *Disturbing Minds* from the windowsill. "It's kind of sad, isn't it? A world-famous philosopher reduced to that type of behavior."

There was so much Evan didn't like about this sentence, he didn't know where to start. "That *behavior,* if he did it, doesn't diminish the man, and certainly not his ideas."

"No? I would think it would."

"Detective, I'm sure you didn't come here to discuss Wittgenstein, did you?"

"I just figured it was a favorite topic of yours, kind of an icebreaker."

"Well, consider the ice broken. What do you want?"

The detective motioned to the swivel chair as if asking for permission to sit. Evan nodded. Malloy stayed standing.

"I interviewed a classmate of Joyce Bonner's yesterday. She has a strong feeling that her friend had a secret relationship going on."

Wittgenstein with a *secret* life, Joyce with a *secret* relationship—Evan wondered how Malloy could hope to link the two. "That must be an interesting lead for you to follow," he said. "On the other hand, girls say things like that sometimes, don't they, to make their lives seem glamorous and mysterious?"

"That's the thing—Joyce *didn't* say anything about it, which is what this friend thought unusual. Normally they shared everything about their lives. But this time Joyce said nothing."

"Then how did this friend divine that a secret affair was taking place?"

"Joyce started behaving differently when she came back from summer camp. She missed work a couple of times, canceled an overnight they were going to have. That wasn't like her."

"I see, well, does all of this have something to do with me?"

"She was at your camp here at Pearce. Spent two weeks."

"Yes?" Evan felt that he had achieved the perfect tone for his response—expressing a little surprise, but giving away nothing.

"I checked the attendance records myself. She was here, all right. You didn't know that, Professor?"

"I didn't know that, Detective. There are a lot of teenagers on campus every summer. It's a way the college builds up a file of prospective applicants."

"And you interacted with these teenagers?"

"A little. Not much, really." Evan thought about the hair and the lipstick. Why hadn't Malloy mentioned them yet? And if he had already interviewed the camp organizers, surely he would have found someone who remembered the threatened thundershowers and the emergency carpool. Evan decided to be forthcoming. "One afternoon I did give a few students a ride across campus, Detective. Is that important?"

Malloy pulled his hand out of his jacket pocket, saw that he was holding a glasses case, and put it back. "Could be, if one of them was Joyce Bonner."

"I can't say one way or the other. They were just four teenagers to me, three girls and a boy."

"So you're not sure if Joyce Bonner rode with you on that rainy day at camp?"

"Actually, it didn't rain. The storm blew over. And that's right, I'm not sure if she was in my car."

"What about at the Sanders Hotel?"

The Sanders—Evan remembered Ellen finding the unexplainable matchbook in his pocket and wondering about it. Could she possibly have called Malloy to inform him of this small mystery? He erased the possibility from his mind. "I don't know what you mean."

"Did you ever go there with Joyce Bonner?"

There was only one reason a man would go to a hotel with a young girl, and Evan resented this implication. "Detective, I don't know why you keep asking me if I went somewhere with her. I went nowhere with her, ever, anywhere at any time." *I went nowhere*. That was such an imprecise statement—meaningless, in fact. Still, it would have to suffice. "Doesn't that cover everything?"

Malloy tilted his head to the side for a beat, which Evan took to indicate a "no."

"It doesn't cover the times you say you don't know about."

"I can't know what I don't know, and I wouldn't think you could hold me accountable for things that happened that I don't know about."

"Fair enough." Malloy licked around his lips in a slow precise way, as if he had been medically advised to do so several times a day. Evan could just see the rounded tip of his tongue. "I've been reading something else interesting—the Bonner girl's diary. There were some entries from the time she was at your camp."

"It wasn't *my* camp. I was an advisor to it, that's all."

"In any case, she wrote about going to Pearce after she graduated because she really liked the professors she met this summer. One in particular."

"And I suppose that was me?"

"She doesn't name him. Just gave a sort of little description."

"What sort of little description was that?"

"She said he had beautiful eyes."

Evan stared straight ahead at the detective. He knew his eyes were reflecting the blue in the carpet, and Ellen would say they looked especially beautiful. She loved his eyes.

Malloy pointed at the illustration on the cover of *Disturbing Minds.* "I like what your Wittgenstein said his goal was in philosophy—trying to show the fly the way out of the fly bottle, right?"

"Yes."

"I guess we're the flies then, eh, Professor?"

Evan nodded at the accuracy of the metaphor. Of all things right now, he did feel like a fly trying to work its way out of the bottle.

CHAPTER 17

Carla gave him a ride home again. He insisted on paying her a few dollars' gas money for going out of her way, and she said she would add it to her Hawaii fund. She still didn't ask what had happened to the Jetta. Perhaps she assumed an accident or breakdown. Perhaps she thought he was too embarrassed to say. He considered her unquestioning acceptance an admirable attribute.

He went in the front door of his house again, called out "Hello" as he had become used to doing, and heard an "In here" from Ellen. He followed the voice to the kitchen, and there she was sitting on the counter, book in hand. He could smell coffee cake baking in the oven.

"Decided you don't like the stools, either?"

"I love the stools. I just thought I would try a change of perspective for reading poetry."

Perspective—that's definitely what he was lacking right now. But where would he go to get perspective on being suspected of kidnapping? What treetop was high enough?

He put his briefcase on a stool. "So, read me a poem and change my perspective."

Ellen turned back a few pages. "Here's part of one: 'This is the secret silent Lazarus would not reveal, that everyone is right, as it turns out. You go to the place you always thought you would go.'"

Evan ducked to see the cover—*Questions About Angels* by Billy Collins. "We go as far as our imaginations can take us— I can believe that. Where will it be for you?"

Ellen hopped off the counter, and he wondered if her perspective had just changed again. Was looking at the world differently just a matter of geography?

She opened the oven a crack, and the aroma of nuts filled the room. "The ultimate elsewhere."

"What?"

"It's one of the possibilities from the poem—'little units of energy heading for the ultimate elsewhere.' That's where I'd like to go." She slipped on oven mitts to take out the cake and set it on the stove. She usually made this dessert only for company, but he didn't see any other signs of guests coming, and it was a school night. He couldn't imagine the occasion. He felt sure they would not be in a celebrating mood after he related his latest news.

Evan reached past her to get a glass from the cabinet and filled it with water from the spigot. "Paul called me this afternoon," he said.

She stuck a toothpick into the cake. "What did he find out?"

"The police apparently discovered some unknown hair in the Jetta. They're testing to see if it matches the missing girl's."

Ellen turned around. "Hair? That could come from anyone. It could have even blown in your window, for God's sake."

"I guess this hair is blond and curly, the same as . . ." He didn't like calling her Joyce. It sounded too familiar. ". . . the missing girl's." He wished he could leave it at that, but there was one more thing to tell. "They also found her lipstick—her *type* of lipstick—under the seat."

Ellen leaned back against the counter and let out a long sigh. "What's going on, Evan?"

"I don't know any more than that."

"I mean with this whole thing? It just keeps getting worse."

"I know. I can't explain it."

She shook her head as if he wasn't getting her point. "I've been trying not to get too upset about this."

"You've done very well."

"But I have to tell you, I don't think I can go through a whole big mess again."

He knew what she was referring to, at least he thought he did. He considered leaning over and inhaling the sweet smell of the cake and then talking of dinner. But that would be ducking her comment, letting it stand out there unchallenged.

"Again?"

"You know what I mean."

"I'm not sure I do, so you better say it."

She took a moment, perhaps debating within herself whether to go on or not, as he had just done. He rarely saw such indecision in her. She always spoke right up.

"Like before, when you were involved with the other girl."

"I wasn't involved with any *other* girl."

"Evan, you even admitted you were."

"If you mean Carol Sparks, I never said I was involved. *She* was involved. She was a desperate student throwing herself at me, and I got distracted by her for a few months. That's what I admitted." He stressed the last word with just enough sarcasm to annoy her.

Ellen tossed *Questions About Angels* onto the marble island. She did not usually treat books so roughly.

"Distracted to the point of having her in your office after hours," she said, "and going on long drives together?"

"*Having* her?"

"She spent a lot of time in your office, that's all I know."

"Wait a minute. Is that what this is all about, something that happened ten years ago?"

"Seven years ago. The boys were just starting day care."

"So seven years ago a suicidal student latched onto me because she had a terrible home life, and I try to help, which gave her the wrong signal, I guess—that I'm some kind of caring teacher—and she gets obsessed with me. That makes me to blame?"

"You weren't a little obsessed with her?"

A *little* panic, a *little* obsession—why was she always mixing up words like this? "No, I wasn't interested in her at all beyond feeling sorry for her and wanting to help. There was nothing romantic or sexual between us."

"That's not what her father thought."

Evan was not prepared for a long conversation about Carol Sparks, but that was exactly what seemed to be coming. One thing was leading to another, and that thing to another. . . .

"Okay, I'll bite—what's her father got to do with this?"

Ellen took the sponge from the sink and wiped away the crumbs from her coffee cake. "He called here one night looking for his daughter."

"And?"

"He said he saw you fondling her in your car when you dropped her off one time."

"Fondling her? He's crazy. He never saw us doing anything."

"He was lying to me?"

"Yes, he was lying. Or mistaken—I don't know which."

"It's not possible something happened back then that maybe you're blocking out?"

"Come on, that's ridiculous. I can't be blocking out something that never happened. Her father was the one who was abusing her—I told you that before. I never touched Carol."

"Never touched her," Ellen repeated. "That's not exactly true."

Exactly true—how many variations could there be on truth?

"I saw you holding her hand, Evan."

"When did you see us?"

"I stopped by your office the night he called. I was pulling into the parking lot, and two people were walking from your building holding hands. You and Carol Sparks."

"So you went to my office to spy on me and saw something in the dark and decided you knew what was going on?"

"I wasn't spying, and I know what I saw." Ellen rinsed the sponge under the spigot, her back to him. "I know you must be tempted dozens of times a year with the young girls in your classes," Ellen said. "That's natural. I've accepted it. But actually doing something like holding her hand—that just . . . well, it really disappointed me."

He wished to see what disappointment looked like on her. He touched her arm to turn her around. "And you assumed the worst? You tell people that the secret of a good marriage is giving the other person the benefit of the doubt. But all of these years you've been assuming the worst rather than just asking me."

"I haven't assumed anything. I'm still not sure I know what went on then."

"Okay, what do you want to know? Ask me anything—whatever doubt has been hiding in your mind all of this time, let it out."

She said nothing.

"Come on, ask me . . ."

"Not now."

"Why not?"

"I'm not talking to you while you're yelling . . ."

"I'm not yelling. I'm voicing my emotions. You always want me to do more of that, don't you?"

Ellen stepped toward the door to the hall. He moved in front of her. "Don't run away. That's what you did then, too. You ran off before we could get everything out in the open."

"Let me by."

He did not say no, but he didn't move. "I want you to ask me what's on your mind. Why was I holding the girl's hand—is that the question? And did I fondle her, like her father so quaintly put it?"

"Please move, Evan."

"Or are you wondering if there were other girls you never knew about? Maybe even Joyce Bonner—would you like to ask if I had some involvement with her?"

Ellen raised her hands.

"Come on, ask me."

She pushed against him, moved him a little, then tried to slip past. He grabbed her arms. "Come on, Ellen, ask me:

'Evan, did you kidnap that girl?' That's what's on your mind, isn't it? Isn't it?"

"Stop it."

"I don't believe this," he said. "You won't even deny it. Some part of you actually thinks I had something to do with that girl."

The thought of her suspecting him raced through his veins like a strong, maddening drug. He couldn't stand her near him. He loosened his grip a little and shoved her away. She fell back, her arms flailing to the sides. She banged against the marble island, took a step forward to steady herself, and stared at him.

He couldn't believe the force that had come from his hands. He couldn't remember ever touching another human being in anger like this, not even as a boy. He reached out to her, but she turned and hurried toward the garage door as if he were chasing her. In a moment she was gone.

When she left he heard steps behind him. He looked around, and there was Zed standing in the hallway. Or was it Adam? Evan reached out again, but the boy ran upstairs.

Evan woke to an uncommon darkness. Thick black air swirled about his head and stung his eyes. He heard a faint rubbing noise, like metal against wood, and sat up in bed. Something else in the room seemed to be breathing. In the shadows a human-like form swayed side to side, as if from one foot to the other. He squinted to make sense of the broad shoulders, absurdly thin body, and shortened arms. It looked like some fantastic marionette.

The figure ceased moving, and the shape melted into the surrounding dark. Evan stretched back on the mattress, inhaling a long breath to compose himself. He hated waking this deep into the night. The sudden consciousness always confused him. What was dream, and what not? He had never been good at distinguishing.

He took another deep breath, sipping in air until his lungs couldn't hold any more, then expelling it like a slow leak in a child's life preserver. A musky scent blew through the open window. The night was growing colder, just as the weatherman had predicted. A storm was winding up the coast. Normally he would curl himself about Ellen, let the heat of her body suffuse into his. Tonight, alone, he reached for the thin blanket at his feet and pulled it to his neck.

He turned toward the alarm clock just as the illumined numbers clicked away the last minute of the hour, 2:59 turning into 3:00. It occurred to him that it was an infrequent event in the digital universe to witness time passing. Sometimes he felt nostalgic for the analog world where the second hand swept past in endless silent circles. With digital clocks, seconds were bunched up into a much larger minute, then disgorged in a single drop of time. What would be dispensed with next, Evan wondered—minutes, hours? Perhaps the digital clock of the future would move just once a day, sweep away twenty-four hours in a short, precise tick.

Time rolled over to 3:01. The night would get no darker but hadn't yet begun to lighten. He felt suspended between the twin worlds of waking and sleep. He didn't want to think, but the unwanted thoughts came anyway. He pictured Ellen in the spare bedroom at Margaret Hope's "charming, surprisingly roomy cape," as Ellen always described it to eligible men. Evan found the place insufferably cute, with embroidered pillows on every chair and cross-stitched clichés hanging like paintings on the wall. He imagined they had stayed up talking for hours as Ellen poured out the horror of his anger. She would wonder how she could ever trust his hands again. Margaret would say, "You may have to face the fact that you can't."

When Ellen called an hour after fleeing the house she had sounded composed and coherent. He quickly apologized—"I didn't mean to push you that hard"—but she didn't acknowledge his words. She said she needed a night away, and she would be home in the morning in time to get Adam and Zed off to school. He felt like saying that he was perfectly capable of performing the morning routine by himself, that she should come back when she wanted to, not for fear things would fall apart without her. But all of that was a complicated point requiring some tact in its expression, and before he could figure the right words she had asked to speak to the boys.

He didn't know how she explained her absence to them. They held the receiver between their heads and listened. They each looked up at him once, then quickly down at the floor again. When they were done they handed the phone back to Evan. He put it to his ear and said, "Good night, I love you." But the line was dead.

Evan shifted onto his back again. A gust of wind spilled into the room, and now the human figure in the shadows seemed to be dancing.

CHAPTER 18

When he came downstairs the next morning, Ellen was already there, breaking eggs into a frying pan. She was wearing an unfamiliar tight red blouse that made him think of a waitress at a diner. He figured the top was on loan from the diminutive Margaret Hope.

"Sunny-side up?"

Her quick question surprised him. He had assumed this morning would begin with tentative glances over the heads of the boys, then, after they'd left for school, move on to mutual expressions of regret and promises to be more understanding. They had never before spent a night apart in anger. There would need to be an accounting of their emotions. Of course, he would vow never to touch her again . . . *like that, I mean,* he would quickly add.

The two eggs crackled in the pan. Ellen looked over at him for his answer in the way she often did with the twins, a certain "I'm waiting" in her expression. He realized that she rarely repeated a question.

"No, over hard." He pulled out a stool and sat on the edge of the seat. "You're not supposed to eat eggs with the yolk uncooked anymore."

She flipped one egg over in the pan and let the other remain with its yellow dome of yolk unbroken. "Who decided that for us?"

"The FDA recommended it a while ago. It's supposed to be on all the boxes." He picked up the empty carton but didn't see any warning.

Ellen slid the spatula under her egg and lifted it onto her plate. "I think I'll live dangerously."

Live dangerously. It struck Evan that this was the perfect example of first-world "living dangerously"—eating an egg over easy. Or trying a new kind of candy, as Carla had suggested he do.

He poured himself some orange juice. "How's Margaret doing?"

It was an awkward question, because they both knew he had no interest in her all-consuming hobby of playing the flute, just as she showed no regard for his writing or teaching. He couldn't think of any member of the opposite sex who attracted him less, and he imagined that she felt the same about him.

Ellen scooped his egg on a plate and handed it to him. "She's giving up the flute."

That was surprising and encouraging news to Evan, perhaps the start to a new personality, one he might relate to in some small way for Ellen's sake. "Oh?" he said, injecting a hint of regret in his voice. "Why's that?"

"She has sensitive lips. They're being rubbed raw from the mouthpiece."

The laughter escaped him so fast that he couldn't even get a hand to his mouth.

"That's funny?"

He pictured Margaret's tiny lips being worn away by her beloved flute, and the image seemed ironically, perhaps even tragically, comical. "No, it was something else I was thinking about."

"You're a terrible liar," she said as she sat at the table. She tore off a piece of toast and dunked it into the yolk. Yellow oozed across her plate.

Evan cut off a piece of his hard egg and ate it. The taste was dry and sinewy, more like the carton than the egg.

"Just as you like it?" she said, and Evan thought he detected a bit of a smile in her expression.

"Delicious."

He was glad that the subject of their sparring was Margaret Hope, and that their fight of the night before was going unmentioned. Perhaps this was the real secret of an enduring marriage—arguing about other people instead of focusing on your own troublesome behaviors.

The boys had come and gone through the kitchen in a matter of minutes. She let them each have a piece of coffee cake. There were no questions, no long looks, no kisses beyond the quick peck-and-run of their usual morning custom. They, too, seemed determined to act as if nothing had happened. Evan thought they might be developing a family trait.

He waited for Ellen at the door to the garage, his hand on the knob, as she hurried about the kitchen collecting her mug of coffee and car keys and pocketbook. She started down the hall toward him, but turned on her heels and went to the sink. She poured herself water and then scooped up her pills from the counter. She dropped them into her mouth, took a quick sip, and swallowed.

He winced at the sight. "How can you do that?" He had asked this question before, so he knew it was a safe subject, in keeping with the commonplace nature of the morning's conversation. It didn't feel to Evan that they were really avoiding dealing with the anger that had erupted in this kitchen only twelve hours before. Rather, it was as if nothing important had happened at all.

For a moment he thought that maybe he hadn't actually shoved Ellen into the island, that he had just tapped her and she had stumbled backward. Why had she run out then? Perhaps at the time she had misconstrued the events as well but now, after a night at Margaret Hope's, she realized that there had been no harm intended, or done.

Ellen set her water glass in the sink. "It's just like swallowing corn or peas whole," she said.

Evan rubbed his throat and felt the hard Adam's apple. "You swallow corn and peas whole?"

"I could. It would be just like swallowing pills."

She was playing with him, circling her logic back on itself in a fine display of nonsense. "Oh, I see now," he said.

The phone rang. She answered, listened for a second, and handed the receiver to him. "It's your detective."

Her choice of words seemed surprisingly right to Evan—it did feel to him as if he had his own personal detective.

"Hello?"

"Professor, it's Robert Malloy. I'm calling to tell you that we're done with your Jetta. You can come pick it up anytime."

The detective's tone was eerily casual, like a car mechanic calling to say that he had finished his repairs. The matter-of-factness of his words seemed out of whack to Evan with the gravity of the situation.

"You don't return the vehicle to where you took it, Detective? That doesn't seem right."

"We could tow it back to the college, if that's what you want."

It seemed a petty thing to do, making Malloy take the car to campus. "Never mind," Evan said. "I'll come by for it in a little while."

"You can sign for it with the desk sergeant. I'll let him know you're on your way."

Lost amid these small arrangements was the central question—had they found anything more incriminating than the lipstick and hair? Evan assumed not, or they wouldn't be releasing the car. He wanted to ask, but not with Ellen standing nearby.

The girl in the front row was smiling at him. It wasn't often that anyone smiled in "Philosophy of Religion," a misnamed course if there ever was one. In his opinion, there was precious little philosophy in religion, a point he was just making when he saw the girl put down her pen, close her notebook, and smile.

"Religion goes beyond what is knowable," Evan said. "It's not cognitive, but rather, finds value on an emotional level."

Her hand was rubbing across her cheek now, as if entranced by the smoothness of it. He saw this out of the side of his eye. If she was this enraptured by her own touch, what of someone else's? He didn't dare look at her directly for fear his eyes would be locked there until she released them by looking away herself. And she might not do that.

"Does religion work? This question occupied William James for much of his life. The pragmatism he espoused emphasized ends rather than means or origins. It follows that religions should not seek authority through canonical texts, reported miracles, or church history. A religion should be tested for its simple ability to cause good in an individual's life."

His gaze swept across the room, and as it passed over the front row, the girl—Miss Robbins—smiled again. He smiled briefly in response. How could he not? A pretty girl smiles at a man, the man should acknowledge the gesture. Or was it a signal? That was the problem for a professor—interpreting the expressions, words, and deeds of his students. He had to be on guard against acknowledging signals from young women. A friendly gesture, that was acceptable.

"The cognitive world of science must be verifiable and sharable among people. Religious faith or vision can spring from personal experience and how one interprets the world. James said that we all live and die individually, so what is real is what is real to each of us individually."

Miss Robbins sighed, and Evan thought of a paper he had read years ago about the erotic nature of teaching. The writer, a distinguished professor of political science, had unabashedly declared the role of Eros in the classroom, particularly between male professor and female student. Eros was at the core of teaching. Eros submerged itself into every thought and look and comment. Eros—

He lost his place. William James . . . pragmatism . . . does religion work? The girl puckered her lips. He looked away from her, over her head into the upper rows of the class, and found a dozing boy to concentrate on.

"God is the name we give to a concept of an infinite being. Yet our minds are finite in scope, so it's futile to contemplate divinity. We can only come to finite conclusions about an infinite being, which seems rather pointless, doesn't it? Our finite minds crave duality, the dialectic that Hegel spoke of. Whatever truth we express has an equally powerful opposite ideal that we must incorporate into our belief system. In religion, for example, good requires evil."

The drowsy boy raised his head and rubbed his eyes. "Why not 'Evil requires good'?"

Evan liked the question and was pleased to see that in his own way, the student had been paying attention. "Yes, both statements make sense. Christianity proposes that God created the good in the Garden of Eden, but the goodness could not survive long on earth without the evil brought there by the serpent and unleashed by the eating of the apple. Perhaps that is why heaven, which is the goal and expectation of millions of religious believers, is so vague in our minds. Most of you have been taught that heaven is a desirable place, yet who has described it for you? Nietzsche proposed going beyond good and evil, but I suggest it's difficult to conceive of any form of sublime or transcendent existence that doesn't include at least the possibility of misfortune or sin or despair."

The girl in the front row lifted her thumb to her mouth and began biting her nail. Her lips opened a bit, and now she seemed to be sucking on her thumb. Evan looked back at the boy, who was resting his head on his arm again.

"We were born with the capacity for every dual emotional

set—happiness-sadness, euphoria-depression, love-hate, charity-malevolence, and on and on. We think in these terms, we act in these terms, we judge others and ourselves in these terms. But whether evil begat good or good begat evil, I leave it to you to decide."

The Jetta had never been this clean. Evan wondered what happened to the gum wrappers wedged in the back ashtray, and the metal flip-tops the boys wiggled off their soda cans, and all of the coins that slipped from his fingers into that annoying little space between the driver's seat and the well. Was everything lying in some police drawer, tagged and photographed, with an explanatory note of its significance? He was sure the evidence would show that he was unusually messy. He would concede forgetfulness as well, for certainly they had found a fistful of yellow Post-it notes that had blown off the dashboard where he put them as reminders of some call to make or meeting to attend.

He was happy to be in his own car again and patted the steering wheel. Carla had seemed a little disappointed that he wouldn't need a ride from her anymore, and she finally showed a little curiosity. "So," she said, "the old Jetta's come back to life?"

The question wasn't specific enough to put him on the spot. He appreciated that she wouldn't do that. He had had the urge to explain the circumstances to her, even share a laugh at the absurdity of the situation. She would certainly have been amazed at the idea of his being cuffed—hands behind his back—and taken away. He could have told the story in an amusing way, how he had tried to wave with the handcuffs on, his mishearing of *Pleasant Run* for *Pheasant Run,* and the scrutiny of the grim Sergeant Killian. They would have had tears in their eyes from laughing so hard.

"It's running like a charm," he had told her, "better than ever." In fact, he was enjoying driving the Jetta so much that he didn't want to go straight home. He came to the end of the interstate and saw the sign for Eastfield State Park. Normally with time on his hands he would turn there without a thought. This day he wondered if there was a reason he shouldn't. Malloy hadn't told him not to. Curry hadn't said that it would be better if he avoided the area. Was it just understood that he shouldn't go there?

Evan turned down the narrow entranceway. The tree branches arching over the road darkened the late afternoon and made him feel suddenly chilled. In a few moments he pulled into the sunshine of the parking lot.

He turned into his usual spot, backing in the Jetta so that he could see the water without getting out of the car. Of course, he had gotten out that day. He remembered scribbling some notes, rereading them, and thinking how worthless they were. He made several more starts at his speech to the freshman class, then gave up. That's when he'd gotten out of the car to stretch. The pad was still in his hand, so he'd torn off the unusable pages and thrown them in the trash receptacle. He could see himself every step of the way now—getting out of the car into the dusty stone lot, reaching his hands into the air to stretch, and tossing the notes into the can in an arc, like a basketball shot. "Swish," he had said to himself, just like one of the twins.

He wondered where these pictures in his head came from. They hadn't been there before, not when the detective questioned him. Now someone was telling him what had happened. All his mind had to do was fill in the details.

Evan looked out at the water, which was as calm as he had ever seen it. What happened to the predicted storm? The surface of the lake looked flat and gray, like ice. He wondered if the police had dragged the bottom. Drowning had to be a possibility for a teenage girl on a hot August afternoon. But then, where were her shoes? No one goes swimming wearing shoes.

Evan got out of his car and walked toward the lake. Twenty yards away, about halfway between the parking lot and the water, he saw the information booth, boarded up with plywood. "Closed for the Season" the sign said. Next summer, what girl would apply for the vacant job of park information aide? He couldn't imagine the parent who would allow it.

He walked down the broad path toward the small square building. The low sun flooded his eyes, and he shielded them with his hand. Twigs snapped under his feet. One wouldn't be able to approach the booth this way without making a sound.

On the red-painted door hung a flyer—"Missing!" It looked like hundreds of pasted-up papers Evan had seen— *Missing,* an exclamation point, then a fuzzy picture of a cat or dog. Here there was a picture of Joyce Bonner in her cheerleading outfit. She appeared to be in mid-cheer, her mouth slightly open, and he wondered what she was about to say. Underneath her picture the small print said, "Anyone with ANY information contact Detective Robert Malloy at . . ." Perhaps it was this flyer that prompted the person to call with the tip—gray Jetta, license EZ-2134, Pearce College sticker on back window.

Evan heard noise in the woods and turned around. A short, dark man was walking in the brush near the lake, jabbing at the ground with a sword-like stick. What about this odd person, for instance? Was he a suspect?

Evan walked to the water's edge. The sand was soft under his shoes. He felt the odd urge to keep going straight into the lake, maybe even dive underwater. He wouldn't surface until he had counted off sixty seconds. Evan tried to think of the most unpredictable, impulsive, craziest thing he had done in his adult life, and he came up with nothing. Thirty years from teenage-hood and he could claim nothing risky, or careless, or irresponsible. It embarrassed him to think of himself as so dull. Wittgenstein had a whole dangerous, erotic life of the flesh to go with his rigorous philosophical investigations. You could see it in his eyes. He wasn't just looking for meaning in words and ideas. There was longing in his eyes, a certain craving, even necessity, for experience. Perhaps that was his balance, to seek order in the metaphysical world by day and gratification in the physical world by night. It would be a rough sort of equilibrium, but equilibrium nonetheless.

Evan turned away from the water. The man in the woods was bent over from the waist. Evan wondered if there were wild blueberries there or some other fruit to pick. He approached to within a few yards and saw the man gather up a handful of pine needles and let them fall through his fingers, as if sifting them.

"Lose something?"

The stranger straightened up. He was holding the stick and a black plastic bag in one hand. "Yes, my daughter."

The words shocked Evan. He couldn't remember ever hearing a sentence—just three words—with more unintended sadness to them. The man bent over again and swept his hand into a pile of dead leaves. He didn't seem to understand the strangeness of what he had just said. How could he insert *daughter* into a sentence where some object, like *keys* or *wallet,* more naturally fit?

Evan gestured back to the information booth. "The girl on the flyer?"

The man nodded and squatted amid some low plants. Evan thought he saw poison ivy there but decided it would be stupid to mention it. The man pushed back the stalk of a small plant with a gentleness that Evan marveled at. If it were Adam or Zed missing, he could see himself ripping out plants, tearing up the whole park looking for clues.

Joyce Bonner's father speared a small bit of blue cloth with his stick and dropped the piece into the plastic bag.

"Didn't the police already search here?"

"Police don't see everything. They don't know what to look for."

Evan watched for a minute. He thought he should just turn away, go back to his car. Surely talking to the missing girl's father was not a good idea. But he was curious. "What do you think you might find?"

"A piece of blouse, an earring, something to show she was here."

Here, there . . . wherever the girl had been, she wasn't now.

Mr. Bonner stood up and arched his back. "You have children?"

"Two boys. I can't imagine losing one of them."

"People say it's the not-knowing that hurts the most. They're crazy. I'm not doing this just to know. I want her back."

It seemed obvious to Evan that a father who truly thought his daughter was alive wouldn't be poking through the underbrush looking for clothes. In his broken heart, Mr. Bonner knew his child was dead. Evan was sure of it.

The man walked a few feet to a fallen tree branch, bent over, and struggled to raise one end. Evan rushed over. "Let me help."

They lifted at the count of three and carried the thick log a few feet away. Evan followed his lead, stepping carefully through the brush, disturbing as little as possible.

They leaned over together to look in the area where the dead branch had been. There was nothing to see except for crushed grass. Evan stood up. Mr. Bonner cocked his head and then reached out to feel with his hand.

"It's kind of strange, don't you think, grass growing under a big log like that. You expect to find worms and snails crawling out of the wet dirt. There shouldn't be grass."

"I guess you're right. What do you think it means?"

Mr. Bonner stood up. "The log was moved there recently, that's what."

And what could that mean? Evan didn't ask. The man was obviously seeking answers from every odd bit of circumstance he could find in these woods. "How long have you been doing this, if you don't mind my asking?"

"Twenty-three days."

Days? Evan had assumed the answer in terms of hours. He counted back—twenty-three days ago was August 25th, two days after the disappearance. It was unbearable to think of this man coming out here every day since then looking for some remnant of his daughter. Would he stop before the snows came? Evan didn't think so.

"Found anything yet?"

"Lots of things—socks, gloves, comics, even a couple of condoms. I wouldn't touch them."

"No, of course not."

"Imagine people out here having sex in the park. Who would do that?"

"People who have nowhere else to go, I guess."

Mr. Bonner grunted and stabbed a candy bar wrapper on

the ground. He lifted it in front of his face, looked at it for a moment, then dropped it in the bag.

"What do you do with all of the things you find?"

"I turn everything over to the police."

Mr. Bonner walked a few yards down the path, then glanced over his shoulder. Evan took it as invitation to come along. "How do you know you're looking in the right area?"

"The information booth's there," he said, pointing with his stick. "That's where she works."

"But this is a fairly busy part of the park, and nobody saw anything. So if your daughter got in a car with someone, he probably would have taken her somewhere else."

"Joy wouldn't get in a car with a stranger, unless she knows him."

One could never know a stranger, of course, but Evan didn't correct Mr. Bonner. It wasn't the time to point out the impossible.

"She wouldn't have gotten in with a stranger if she had a choice, but maybe she didn't have a choice. Your daughter wasn't very big, was she?"

"I don't use the past tense, Mr. . . . ."

"Oh, sure, sorry. I'm just saying that she probably didn't put up much of a fight, not enough that people would see."

"She's a fighter. She doesn't give in."

"But a man of my size, or yours even, coming up behind her, could have gotten her in his car and taken her somewhere more remote in the park. He wouldn't take the chance of being seen around here."

Mr. Bonner looked out over the lake, then to the right where the land rose up a hundred feet. "I don't know the park, never came here except to drop Joy off a few times in the parking lot. My wife picks her up."

"It's a pretty big place, bigger than you'd think from standing here. The Ledges are to your right." Evan pointed to where the land rose up about a hundred feet. "They're mostly granite. Beyond them are the wetlands filled with skunk cabbage and sticker bushes. You can't really walk in that area. On the other side, beyond a really beautiful stand of birches, are some open fields. Kids play ball there. But a stream runs through the middle and overflows a lot, so it gets pretty muddy sometimes."

"You seem to know the park well, Mr. . . . ?"

"My name's Evan. Yes, we used to bring our boys here when they were younger. I don't get much beyond the lake anymore."

"Well, maybe tomorrow I will start looking in these other places you mention. I've done about as much as I can here."

Mr. Bonner continued along the path, his shoulders rolled forward, his head hanging. Evan wondered if he had always been hunched over like this, or if the weight of recent events had worn him down. He seemed now like a man who would be looking downward for the rest of his life.

"Good luck," Evan called after him.

Mr. Bonner waved without turning around.

CHAPTER 19

A s the fourth week of September commenced, Evan became increasingly uneasy. After some reflection, he traced this feeling to an unexpected source: the absence of Robert Malloy. The detective had not been heard from in six days. Evan wasn't anxious about the tangled threads of supposed evidence—the hair and lipstick, for instance—left hanging. He assumed his explanations had been convincing or Malloy would have come calling immediately. That's what Paul Curry thought as well, an opinion he shared from his beachside vacation home. "Just sit tight," he said. "It's their move."

Evan was not averse to sitting tight. He had no desire to spark up the investigation in any way. What would he say,

"Hello, Detective, I was just wondering, have you come up with any more damning information about me?" It would be a foolish question.

Still, he did feel a strange urge to have the detective pop up again. It was, he said to Ellen as she stood at the stove preparing dinner, as if he were starring in his own mystery movie when Malloy appeared. Evan thought this an interesting observation about the power of the psyche to reframe experience. She wiped her forehead with her hand and said that perhaps he was demonstrating the power of the ego to plow its way into the center of someone else's story—Joyce Bonner's disappearance, for example.

"I'd be glad to bow out of this story at any time," he said. "This isn't the role I was expecting to play at this time of my life." He thought his movie metaphor surprisingly apt.

"I know," she said. "Sometimes we find ourselves in situations we never dreamed for ourselves."

He waited for her to elaborate. What role had she never dreamed for herself—the Accused Man's Wife?

"Can you get out plates and utensils for two, Evan?"

"Two? The boys aren't eating with us?"

"I dropped them off after school at a birthday party for Kenny Marshall. They'll be back at nine."

It surprised him to realize that his sons weren't upstairs. He had felt their presence in the house and the comforting completeness of the family being all together. Now there were two loose ends.

He went to the cabinet beside the sink and took out dinner plates. As he did he gazed through the front window and saw a car across the street. It had not been there when he came home, he was sure.

"Use the blue plates in the dining room," Ellen said.

Evan put back the everyday plates. "That car out front," he said, "was it there when you came home?"

"What car?"

He parted the curtains for her to see.

"No, I don't remember any car."

"You mean it wasn't there?"

She pulled away from the window. "It could have been."

Her uncertainty puzzled him. How could she not have noticed a car parked on the street in a neighborhood where everyone used their driveways?

She took the lid off a large pot, looked inside, then put the lid back on. "Who do you think it is?"

"I have no idea."

"Probably someone visiting Mr. Grayling."

"The only one who visits the old man is his daughter, and she drives a light blue van. This is a dark foreign car, like a Honda or Toyota, and the driver is just sitting there."

"So maybe he's lost."

"People don't sit in their cars if they're lost, they ask for directions or drive to a gas station." Evan looked again. The car was still there. In the falling darkness, he could just make out the face of the driver turned toward the house.

"Why don't you go offer your help?" Ellen said.

There was that option. But was it wise to knock on the window of a car without knowing who was inside? He could call the police, but what would he say—there's a car parked across the street? In the range of possible threats in the world, that one didn't sound too menacing.

"Dinner's ready." Ellen picked up the tray of food, and he followed her into the dining room. He bent down to get the blue plates from the cabinet, and she said, "Bring out the candles, too."

"Candles?"

"I thought we could use a little different atmosphere to-night. It's not often the boys are gone."

Evan set the plates and candlesticks on the table. She went to the kitchen and returned with a matchbook in her hand. He saw the cover—The Sanders Ballroom, with the little top hat. He had forgotten about these matches.

"I'll light," he said.

"That's okay." Ellen struck a match, but it went out as she moved her hand toward the candle. The second one did the same.

He reached for the matchbook. "Really, I'll do it."

She pulled off another match and held the head to the strik-ing strip, but her hand didn't move. She looked up at him for a few seconds, and he thought she was going to say some-thing, perhaps explain what she had in mind for after the can-dlelight dinner, but she struck the match and held it against the wick. He watched the fire burn close to her fingers, and then the candle finally ignited.

He sat at his usual place and began spooning out aspara-gus. She sat opposite him and picked up the salad bowl, then put it down. "Evan," she said, and he knew she was about to say something serious or awkward, because she always led with his first name on those occasions. "These are the matches I got from your pocket a few weeks ago when we came home from my mother's."

"Right, I remember."

"I just looked inside the cover. It says, '7 at fountain.'"

"Really?"

"Did you meet someone at The Sanders Ballroom fountain?"

The question seemed ridiculous to him. Why would he arrange a meeting with someone through a matchbook? "No, of course not. I can't even remember the last time I was there."

"Then how did the matches get in your pocket?"

"Didn't you ask me that before? I have no idea."

"I assume you didn't pick them up to light a cigarette."

"No, I'm not a secret smoker, if that's what you're asking."

"And you say you weren't at The Sanders?"

Evan set down the plate of asparagus. "I'm not just saying it, it's a fact. Years ago I might have stopped in there for some reason—I think one of the philosophy associations held a meeting in the ballroom. Maybe I picked up some matches then."

"So you don't know what this note means?"

He shook his head. "Let me see it." He extended his hand across the table. She opened the cover and turned it his way. He stood up and leaned between the candles for a closer view, but still the writing was indistinguishable. "I can't see it, the way you're holding it." He put his hand out again.

"It just says '7 at fountain.' That's all."

He left his hand outstretched in front of her, palm up. "You won't let me have it?"

She put the matches in her shirt pocket. "I'm really trying to have a nice dinner, Evan. I don't want to argue."

"I'm not arguing. I just asked you a question."

"Have some applesauce," she said and lifted the bowl to his hand. "Margaret made it."

After a few moments he took the applesauce. The matches bulged a little against Ellen's breast.

Later, in his study preparing lecture notes, Evan heard a shout from the second floor, then thumps against the ceiling above him. He remembered Ellen and the boys passing his door to go upstairs earlier and so waited for her to quiet them. The banging continued, and then came a yell like he had never heard before from the twins.

He ran to the base of the stairs. "What's going on?"

There was silence for a moment, then another round of shouts and thumps. He ran up the steps and turned the corner into the boys' room. The two of them were rolling over each other on the bottom bunk, pounding their fists into each other's backs. He couldn't tell which was which. One of them was biting, the other scratching.

He grabbed the twin on top—Adam, he thought—and hauled him off the bed by his shirt. The squirming boy got in one last kick, and the toe of his sneaker struck his brother in the mouth. The scene stopped for a moment. They looked at each other, as if waiting for some cue as to who should react first.

Zed screamed and clamped his hand over his mouth. Blood ran through his fingers. Evan pulled the boy off the bed and into the bathroom. The face was so bloody he couldn't tell how much damage had been done.

Evan turned on the cold water spigot. "Wash yourself off."

Zed cupped a handful over his mouth, and the water turned red as it dripped from his chin.

"Let me see now."

The boy twisted away.

"I have to see if your teeth are all right."

Zed spat in the sink, splattering blood over the white porcelain, then turned his mouth upward. Evan reached in with his finger and brushed it gently over the edges of the teeth, top and bottom.

"Everything looks okay. You didn't lose any."

Zed pulled away and spat again. Evan opened the linen closet and grabbed a red towel. He ran the edge of it under cold water and then pressed it against his son's mouth. "Hold this tight against your lip. If that doesn't stop the bleeding we may have to take you in for stitches."

"I'm not getting stitches," Zed cried.

"Then keep pressure on it."

He sat on the edge of the bathtub, holding the towel to his mouth. Evan ran the water to wash away the blood from the sink.

"What happened? You two never fought like that before."

Zed took the towel away from his mouth as if he were going to answer, then put it back against his lips.

Evan turned and saw Adam standing in the doorway. His hands were balled up in front of him, a pose he had never struck before. Was this the look of violence?

"I want to know what happened, Adam. Why were you fighting?"

The boy shook his head. His lips stayed shut.

"If you don't talk you're facing worse punishment. You know how it works around here."

The boys glared at each other. Evan figured he could coax one or the other to tell what had happened, but not if they were together.

"Okay, you've each lost your computer time for a week."

"That's not fair," Zed said. "I'm the one who got kicked."

"You don't decide what's fair in this house. Adam, get your things, you're sleeping downstairs in my study tonight. I don't want any more bloody fights."

"Why do *I* have to move? Zed started it."

"I didn't."

"I don't know who started it, but you got in the last kick, so you get moved."

Adam turned back into the bedroom and grabbed his bookbag from the hook on the door. Evan followed him.

"That's it? You don't need pajamas or anything?"

"Pajamas? Come on, Dad."

Evan nudged Adam toward the door. "I'll be back up in a minute, Zed. Keep the towel pressed against your lip."

Evan walked his son downstairs, and when they turned into his study he said, "Okay, I want to know what happened."

Adam dropped his bookbag to the floor. "Z. said something, that's all, and I got mad."

"What did he say?"

"I can't tell you."

"Are you going to be able to forget about it by tomorrow?"

"If he takes it back."

Evan tossed the sofa cushions in the corner and pulled out the bed. Adam sat back on it, his sneakers just hanging over the side.

"Dad?"

"Yes."

"Can I tell you something else?"

"What?"

"I'm not supposed to."

Evan was losing patience. "Do you want to tell me or not?"

"Sort of."

"Then what's stopping you?"

Adam shrugged. "Nothing, I guess." He sat up on the sofa. "Okay, I'll tell you this, but you can't say I did, okay?"

"I don't make promises like that, but I'll try to keep your confidence."

"Well, yesterday, Mom came into our room, you know—"

"No, I don't *know*."

"Sorry, I mean that Mom came into our room to talk to us. She sat in our beanbag chair. She never does that. So then she started asking us questions."

"About what?"

"That day at camp, you know—I mean, that day you picked us up."

"What kind of questions?"

"She was like, was Dad on time and did we drive straight home and were you like usual?"

"Like usual—how would that be?"

"You know, sort of how you ask us crazy stuff, like you'll say, 'How was work?' when we come home from school. Or like, 'You want to go swimming in the lake?' You asked us that on Christmas, remember? It was snowing outside. You even put on your bathing suit. Mom said you were acting stupid."

Evan remembered the moment, walking into the living room in his bathing shorts, pretending surprise—"How come nobody's ready?" And then Ellen's comment as she sat on the sofa reading, "You're acting stupid, Evan." He had thought he was acting funny for the kids' sake. Her words made him feel pathetic, as if he were some odd uncle who would go to any extreme to humor children.

"Dad?"

Evan looked down at Adam lying back on the sofa bed. In the dark light, he seemed like a much younger child. "Yes."

"You're not mad at me, are you?"

"Of course I'm angry at you. You could have knocked your brother's teeth out."

"I mean for talking to Mom."

"No, I'm not angry about that."

"'Cause I didn't tell her anything."

Anything—what did he mean by that? What did his son think he wouldn't want him to say? He felt a strange reluctance to know.

"Why was she asking us that stuff, Dad?"

Because she was suspicious and untrusting—that was the truthful answer. He had the powerful impulse to be perfectly honest, for the first time to say something negative to one of the boys about their mother. He would be justified, too, because she had sowed this uneasiness in their minds through her questioning.

Adam reached under his T-shirt to scratch his arm and then pulled his hand out and rubbed his head. Evan thought of lice. But that didn't seem possible. If anything, the boys were too clean. He had to pound on the bathroom door to get them out of the shower.

"You know your mother," he said. "She's always trying to keep track of us guys."

"Yeah, she's like all over us sometimes when we go out to know where we're going."

"It's because she loves you, that's why she's asking," Evan said, and he felt a bit noble for conquering his instinct to speak ill of her. Of course, she would never know.

"It's just we're getting kind of old for that," Adam said.

"I don't think you're ever going to get so old that Mom won't be checking up on you. Where is she, anyway?"

"She went for a walk."

"A walk?" Evan turned toward the window. "It's pitch-dark out. Why's she taking a walk?"

Adam shrugged. "She said she needed air. I gave her my flashlight."

Air. People were always going out for it when they felt the world tightening around them. But what curative powers could the night air bring when a person was plagued with suspicion?

CHAPTER 20

They arrived at Eastfield Middle School in separate cars and parked next to each other. She walked across the lot one step ahead of him, in short, quick strides, as if they were late. He checked his watch—they were early for their 9 A.M. appointment.

"What's this all about, anyway?" Evan asked to slow her down.

Ellen spoke over her shoulder. "I told you all I know. Zed's homeroom teacher wants to speak to us. It sounds like he's getting in trouble."

Inside the building she stopped a boy or girl at every turn in the hallway and asked directions. He thought the way to go obvious but didn't say anything. In a few minutes they were entering the doorway marked "Ms. Greeley," and there was Zed sitting in the front row, his head propped up by both hands, staring at the teacher at the blackboard. The seats all around him were empty.

The woman who turned to greet them was so young and pretty that Evan could understand why his son was staring. Perhaps she was the source of Zed's inattention in class.

"Mr. and Mrs. Birch," she said, "I'm Jane Greeley."

They shook hands all around.

"Please sit."

They sat on either side of Zed, squeezing into the small desks. He gave each of them a little wave. His lower lip was still swollen from the fight two days before, but he didn't seem self-conscious about it. Perhaps he was proud. It was his first visible injury.

Ms. Greeley sat behind her desk, with the huge American flag hanging just a few inches above her head. Evan thought that would be annoying.

"Thanks for taking the time to come in this morning," she said.

"Of course we'd take the time," Ellen said.

"You'd be surprised how many parents won't. If it happens at school, it's our problem."

"That's not our philosophy," Ellen said.

"I asked you here because Zed has been getting into some uncharacteristic trouble the last couple of weeks—late for classes, talking back to teachers, that sort of thing. I'd like to get a handle on this before it gets any worse."

"That sounds like a good idea," Evan said.

Zed slumped in his seat, threw his head back, and stared at the ceiling. Ellen tapped his arm. "Pay attention." He straightened a little.

"I've checked with all of Zed's teachers, and none of them sees any school-based reason for his misbehaviors. His grades have only suffered a little. He still turns in his homework every day. But he seems to be seeking out the habitual troublemakers. He's changed his table in the lunchroom to sit with them. He and Adam used to be inseparable during the day. Now they come in and leave together—that's it."

Evan leaned forward. "Shouldn't we be having this conversation in private and then bringing Zed in?"

"I'm completely open with my students, Mr. Birch. Zed knows he's been skating on thin ice lately. And he has to understand what our expectations, and your expectations, are for his behaviors."

Evan sat back. "Okay."

"Oftentimes there are things happening at home that distract a child, things he may not even comprehend. They can cause him to be anxious or unhappy and lead him to make wrong choices."

Ms. Greeley looked from Evan to Ellen and back to him again. Her question was clear: Was there anything going on at home to explain Zed's deteriorating behavior?

Evan turned his hands up, a noncommittal gesture, neither yes nor no. Ellen opened her pocketbook, pulled out her small water bottle, and took a swig. "There are always things going on," she said. "It's hard to know what might be causing a child anxiety."

Ms. Greeley picked up a pencil and tapped it on the desk, pushing it through her fingers. "I'm talking about something unusual, something that might particularly upset a ten-year-old."

She was implying marital tension, of course, perhaps talk of divorce that a youngster might have overheard. She would not be imagining a father being hauled off by the police in front of his sons for kidnapping a sixteen-year-old girl.

"We'll have to give it some thought," Evan said.

He looked across Zed, and Ellen gave a quick nod of her head. He was to go no further explaining.

"I'm not asking you to discuss any such matters with me," Ms. Greeley said. "I asked you in so we all understand there's a problem here, and you need to talk it over with each other and with Zed."

The boy yawned, his mouth getting wider and wider, and Evan realized there would be a lot to talk about.

The headline in the campus paper said, "Police Eye Pearce Professor in Girl's Disappearance." Evan saw it as he walked the main hallway of the Student Union with Professor Ivan Malov, the newly named chairman of the physics department, a man of so few words that Evan had given up trying to coax conversation out of him. Malov did, however, know how to grunt with great meaning, and he did so now at the bundles of *Pearce Banner*s lying on the floor. Evan interpreted the sound and slight nod of head as a desire to see the paper, and so he bent over to get a copy. He held it out to Malov, but the elderly gentleman kept his hands behind him and read the story as they walked.

When they reached the doors Malov shook his head and said, "Unfortunate, I think."

Evan nodded. It was the kind of comment he felt comfortable assenting to, one that could be taken many ways. He opened the door, but before either of them could go out, a German shepherd came trotting in. Malov tipped his hat to the dog and said something in Hungarian. Then he shuffled through the door and veered off toward the science building.

Evan slid the paper into his briefcase. He was curious, of course, to read the story but did not want to do so in the open. He knew from scanning the first paragraph that the professor "being eyed" was unnamed. That was the most important thing.

When he reached the Humanities Faculty Building, Evan entered by the back stairway and took the *Banner* from his briefcase. In the dim light he leaned against the cold cinder block wall and began reading:

"A professor at Pearce College is under suspicion by local police in the disappearance of sixteen-year-old cheerleader Joyce Bonner, who was last seen working at the information booth at Eastfield State Park on August 23. The *Banner* has learned that police have come on campus several times to question the professor.

"Dean Mark Santos refused to comment on this report except to say that it was the policy of the college to cooperate with local authorities pursuing any criminal matter related to any member of the Pearce community.

"Speculation is running rampant on campus as news of the investigation spread.—'Sure I believe a professor could be involved,' said Donald Klein, a sophomore business administration major who was eating lunch outside Burt's Dogs. 'Professors commit crimes, too, don't they?'"

Yes, Evan said to himself as he stuffed the paper back in his briefcase, they do. He didn't need to read any more insightful quotes from sophomores eating hot dogs at Burt's and so headed up the stairs. When he reached the reception area, Carla jumped up from her desk, shaking the paper in her hand.

"Did you see it, Professor?"

"Yes, I saw it."

"I bet it's Professor Rothvan in Poly Sci. Doana said he's been acting stranger than usual."

"Doana?"

"Doana Moore—the receptionist in government. Five o'clock comes, she's out of there. She wouldn't be caught dead working overtime for him. He always gave me the creeps, too."

"Past tense?"

"Huh?"

"He doesn't give you the creeps anymore?"

"Sure he does. I wait outside when I pick up Doana for lunch. He always brushes into you when he goes by and then says, 'I'm very sorry to have encroached upon you.' *Encroached upon you*—who talks like that?"

"Jack Rothvan may be a bit eccentric, but that doesn't make him a criminal. And it's not a good idea to speculate about people. Reputations have been ruined on less."

"But everybody's talking about it. You can't stop everybody."

"You're right. People seem to have an insatiable appetite for the tribulations of others."

"I don't know about that," she said. "It's just interesting wondering. Lord knows nothing else interesting has happened on this campus for years."

"A girl disappeared, Carla. That's terrible, not interesting."

"It's terrible and interesting, Professor."

Evan found himself nodding at her observation. It—the disappearing girl, the suspected professor—were terrible and interesting in about equal measures.

"Jackie in the cafeteria remembers seeing a car towed

about a week and a half ago. They never tow from the faculty lot, you know? She thinks that had something to do with it."

Evan looked at Carla. He didn't see any guile in her face, no probing, no knowledge of these events other than what she was relating. She obviously wasn't testing him. Still, she might find out later that it was his Jetta that had been towed, and then she would wonder why he hadn't admitted it to her. That would be awkward to explain.

"That was my car they towed, Carla. Remember that's why I needed you to drive me home for a few days? My car was out of commission." He phrased this admission carefully, without even a hint of a lie.

"Oh," she said, and the excitement vanished from her face, "I don't remember you telling me that."

"I'm pretty sure I mentioned it," he said.

Carla shook her head. "No, I would have remembered, 'cause I was thinking that maybe Jackie was right, the towing had something to do with this."

Evan reached into the bowl of candies sitting on top of the dividing wall and took one. He thought of Carla's advice— *live dangerously.* "Well, how do you know it doesn't?" He unwrapped the peppermint and popped it in his mouth. He waited for the bitterness to overtake his tongue, but the taste wasn't so bad this time.

Carla walked around the partition, back to her desk. "You mean, what if *you* were the professor the paper wrote about?"

The note of incredulity in her voice surprised him. Of course, she had only worked there for four years, so she wouldn't know that he had been called Professor Romeo by the coeds in his first years of teaching. Girls used to take his courses just to stare at him—he learned that by reading the *Banner*'s annual survey of favorite professors.

"Yes, me," he said. "It isn't conceivable to you that the police think I'm involved in this somehow?"

Carla waved the paper in the air again. "I know people," she said, "and this isn't you."

On his way home from the college, Evan stopped at the Eastfield Memorial Library. He was fond of the brick building, in particular its circular main reading room, which had the pretention of a rotunda. When it was too cold or rainy to go to the lake, he often pulled in there, grabbed a book, and sat in one of the large easy chairs. Sometimes he dozed off.

This day, though, he had more purpose in mind than relaxation. He intended to read about Joyce Bonner. It surprised him that he hadn't thought to do so before. If one were accused of some criminal act, he should learn as much as possible about the alleged victim involved. Evan knew little, he realized, beyond what Detective Malloy had told him.

Evan carried a stack of *Eastfield News* papers to the photocopying machine. He thought it better that he read about Joyce Bonner at his home or office. He began with the day after the disappearance, August 24—"Teen Found Missing from State Park." *Found Missing*—the wording amazed him. Was the headline writer being ironic on purpose or by accident? Evan suspected the latter.

As he copied the article from the 24th, he read the headline for the next day, August 25—"Foul Play Suspected in Girl's Disappearance." Why, after one day, were the police assuming a crime? Surely in a town like Eastfield more teenagers ran away than were abducted. Joyce could have run off with her secret love, the one she wrote so obscurely about in her diary.

It was a possibility worth considering. He thought he would suggest it to Malloy.

August 26—"Police Try to Re-create Bonner Girl's Last 24 Hours." Evan thought *last* an unfortunate choice of words, at least without the qualifier, last 24 hours *before disappearance.* Maybe he was thinking like Mr. Bonner now—the girl deserved to be referred to as if she were still living.

August 27—"Volunteers Search Lake Area for Clues." In the accompanying picture, dozens of people were standing in the parking lot talking. In the front, two men were grimly shaking hands. In the background, a boy was patting a dog. There were no police in the picture, no one giving orders, no one seemingly in charge. The caption said, "Twenty turn out to look for Joyce Bonner yesterday." Evan couldn't tell if these people had just come from the search of the lake or were about to go on it. He thought it odd that two vastly different experiences—heading off with great hopes to search for a girl and coming back unsuccessful—could appear the same.

August 28—"Divers Scour Eastfield Lake for Missing Cheerleader, Find 1984 Camaro." There was certainly more to Joyce Bonner's life than cheerleading, yet it was the only adjective applied to her in article after article. She was destined to be remembered forever as "that cheerleader who disappeared at the lake." Few people would recall her name, but they wouldn't forget the three-column picture of the sludge-covered Camaro being hauled from the water.

August 29—Nothing. Evan scanned the issue a second time but still couldn't see any mention of Joyce Bonner. Was six days the life span of this story? At the least he expected a small item, perhaps only a sentence or two, saying, "Police remain baffled as they continue their search for the missing teenager . . ." Evan was sure the police were baffled, and he thought they should admit it.

August 30—"One Week After Disappearance, Parents Make Plea . . .'Let Our Daughter Go.'" On page one, there was Mr. Bonner, his arm around his wife, a woman at least a half a head taller than he. They seemed—

"Terrible case, huh?"

Evan felt the voice on the back of his neck. He looked at his hands holding the newspaper. Would it seem odd for him to be photocopying so many articles about a missing girl? "Yes, terrible," he said turning his head half around. He caught a glimpse of a man in a dark flannel shirt. The cuffs were frayed—almost shredded. Evan wondered what kind of work would cause that.

The man's thick finger poked past Evan's face, pointing at the top story—"Parents Make Plea . . .'Let Our Daughter Go.'"

"Were you part of that big search they had a few days ago?"

"No, actually, I haven't been following the case." Evan realized that his answer sounded ridiculous, given the newspapers in front of him. "I'm just catching up," he added.

"It's a sad one. A girl disappears just like that"—the man snapped his fingers near Evan's ear. "It makes you sick to your stomach."

Evan pressed the start button of another copy. Of course the girl had disappeared in the snap of fingers. How could one disappear slowly?

"Without a trace," the man said.

"Excuse me?"

"She disappeared without a trace—that's what the police say. Except for the stranger in the gray car."

At first Evan thought the man was referring to someone else—a new lead. Then he realized, the stranger was him. He took one article from the copier and replaced it with another. "I haven't seen anything in the papers about that."

"My brother-in-law, he works in the district attorney's office. He heard there was some guy watching the girl right before she disappeared."

"Watching's a crime now?"

The man didn't answer right away. Evan supposed he had sounded too flip.

"Well, no, of course not. But a man's watching a pretty girl and she disappears, it's kind of suspicious, that's all I'm saying."

Evan placed the last article on the copier. He wondered if little chance conversations like this were happening all over Eastfield. If one man knew of the suspect in the gray car, surely dozens of others did, too. "I hope they find him," he said as he gathered his papers. He liked the irony of wishing out loud that the suspect—he himself—would be found.

"Oh, they already know who he is," the man said. "They're watching him 24/7, that's what my brother-in-law says."

Evan spun around, saw the young librarian behind the checkout counter, saw an old man lifting the current day's *Eastfield News* from its bin, saw a man on a ladder pushing up a panel of the fake ceiling, saw teenagers at the computers and women holding children by the hand. At that moment, it seemed to Evan, they were all watching him.

He left the library with the photocopies under his arm. For the first time since he had been pulled over by the trooper, he felt like more than just an idle suspect. He would have to accept the realization that he was indeed a pursued man, the person presumed guilty of a shocking crime. People were talking about him, if not by name then at least by description. And the police were apparently watching him. He waited for a minute on the brick walkway, but nobody followed him out of the library. He scanned the parking lot. The cars all appeared empty.

Zed wouldn't talk. He said nothing was wrong and that was the end of it.

Ellen threatened to take computer time away and he just shrugged. Evan threatened to cancel sleepovers for the next month. Zed said, "I like my own bed better anyway."

They asked if he was having trouble with a kid at school or a teacher or anyone else—no, no, no. They asked again why he had fought with Adam—he squeezed shut his lips. Finally they left him with a warning: any more calls from school and they would take away his PlayStation for a month. "Fine," Zed said, "I've beaten all the stupid games anyway."

CHAPTER 21

D etective Malloy showed up the following day at 2:15, when Carla took her break. Evan figured he had timed his visit to avoid her, perhaps to save explaining his purpose to a receptionist who would surely ask questions. That was very considerate of him.

Evan hopped out of his chair, extended his hand, and grinned. "Well, Detective, long time no see."

Where had this trite greeting come from? He remembered hearing the phrase in his childhood, but he didn't think he had ever used it himself. Malloy was apparently evoking a certain quaintness in him.

"Investigations take time," the detective said as he entered the office. His head swiveled from side to side, as if there might be evidence lying right out in the open for him to take in. "When you rush you make mistakes."

Evan picked up the *Pearce Banner* and shook it dramatically in the air the way Carla had. "It wasn't a mistake to announce to the college newspaper that a professor is under suspicion for kidnapping?"

Malloy shook his head. "We don't do any announcing like that. To be honest, we don't know how they got their information. We're investigating."

"You're investigating the investigation now? That must get a little complicated for you."

"We'll sort it out. We always do."

The surety of these words surprised Evan. "You mean there aren't any unsolved crimes in Eastfield, no unpunished leaks of information like this?" and here he waved the paper again. "I find that hard to believe."

"Oh, we have our share of open cases, about average for a town our size."

The detective smiled when he said this. He seemed to be cheerily admitting the opposite of what he had just claimed. They did *not* always sort things out.

"So what is it this time—you have a warrant to search my house or dig up my backyard?"

"No, no warrants today, Professor."

Evan picked up the trilobite from his desk and thought about this simple life-form fossilized hundreds of millions of years ago. Humans encased themselves in wood or metal caskets to preserve themselves for a few years. But the lowly arthropod retained its form for eons without any intention at all.

"I have a question, Detective. How would you dispose of a body?" Evan realized this was a strange subject for him to bring up, given his situation. Still, he had always thought that murderers went to far too much trouble to get rid of their victims. Now he had the opportunity to get a professional's opinion.

Malloy leaned against the window ledge. The afternoon sun created a fringe of orange light around his head. "Oh, I don't know."

"You must have thought about it. It's like a philosopher playing God, imagining how he would have created the universe differently."

"Well, I wouldn't dispose of a body, I'd dispose of a person. Go out on a boat with him at night, an accident happens, he goes overboard."

"Your potential victim might not always go on a boat ride with you."

"As long as he'd go *somewhere* with me," Malloy said, "I could take care of him." He opened his notepad. "Now I have a few questions for you, if you don't mind."

"Does my minding or not minding make any difference?"

The detective shrugged. "I'd prefer you didn't mind. It makes things more pleasant."

"I suppose we should at least go through the do-I-need-a-lawyer-here-while-I'm-talking-to-you routine again."

"That's up to you. You were read all your rights, which include not talking to me, and you've talked before. But you can certainly call in your lawyer, if that's the road you want to go down."

Evan detected a slight downward slide in Malloy's tone, implying something ominous at the end of *that* road, perhaps a break in their cordial relationship. The sudden shift from friendliness to vague threat was a little unsettling. "Why don't you tell me what the subject is today," Evan said, extracting the pleasantness from his own voice, "and then I'll decide?"

"Books."

"Books? Like *Disturbing Minds?*"

Malloy's cheek twitched, a quick flutter of a muscle to the right of his mouth, and he slapped his face at that spot. "Not exactly," he said without explanation, without showing any awareness that he had done something odd. Evan couldn't imagine what he would have thought if he hadn't seen the twitch. How would he have interpreted someone suddenly slapping himself? The bizarre behaviors kept mounting.

"Have you heard of *Death Makes a Comeback,* Professor?"

"I'm familiar with the title."

"Read it by any chance?"

Obviously the detective knew Evan had checked this book out, otherwise he wouldn't have asked the question. The title sounded peculiar, of course, and so, by extension, anyone in possession of the book might be considered peculiar. There was a perfectly logical explanation, though: He had chosen it randomly—by *chance,* just as Malloy had asked. Sometimes Evan did that, walked down an aisle of nonfiction, stopped halfway along, and reached for a book. Often he closed his eyes so as not to be influenced by the cover design or author. That's what he had done in this case, blindly reached into the shelf and pulled out *Death Makes a Comeback.* The title amused him, and so he had taken the book home.

"No," Evan said, "I haven't read it."

"No?" the detective repeated. "You checked it out of East-field Memorial Library, isn't that so?"

"I check out a lot of books. I read some, skim others, and don't get past the first page of a few. That's what happened with *Death Makes a Comeback*—I didn't get past the first page."

Malloy's face softened into its familiar, easygoing facade.

"That happens to me, too. The wife brings home books and tries to get me to read in bed. But after a few pages I'm snoring away."

"I don't snore," Evan said. "I talk sometimes in my sleep, though—perhaps you'd like to tap my bedroom at night, listen in."

Malloy laughed, and Evan realized that it was this good humor, this conviviality, that he liked so much about the detective. It was as if they were having a friendly conversation about some mysterious happening at the college—a chalice missing from the chapel, perhaps.

"I don't think we'll need to do that, Professor. But I am curious about your visit to the library—on August 20th, I mean. Did you go there specifically to get *Death Makes a Comeback?*"

Evan couldn't recall why he had gone to the library that day, but it certainly wasn't to get that or any other particular book.

"No, I didn't go specifically for *Death Makes a Comeback*. And I have to ask, is it customary for librarians to tell you what books people check out?"

"They generally cooperate with us when there's a good reason."

"And what reason did you give them this time?"

"The investigation into a sixteen-year-old girl's disappearance."

That was sufficient cause, Evan had to agree. He certainly wouldn't want to hear a librarian claim confidentiality if one of his own children were missing.

"You've got that nice new library on campus, Professor. Cost a million dollars to renovate, didn't it?"

"Almost three million, actually."

The detective let out a whistle—a cliché reaction, Evan thought. He was disappointed.

"So why would you go to our little town library that specific day?"

"It's pretty simple. On campus I inevitably run into my students or fellow professors. Sometimes I like to get away from the college and everyone in it, if you want to know the truth. The town library has a pretty good catalog, and of course, it's open stacks."

"Open stacks?"

"The nonfiction books are all out on the shelves on the basement level. You don't have to know what you want. You can just wander around and pick out something."

"In the basement, huh? I've never been down there—I guess I shouldn't admit that. It's pretty private, I imagine."

"Private?"

"Not a lot of other people walking around."

"I run across a few people from time to time."

"Did you run across anyone on August 20th?"

"I think I did, yes."

"Anyone you remember?"

"There was someone making noise—like laughing, I remember that, because I thought it out of place. But I didn't see her face."

"Her?"

"Yes, it was a female voice. And I was aware of a man walking past the aisle when I came in."

"Did you speak to any of these people?"

"No." Evan said this quickly and firmly and then realized he was mistaken. He had said "Excuse me" when he first entered the basement as he almost bumped into the man crossing in front of him. Evan remembered distinctly thinking that by the circumstance, the man should have apologized to him. Still, "Excuse me" was trivial speech, so he let his answer stand.

The detective checked his little black notepad. "How about *The ABCs of Love*—you know that book?"

"No, I'm glad to say I've never heard of it."

"It happens to be on the other side of the stack from *Death Makes a Comeback*."

"If you say so. It sounds like you're actually more familiar with the layout of the basement than I."

"I'm just taking the word of the librarian. I talked to her on the phone before coming over."

"Tell me, Detective, is all of this important somehow?"

"Well, the person who checked out *The ABCs of Love* at 5:32, two minutes after you checked out *Death Makes a Comeback*, was . . ."

Evan did not need to hear the name. It seemed like every story now—the girl missing from the park, the girl putting on lipstick in his car, the girl checking out the book—ended with Joyce Bonner. He wondered how many other times in his life he had crossed paths with this disappearing cheerleader.

He was late getting home. Ellen would be angry at him for leaving the boys unsupervised, even for a half hour. He thought they had reached a wonderful age—old enough to stay alone for short periods, particularly since there were two of them, yet not old enough to get into drugs or sex. But she insisted that kids were most tempted into trouble when left unmonitored in their own homes after school. So he'd promised to make sure he would cut short his office hours any afternoon he was needed.

Of course, he couldn't have predicted that Malloy would show up. The detective's surprise visit would make a perfectly good excuse, but Evan didn't want to mention him again to Ellen. So he drove home faster than usual, fifteen or twenty miles over the speed limit, and asked himself why some policeman didn't pull him over now, when he was so obviously guilty of breaking the law.

When he came into the kitchen he saw the boys' bookbags lying on the floor next to the refrigerator. Clearly they had remembered the key hidden under the rock by the hydrangea bush out front and let themselves in. He made a mental note to check that they had returned the key to its hiding spot.

He brushed graham cracker crumbs into the sink and put away the container of milk. Then he went to the back staircase. He heard only faint music upstairs, which surprised him. Why weren't the boys blasting out their songs now that they had the house to themselves?

He took the steps by twos and turned into their room. Adam was sitting at the computer. He didn't look up. It concerned Evan a little that his son wouldn't notice who was running up the stairs. Maybe Ellen was right—they weren't old enough to be left by themselves.

"Adam?"

"Hey, Dad."

Evan checked the image on the computer screen to make sure it wasn't inappropriate. Then he looked into the boys' bathroom. "Where's your brother?"

Adam shrugged.

"You don't know where Zed is?"

"Not exactly."

"Where is he inexactly?"

"Riding his bike."

"Where is he riding his bike?"

"He didn't say exactly."

Sometimes, in a strange way, Evan liked this kind of precise vagueness in his sons' responses. It showed a facility with words and language that implied a flexible mind at work. Today he was just annoyed.

He moved next to Adam, casting a shadow over the monitor.

"Did you two get into another fight?"

"No."

"Well, I'm not interested in any more word games. Tell me where Zed is or I'm turning off the computer."

Adam put his hand over the on-off switch. "You can't do that. I'll lose everything."

"Then tell me."

"I think he went to the park."

"The state park? He knows Mom said not to go there."

The boy shrugged. "I think he forgot."

"That would be convenient forgetting, wouldn't it? Why didn't you go, too?"

" 'Cause we're not allowed."

"Then he couldn't have forgotten, could he? Why did he still go?"

Adam squeezed his eyes tight shut. He did not want to lie. "He went to look for something, okay?"

"No, it's not okay. Look for what?"

Adam twisted his head around to face Evan. "Her!"

"Her? Mom?"

The boy looked up with a strange expression. "No, *her*— the stupid girl that's missing."

Evan took his son by the shoulders and spun him around in his chair. "Why is he looking for her?"

"I don't know."

"Yes you do—you two always know what the other's thinking."

"Stop shaking me, Dad."

"I'm not shaking you. Tell me why he's looking for her."

Adam squirmed free and jumped from his chair. Evan stepped toward him. Adam backed himself against the wall. "Okay, I'll tell you. Just don't shake me anymore." He rubbed his bare arms, raising up a line of fine white hair. "Z. thinks you did it."

"Did what?"

"You know . . . with the girl."

It took Evan a moment to understand, and when he did, the thought shocked him. "Zed thinks I had something to do with the cheerleader's disappearing?"

Adam nodded.

"Why does he think that?"

Adam glanced toward Zed's bunk.

Evan looked there but saw nothing but a heap of pillows and blankets. "What?"

Adam went over to the bed and reached under the mattress. He pulled out a chrome lighter. "That day you drove us home from camp he found this in the backseat."

Evan took the lighter and turned it over. The initials *JB* were scratched into the side as if by some rough tool. The lipstick, the lighter—what had the girl done, dumped out her pocketbook in his car?

"Why didn't he show this to me, Adam?"

" 'Cause you would have taken it away."

"So all this time he's been thinking I kidnapped the girl?"

"No, he didn't think anything until Mom started asking questions. Then he was playing with the lighter that night and kind of figured it out."

"There's nothing to figure out, Adam. I gave a ride to Joyce and three of her friends during the arts camp this summer. I didn't even know her name then. Her purse must have spilled because she left her lipstick in my car, too."

Adam nodded. "Yeah, I told Zed there was a reason. But he wouldn't believe me. He always makes up stories, you know."

"Yes, I know. I'm going to the park to find him. If Mom comes home early, tell her I went to the store with Zed."

"You want me to lie to Mom?"

"I want you not to upset her, that's what. So just say what I told you."

Evan saw the overturned blue Huffy lying next to the bicycle stand at the edge of the parking lot. He stood still for a moment. Birds were calling to each other in the trees, and he had a sudden wish to be able to distinguish one from another. There was the vague hum of cars on the main road and the slight rustling of leaves in the wind. Nothing sounded like the careless noise of a boy.

Evan set the bike in the bushes where it wouldn't be easily seen and hurried toward the information booth. The "Missing" flyer for Joyce Bonner was ripped at the top and folded over. He pressed it back up and saw that the girl's eyes were blackened out, which made her look dead, even in mid-cheer. Evan imagined Mr. Bonner seeing his beautiful daughter like this. It would not take much to break down this man. Evan ripped the flyer from the door and put it in his pocket.

He turned toward the lake and blotted out the afternoon sun with his hand. Just twenty yards in front of him was Zed, skipping stones over the water. Evan started to call his name and then just walked toward the lake. He got within a few feet and was amazed that this son, too, could ignore someone approaching.

"Zed?"

The boy didn't turn around.

"What are you doing here?"

He picked up another stone and flicked it across the smooth surface of the lake.

"I asked you a question."

"Throwing stones."

"Why did you come to the park?"

"I just did, that's all."

"Were you looking for someone?"

Zed whirled about. "Did A. say that? Did he?"

"Settle down. I made him tell me where you went. You know you're not supposed to come here alone."

"So?"

"What's that supposed to mean?"

"It's not against the law to ride my bike in the park."

"You tell that to Mom tonight and we'll see what she says." Evan put his hand on Zed's shoulder. "Come on, let's put your bike in the car."

The boy ducked away. "I'm not done."

"Not done what?"

"Nothing."

"I think you're done doing nothing, Zed."

The boy stomped his foot. "I hate that. You always twist words up like you know everything."

"You weren't being logical, that's—"

"I don't care about your stupid logic, okay?" He kicked at a rock embedded in the ground, once with his toe and twice with his heel. Then he bent over and dug the rock out of the soil.

"You shouldn't be throwing something that big in the water. You might hit a fish or duck."

The boy shrugged and swung back his right hand in a throwing motion. Evan reached forward and knocked the rock out of his hand. "I told you not to throw that."

"You don't do everything right, so why do I have to?"

Evan didn't know how to answer. To be truthful, he would have to first deconstruct the question to define "right," then deal with why it was in the best interest of a boy to seek it. Ethics was not a subject hastily discussed by the side of a lake on a chilly afternoon.

"Zed," he said, "if there's something bothering you, we can sit down at home and talk about it. Now let's go." This time he took the boy's arm and pulled a little.

"No," Zed shouted. "You can't make me."

The bold defiance angered Evan. He and Ellen had agreed that they would never use force with the boys, but force is exactly what he felt rising through his arms. "Yes, I can make you," he said and yanked Zed off his feet a little. Then he heard rustling in the woods and turned as a man carrying a fishing pole and tackle box came toward the shore. Evan wondered how much he had seen.

The man came closer. "What's going on?"

"It's okay—he's my son."

The man looked at Zed. "Is that right, kid?"

The boy kicked at another big stone in the ground. Then he stooped down, licked his finger, and rubbed a smudge mark off his sneaker.

"Zed, tell the man."

"Yeah."

The stranger stepped nearer. He was only a few yards away now. "You sure?"

Evan touched the man's shoulder. It was an intimate thing to do, and he wasn't sure where this gesture came from. He wasn't in the habit of touching men, even casually. He thought of Wittgenstein in a park like this at night, groping for the hands of strangers. How would he justify these encounters to himself? And would he go home feeling fulfilled or demeaned?

"I appreciate your taking an interest in this," Evan said. "As a matter of fact, I did the same thing about two weeks ago with a little girl and her mother—actually, it turned out not to be her mother. I don't really know who she was. I just saw her dragging this child down the street, and—"

Why was he babbling on like this? The man didn't need to know his whole life story.

"My point is that I intervened—asked a question—like you just did. You were right to wonder what was going on. I was just getting a little angry at my son because he's not supposed to come to the park alone."

The man shifted the gear in his hands. "I used to let my kids come here whenever they wanted, but no more. Not after what happened."

Zed stood up. It seemed as if he were about to speak.

"I know," Evan said, "you can't be too cautious nowadays."

"It's a terrible world when kids can't go out of your sight without you worrying about them."

Was it a terrible world? Evan hadn't thought so. A frightening world sometimes, a worrisome world, an irritating world, certainly, but he wouldn't have said it was terrible.

The man walked off toward the parking lot. Evan waited until he was out of earshot before turning to Zed. "Okay, I don't want any more shouting or disobeying. We're going home right this minute." He laid his hand on Zed's shoulder again. It was a risky move. If his son said no and pulled away, what could he do except start laying out punishments, which had already proven ineffective? He didn't feel like coercing Zed with threats, anyway. He wanted to be obeyed simply because that was what a son was supposed to do for a father.

Evan's hand slipped off Zed's shoulder. He walked down the path a little, toward the parking lot, listening for scuffling in the leaves behind him. He heard nothing. He took a few more steps. When he turned he saw Zed still standing at the lake, facing him. It seemed to Evan like a scene from an old western, two gunslingers staring each other down. Who would draw first?

The boy took a step, sideways, then another. Evan didn't know how to interpret the movement.

"Zed?"

He broke into a little trot along the edge of the water.

"Zed!" Evan charged after him. The boy zigzagged onto the walking path and then down to the water again. Evan brushed away tree limbs and ducked and ran. He felt as if he were observing himself in this chase, and he was sure he was playing his role badly. The wise father would never get into the ridiculous position of chasing his son through the woods.

Zed stopped. Evan pulled up a few yards away and saw that the shoreline was blocked by a tangle of bushes and limbs. The boy whirled around, then glanced at the water.

"No, Zed, come on. The game's over now."

Zed lifted his right foot over the water's edge as if dangling it over a ledge. Evan folded his arms. He would wait out his son. Zed folded his arms, too—a mocking gesture—then splashed into the lake, heading around the bushes. Evan rushed at him and in a few seconds, caught hold of an arm. They fell together in the shallows, and the coldness of the lake surprised Evan because it felt so good. He lay there letting a foot of water soak into his clothes.

Zed jumped up and stood over him. "Dad, you okay?"

The sky looked strange to Evan, more purple than blue. He remembered reading that astronomers had determined the universe was actually a vast sea of beige, if you could move back far enough to see it. That seemed like the ultimate perspective to Evan, to see the color of the universe. But who could stand that much beige?

"Dad?"

"Yes, Zed."

"Aren't you going to get up?"

"In a minute."

"You're getting really wet, you know."

"I can't get any wetter than wet or colder than cold."

Zed kicked his foot into the sand. "Stop it, stop it!"

Evan rose from the water, and suddenly he did feel very wet and cold. *Stop it, stop it!*—whatever he was doing wrong, he wished he could stop it just like that, by merely willing himself to. Zed stood shivering in front of him. Evan opened his arms, and the boy stepped inside them. His body felt harder than Evan remembered.

"I thought, for a second I thought . . ."

Evan pulled away a little. "What?"

"I thought like maybe you were dead 'cause you were looking so weird."

"No, Zed, I'm not so fragile that I'm going to die from falling in a little water."

The boy hopped from one leg to the other and shook his head. Water flew off his hair.

Evan squeezed his pants, and a pocketful of water burst out. "We must be quite a sight. Your mother is going to have a few questions."

Zed grinned. "Yeah, she'll probably ground both of us."

"I've got some blankets in the car we can wrap ourselves in. Are you ready to go with me now?"

"Yeah."

"Yes, *yes*—not yeah."

"Okay, Dad, yes."

Evan put his hands on his son's shoulders. "First I want you to tell me, how can you think I had anything to do with the girl disappearing?"

"I don't know. I guess 'cause everybody does—the police, Mom."

"Not everybody. Adam doesn't."

Evan wished he hadn't said that. No matter how hurt he was by Zed's lack of faith in him, it was wrong to make one son feel bad by comparison to the other.

"He believes everything," Zed said. "You could tell him you're really Superman and he'd believe you."

Evan touched his son's chin to raise his eyes. "I'm not Superman by a long shot. I'm just your father, and I hope you'll believe I didn't have anything to do with that girl."

Zed wiped his wet arm across his face and nodded.

CHAPTER 22

An old saying ran through Evan's head: in the physics lab, don't look; in chemistry, don't taste; in biology, don't smell; in medicine, don't touch. And the philosophy classroom? The appropriate admonition suddenly came to him—don't listen. Thoughts were dangerous, a fact his "Introduction to Philosophy" class of seven apparently knew well, because barely any of them had stirred for the first forty-five minutes. He thought of Keynes's description of a university education—"the inculcation of the incomprehensible into the indifferent by the incompetent." Obviously sometime in the past few years he had lost his power to command his students' attention. Was that his incompetency or their indifference?

Evan slapped shut his lesson book. He decided to extemporize.

"Okay, students, any of you still awake, what do you know?"

He sipped from his large container of cold black coffee as he let the question float over the classroom.

"And how do you know it?"

After a minute, during which Evan wondered why he always let his coffee go cold, a lazy hand raised in the rear row. He nodded in that direction.

"I know that I'm sitting in a classroom at Pearce College listening to you, Professor Birch, lecture on how we know and stuff."

"Okay, we're here in a Pearce College classroom and I'm Professor Birch lecturing on how we know . . . and stuff. Everyone agree with that statement?"

Enough heads nodded for him to continue. "Mr. Winokur perceives that he is sitting, and I suppose if we consider slouching sitting, then he's correct. He does appear to be listening now, because he just straightened up, and I assume we all agree that this is a classroom. But are you sure we're at Pearce College, Mr. Winokur?"

The young man held up his notebook with PEARCE boldly stretching across the top and a musketed Patriot underneath.

"Colleges change their names sometimes. Are you sure Pearce hasn't gotten a hundred-million-dollar donation this morning on the condition that it change to the donor's name? Isn't it just possible that you're going to Bill Gates College now?"

A few students laughed, which pleased Evan until he realized how rare laughter was in his classes. He wished he had a joke to tell, something funnier than Wittgenstein and the

Frenchman. He thought of Zed's riddle—what do Attila the Hun and Winnie-the-Pooh have in common?—and decided against using that, too.

"It's very difficult 'to know' in any rigorous sense of the verb for many reasons, such as the infinite possibilities for change occurring beyond your immediate knowledge base."

"We can't even know we really exist," a girl said. Evan picked up his coffee container and dropped it in the trash. As he did he glanced at his class book to remind himself of her name. It was Mary Grinaldi in her customary seat, last row, far left.

"This could all be a dream, right?" Evan said and waved his hand around the classroom.

She had never spoken before, and he didn't want to stifle any future participation, so he phrased his response encouragingly. "Thank you, Ms. Grinaldi, for bringing up this subject, because I do want to deal with it. Is life a dream? Wittgenstein said that if a man should stumble upon a group of philosophers arguing this question, he would think them insane. Why did he say this? First, it's not conceivable that we're all dreaming the same dream, so I assume you mean that perhaps you, Ms. Grinaldi, are dreaming this classroom, this lecture, dreaming me standing here lecturing on dreams. You would be, in effect, the creator of this whole world you perceive. If you are dreaming—for *dreaming* to have the commonly accepted meaning—there must be a non-dreaming state that you would consider reality, and so at some point you will presumably wake up and be able to distinguish between the two states, at least in description of them. If you never wake up, then your sole state of existence is this dream state, so 'dreaming' in this universe of your creation is your reality."

Mary Grinaldi's head lowered at each sentence, as if he had

been raining blows upon her. Evan was sorry that she took his arguments personally. He simply wanted to dismiss the soph-omoric notion that "this could all be a dream" as quickly and completely as possible. If life were a dream, then the dreamer was essentially his own God creating his own world. The evi-dence to the contrary seemed obvious to Evan—he would cer-tainly not create a world for himself in which he was the accused.

As he left the Arts Building, a young man with a camera strapped around his neck walked to the foot of the steps and aimed his lens upward.

Evan instinctively raised his arm to block his face. He heard the click of the picture and lowered his arm. "What are you doing?"

The boy let the camera fall to his chest. "Taking pictures, do you mind?"

"Yes, I mind. Who are you working for?"

"What?"

"Who are you working for—the *Banner*?"

"Look, mister, I don't know what you're talking about, but how about moving out of the way?"

Evan looked behind him and saw "Pearce College" in-scribed in the stone, and then "1887." "Sorry," he said and hurried down the steps.

When Evan opened the Humanities Faculty door, two an-thropologists were coming out. "Good afternoon," he said cheerily. They passed by him with what he judged to be per-functory nods.

He climbed the stairs and turned into the reception area. He couldn't see Carla and peered over the partition. She was hunched over the newspaper.

"Something interesting?"

"Oh, Professor," she said, "I didn't hear you come in."

"I'm sneaky sometimes. Any messages?"

She reached up with a half-dozen pink slips, keeping her right arm across the newspaper. It was obvious that she was hiding something. He feared someone had died. Then the more likely possibility came to him—the news was about him.

"May I take a look?"

She handed him the paper, back page up. He turned it over as he walked into his office and saw the headline: "Popular Philosophy Professor Questioned in Girl's Disappearance"

The wording surprised him. If he was so popular, why were so few students taking his courses? In the accompanying picture, a dark, indistinguishable car was being towed from the faculty parking lot. On the right stood a man—Malloy, perhaps—directing the operation with his hand in the air, mid-gesture. In the background, two uniformed officers leaned against their squad cars.

Evan walked into his office and set his briefcase on the back shelf. He took off his jacket and hung it on the door hook. He hit the "Daily Schedule" icon on his computer screen to see if he had any meetings that afternoon. There were none. He settled into his chair and loosened the laces on his shoes. Then he read.

"Eastfield Police came on campus September 10 and impounded the gray Jetta belonging to Philosophy Department Professor Evan Birch, the *Banner* has learned. The action is apparently part of the ongoing investigation into the disappearance of a local cheerleader. Sixteen-year-old Joyce Bonner was last seen working in the information booth at East-field State Park on August 23. She has not been heard from since.

"According to sources, the Jetta was taken to the State Crime Lab for evaluation and returned to Professor Birch less than a week later. It is not known what evidence may have been gathered. Further, it is unclear what connection exists between Joyce Bonner, an Eastfield High junior, and Professor Birch, or why police wanted to look at his car.

"The professor, the father of twin boys who lives in the Pheasant Run development, has taught at Pearce for the last twelve years. While other full-time philosophy faculty have moved on in recent years because of the downsizing of the department, Professor Birch has remained.

"Longtime Humanities secretary, Carla Caruso, said, 'I don't know anything about this except I shouldn't be talking to you.'

"Encountered in the Arts Quad on his way to a meeting of trustees, Dean Santos said, 'I have nothing to say' to repeated questions about the investigation.

"Attempts to reach Professor Birch for comment about the cloud of suspicion hanging over his head were unsuccessful."

Evan laid the paper on his desk, facedown. Attempts to reach him? By what method had the *Banner* tried to contact him? He had been reachable all day, and he resented the implication that he was unable to be found, like someone running for cover.

And "cloud of suspicion." He would have preferred to be under a canopy of suspicion, or the purple sky of suspicion, something more evocative than the common cloud.

The phone rang in the reception area. "It's Dean Santos," Carla called in to him. "Again."

Evan flipped through the message slips. The top four were from Santos. Evan picked up the phone. "Hello, Dean."

"Birch, this story in the paper, is it true?"

"Somewhat, yes. I have talked to the police, a Detective Malloy."

"What do you have to do with this matter?"

"It seems I stopped at the lake the day the girl disappeared."

"They talked to you because you might have seen something, is that it?"

Evan could hear a desperate hopefulness in the dean's voice that he was a mere bystander, perhaps even a witness, to the crime, but surely not a suspect. "I guess that's part of his reason, but there are some other connections."

"What other connections?"

"The girl, Joyce Bonner, attended the Arts Camp here in August, and apparently I drove her and a few friends a short distance to the library."

"That girl was on our campus?"

"It seems so."

"And the police impounded your car because you gave her a ride?"

"And because I was at the lake. Those appear to be the only reasons."

"This isn't good," the dean said. "Publicity like this isn't good at all for the college."

Isn't good—why did people prefer to characterize a situation as the negative of the positive rather than the negative itself? He supposed the latter was a little too daunting to face.

"We're stretched thin as it is," Santos said. "Otherwise I'd pull you off teaching till this clears up."

It wasn't comforting for Evan to hear that only circumstances were preventing the suspension of his teaching duties.

He wasn't even sure he could be removed simply because of an accusation. Certainly he would grieve any action.

"When will this situation be resolved?"

"I can't say exactly, Dean. I've told the detective everything I know, which isn't much. I would have thought the investigation would be over already."

"All right, just keep me informed," Santos said. "I don't like surprises."

"I don't either," Evan said. "They rarely bring good news."

"They never bring good news," the dean said and hung up.

Evan was late again getting home, but only by a few seconds. The school bus was just pulling away to reveal a van marked "Channel 4" parked in front of the house. On the lawn was a woman holding a microphone. Behind her stood a large man with a camera mounted on his shoulder. Between them were his sons.

Evan honked his horn and swung into the driveway. He put the car into park and jumped out. "Adam, Zed—come here!"

The boys looked over and waved.

"Right now," he yelled.

The twins hurried over, their bookbags swinging from their hands. "What's up, Dad?"

"Get inside the car."

"But that woman wants to talk to us."

"Inside," he said and opened the back door. They jumped in as the reporter ran up to the car.

"Professor Birch, can I ask you a few questions?"

He stopped halfway into the driver's seat. "You come out here and start questioning my sons without my permission and then ask to talk to me?"

"We just wanted to know—"

"Get off my property," Evan said, "or I'm calling the police." The irony occurred to him—he, a suspect in a kidnapping, calling the police to protect himself.

"You want me to shoot this?" the cameraman said to the reporter.

The woman shook her head.

"Thank you," Evan said. "Now please leave."

The boys ran ahead of him up the stairs and into the house. When he reached the hall he saw them crouched at the window in the sitting room, their heads just a little above the sill.

"The woman's getting in the van, Dad. Are you still calling the cops?"

Evan looked through the drapes. "Not if they're leaving. Come away from the window."

"Why'd you get so mad?" Zed said as he hopped to his feet.

"Because you're not supposed to talk to strangers. We've told you that a hundred times."

"You told us to be polite a hundred times, too, Dad."

"You can be polite to strangers by saying you're sorry, but don't talk to them."

"She just wanted—"

"It doesn't matter what she wanted. Don't talk to strangers."

"Okay."

Evan looked outside again. The cameraman had stopped on the other side of the van and turned his camera back on the house. He scanned left and right, then up and down. Evan imagined the story on the evening news . . . "Inside this pleasant middle-class house in the pleasant middle-class subdivision of Pleasant—that's Pheasant—Run lives Professor Evan Birch, teacher, father, suspected kidnapper."

"Dad?"

Evan turned. The boys were standing side by side, their backpacks slung over their left shoulders. He did not know which one had spoken. "Yes?"

"That woman," Adam said, "she was asking about the day you picked us up at camp."

Evan tried to appear calm. But if the reporter was asking about that day, she knew much more than he had hoped.

"That's what Mom was asking about, too," Adam said.

"What did you tell her—the reporter, I mean."

"Nothing. You just came and got us and we drove home, that's all."

"He was late," Zed said.

"No he wasn't."

"We were standing there for like an hour."

"We were not. You don't even have a watch, so how would you know?"

"I can tell time without a watch."

It seemed surreal to Evan to hear them referring to him as some third person. Did all of their conversations about him sound this way?

"Okay, stop the arguing. It's hard enough to remember what you did yesterday let alone weeks ago."

"Yesterday we fell in the lake," Zed said.

"That's true," Evan said. "Some days are easier to remember than others."

CHAPTER 23

I t was the Saturday of the fall open house at the Institute for Primate Studies, and Evan had forgotten.

"I'm sorry," he said for the third time as they weaved back and forth across the bedroom getting dressed. "I've had a lot on my mind lately."

Ellen sat on the bed and pulled on stockings, a dark pair that he was sure would make her legs look black. He wondered how formal this occasion was but didn't want to ask. She had no doubt told him already.

"You haven't forgotten the classes you teach, have you? Or your office hours? So why did you forget the one important event of my work life this fall?"

"I guess I'm just a rotten husband."

"Insulting yourself isn't an answer."

"I don't know why I forgot. What difference does it make anyway? It's not as though I scheduled something else. I'm getting dressed to go with you in plenty of time."

"The difference is that I'd like you to remember, that's all."

"Okay, from now on I'll try to be better at remembering things like this. I promise."

Her head was in the closet now, and he didn't know if she had heard him.

They went downstairs to the kitchen. It was two o'clock, a half hour before they needed to leave, so Ellen put on hot water for tea. The *Eastfield News* sat on the table, rolled up in its plastic sleeve. Ellen hadn't taken it out yet, as normally she would. She hadn't turned on the TV news that morning either.

"You don't want me to open the paper, I presume?"

"That's up to you," she said as she wiped the counter with a sponge.

He left the paper where it was. Through the orange plastic he could see *Rampage* in large, headline type. He couldn't imagine that the word referred to him. At least he wasn't the lead story.

Ellen reached alongside the refrigerator for the broom and began sweeping the tile floor. He thought that a strange thing to do now that she was dressed in her crisp black skirt and purple silk shirt.

"You want me to do that?"

"No, thanks."

The steam rose from the kettle. She put the broom back next to the refrigerator and pulled out two Soothing Moments Golden Honey Lemon tea bags. Apparently he didn't get a choice.

"Where are we dropping the boys?" he said.

"Nowhere."

"They're coming with us?"

"They're staying here."

He wanted to ask why they were suddenly old enough to stay by themselves, but she was in her brisk manner that did not tolerate questions.

"I'm sure your presentation will go well," he said. "It's not like Tyco has to perform live. All you have to do is introduce the video. There's no reason to worry about it."

She turned off the heat to the kettle and poured water into the cups. "You think I'm worried about that?"

Yes, no—he didn't know the right answer. In such cases, it was his habit not to say anything at all.

About a hundred people sat in folding chairs in the large oval reception room. The director, a thin, gangly man, described his great goals for the Institute in the coming years and the unfortunate meager levels of funding. He asked those in attendance for their generous support and beseeched them to give to the limits of their ability—"to open their purse strings wide in these dire days."

Evan had never seen a more pathetic display of begging. He nudged Ellen and rolled his eyes. He was sure she would be uncomfortable, too. She turned away.

The director introduced the main researchers one after another, and Ellen wasn't among them. Evan reached over to hold her hand and felt her fists clenched on her lap. Despite what she had said, he believed that she was nervous about speaking in public, and that surprised him. Self-confidence was one of her strong points, even to a fault.

The director lowered the lights and showed slides of chimps in the wild. Their numbers in Africa had dwindled, he said, from two million one hundred years ago to fewer than 150,000 today. Not only were they losing habitat, but they were often shot for bushmeat or trapped for medical research. The chimps at the Institute, he hastened to add, were orphan infants, rescued after their mothers had been killed.

With the lights still dim, the director introduced Ellen as a project assistant working in the field of animal intelligence. She hurried to the podium and set her notes in front of her. She looked down but then didn't speak, and he worried that she couldn't see her speech. When she looked up she began describing her work with Tyco—how it began, how she had almost given up, and then the breakthrough when the chimp became eager to count for her.

After a few minutes she cued the video man with a wave of her hand, and the screen filled with Tyco bounding around her large cage, her thick fingers grabbing the bars. Evan thought this a poor choice for an opening shot. Why remind people that these chimps lived unnatural existences solely so that humans could study them?

Then Ellen came into the picture, on the other side of the bars. It appeared that she was in a cage of her own. Her hair was pulled back, fixed on both sides with silver clips, which gave her an angular look that he didn't like.

But Tyco apparently did because she pressed herself against the bars and hooted and grinned. Ellen put the chimp through her paces. Tyco pointed at the correct numbers on an electronic touch pad when presented with two objects, and then five. She picked out three apples when shown a paper with the numeral 3 written on it. On the touch pad she punched in the numbers from 1 through 6. After each success Tyco sat in front of Ellen to receive a pat on the head and then twirled and hooted.

The video dissolved on the image of Tyco grinning, and the audience clapped enthusiastically. Ellen acknowledged the response with a smile and resumed her seat. He put his hand on her leg and said, "That was great. Way to go."

The director took center stage and asked again for money "to continue such groundbreaking research." Then the program was over, and everyone stood up.

"What do we do now?" Evan said.

"Mingle awhile," she said. "Act friendly."

"*Act* friendly?"

She walked toward the open reception area. He followed vaguely behind her. A young girl in a white shirt and black pants passed by, and he swiped a glass of wine from her tray, which tipped it out of balance. He pictured all of the glasses sliding to the floor and everyone turning to see that he was the cause. But the girl's free hand re-centered the tray, and she walked on without a glance at him.

Ellen was shaking hands, her back to him. He was on his own. He considered going outside and walking the grounds for a while, but if she saw him head through the door she would certainly accuse him of disinterest in her work.

So he would *act* friendly. He spotted an opening in a group of three and moved in. The man in the little group acknowledged his presence with a nod. The women did not.

"I was just saying that this is the first time I've seen a film on a big screen in years," the man said. "I don't go to the movies anymore. Why would I pay nine dollars to sit with a bunch of kids yapping the whole time? Who needs that?"

The two women didn't seem to be paying attention. Perhaps they didn't even know the man. "I can see your point," Evan said.

"We rent twice a week, the wife and I. Her choice on Fridays, mine on Sunday."

"Excuse us," the women said and turned away.

Evan had always thought some stated reason was necessary in these situations—an "I have to speak to someone" or "I need to go to the restroom" kind of thing. Simply saying "Excuse us" and leaving seemed rude. Still, they hadn't left him alone. "What did you see last night?"

The man shook his head a little, evidently not pleased. *"The Maps of the World."*

"A Map of the World?"

"I guess. I never could figure out the title. Not much action, you know? The acting was good, though. It had that woman in it. I like her."

"Which woman is that?"

"Her name is . . . Ripley, that's it, from *Alien.*"

"I don't know her."

"Sure you do . . . *Ripley.* The thing comes out of her stomach."

"Sigourney Weaver?"

"That's it. Her husband is a farmer, the strong silent type. Hold on." The man tapped the arm of the woman behind him. "Who was that guy in the movie we just saw, the one who watches his wife fall apart?"

"David Strathairn."

"That's it, David Strathairn," the man said over his shoulder to Evan and then turned into the conversation with his wife.

Evan was left standing by himself in the middle of the room. He sipped his wine. He couldn't tell if it was merlot or cabernet sauvignon. Wines—there was something else he had never been good at distinguishing. Whichever it was it tasted expensive. The Institute obviously had enough money to spend on fine wine.

He looked about, rising up on his toes a little as if searching for someone. He thought he would appear purposeful doing this, as if he had just momentarily misplaced his companion. He saw Ellen at the end of the buffet table, in a circle of what appeared to be admirers. She was nodding her head. He could read her lips saying "Thank you" several times. He didn't want to interrupt her moment of praise, but still, when she glanced his way, he winked. It was their agreed-upon signal for one to come rescue the other at a party like this. At the least she could bring him into her conversation. But Ellen looked away as if she hadn't seen him.

He moved quickly across the room, again appearing intentional. He didn't know why it bothered him simply to be as he was—an unattached person in the crowd. He didn't really mind not talking to anyone. In fact, he preferred not talking to anyone. A few people turned his way as he passed. He thought they were about to speak to him. Perhaps they recognized him as Ellen's husband. They nodded but said nothing. He nodded and moved on.

He reached the large windows and looked out on the grounds, thinking about where Tyco and her fellow chimps were kept. He wondered how much time they got to play outside. He wondered what happened to the ones who showed no special abilities. Was it only the smart who survived? He had never asked Ellen these questions. She was right, he supposed—he didn't take her work seriously enough.

He drifted to the back of the room toward the cheese table, feeling better now out of the din of the conversation. There was only one other man there, leaning over the various cutting boards, his hand poised to choose. He looked up. Evan nodded.

The man turned and extended his hand. "Bill Mathers," he said.

Evan shook the hand. The fingers felt sticky, as if coated with the residue of some oily food. "Evan Birch."

"I'm at GE, in engineering."

"I'm at Pearce," Evan said, "in philosophy."

"A professor," the man said. "Not the one they're investigating, eh?" He laughed at the possibility.

Evan laughed, too. "Never know."

"That's really true," the man said with sudden enthusiasm. "A relative of mine, Uncle Don, my favorite uncle as a matter of fact, he used to bring us a bag of toys every Christmas Eve because my parents didn't have the money. Turns out he was a cross-dresser. Loved high heels, can you believe it? Most women wouldn't be caught dead in them nowadays."

It occurred to Evan that he had never seen Ellen in high heels. He didn't believe she owned any. "You're right about that."

"Sure I'm right. But my point is that I never knew about Uncle Don's predilection, shall we say, till he came out of the closet. I mean literally—he walked out of my aunt's closet one day with a dress on. He didn't know I'd come over and let myself in their back door. It was kind of a shock."

"To him or you?"

"Both of us, I guess."

"What did he say?"

"He just smiled and turned up his hands like, 'Well, here I am.' He could have said he was trying on a Halloween costume—I would have believed him. But nope, he just told

237

me to go downstairs and wait for him. Then he never mentioned it again."

"And you didn't either?"

"Oh I mentioned it all right. I ran home and told my mother. She said everybody was a little weird in some way, and this was Uncle Don's way and I shouldn't worry about it."

"That was a very enlightened reaction."

"My mother was like that. Live and let live."

Evan pulled off a few purple grapes. The man did also and then nodded toward the crowd. "You taken in by this stuff?"

Evan had been expecting a more typical question, such as, "What brings you here?" or "Nice spread, huh?" Apparently this man enjoyed lobbing curveballs into the conversation.

"I find the research interesting," Evan said. "Especially that chimp counting," he added.

"Tyco? Strange name for an animal, isn't it? She's new this time."

Evan picked up a square of cheddar and popped it in his mouth. "So, you've attended this open house before?"

"They invite me every year, and every year I stand back here making sarcastic comments. That's why nobody talks to me."

The man didn't seem to realize that he had essentially called Evan "nobody." He didn't mind, though. At this reception at this moment, he did feel like nobody. "Why do they keep inviting you?"

The man tapped the wallet in his back pocket. "They know my wife and I have money, and they'd like some of it. They've already convinced her."

Evan picked out a different cheese, one he could not identify by sight. "That film of Tyco counting didn't intrigue you?"

"All I saw was a chimp pointing at the right numbers up to six."

"She also picked out three apples when shown the numeral three."

The man took the same cheese as Evan had. "Sure, but does that mean she's thinking?"

"I don't know. Animal awareness isn't my field. I'm sure my wife would have an opinion, though." Evan glanced around, but Ellen had disappeared from view. He reached for a sesame cracker. "Of course, I can't really say I know what *I'm* thinking."

"You can't? That seems odd."

"Not really. You don't feel pain—you just hurt. In the same way, you don't think about what you're thinking, you simply think."

The man reached for a cracker. "If you say so."

More accurately, Evan thought, it would be that Wittgenstein said so more than half a century ago. The two men stood there for a moment, facing the food table. Evan wondered if this fellow were deliberately copying what he ate or was merely highly suggestible. Evan speared a cube of pineapple from the buffet table and stuck it in his mouth.

The man reached for a toothpick and stuck it through two pieces of pineapple. "All I'm saying is that animals can be trained to do certain things after you work with them for years and years. But they don't know what they're doing."

"Half the time I don't know what I'm doing," Evan said as he picked up a round, dough-like hors d'oeuvre. It was the last on the plate. He wondered what kind of anxiety this might provoke in the engineer.

The man set his paper plate on the buffet table and wiped his lips with the back of his hand. Evan offered him a napkin, but he waved it away.

"At least you know half the time. That chimp doesn't

know what he's doing *all* the time. It's like with that one they called Nim Chimpsky—you remember him?"

"I know something about him."

"They found out he was a fraud. He could only use signs when his trainers were around to interpret him. Put him with strangers and he didn't make any sense at all."

"That's not surprising. Language is a social skill. It's acquired from parents and friends and siblings."

"Sure, but then you can use that skill whenever you want to. Nim couldn't, and I bet this Tyco can't count for anybody but that woman, Ellen something."

"Birch."

"Birch? That's your name."

"Yes, she's my wife."

The man coughed into his hand. "Oh, sorry, I didn't mean anything by it. I just get going sometimes. My wife says I'm a professional skeptic."

"That's okay. You're free to believe what you want and not believe if you want."

"I believe the chimp can count. I'm not saying it's a trick or anything. I just think counting to six is no big deal. Let's see that animal add or subtract. Or learn zero—there's a good test. If she can do that, I'll open my wallet."

Evan liked this subtle measure of thought. He sipped his wine and looked toward the doors. Ellen was walking up to an elderly couple at the literature table. He caught her eye again and winked twice. That was about as emphatic as he could be. She said something to them and then came over.

"Well, Evan, where did you get to?"

He assumed she was being ironic and took her arm. "Ellen," he said, "this is—" He couldn't remember the name, of course. He never remembered names. It was stupid of him to construct a sentence as if he would recall the name. "I'm sorry, I'm afraid I'm not very good at—"

"Bill," the man said. "Bill Mathers."

"Ellen, Bill here has suggested the next challenge for you. He says he'll be convinced Tyco's thinking when she learns how to use zero."

Ellen looked at Bill with an expressionless expression that Evan found unsettling. He would have expected at least a forced smile. "There's already a researcher who claims her chimp does that," she said, "but it's still controversial. Of course, using zero doesn't prove intelligence. The Greeks got along fine without it. In fact, the Mayans didn't discover zero until about two thousand years ago."

"Discover it or think it up?" Evan said.

"However you want to phrase it."

"I just mean it's an open question whether numbers in general and zero in particular exist on their own or were created by us."

"I thought it was the Egyptians," Bill said. "Didn't they come up with zero?"

"It was the Mayans," Ellen said flatly. "That's what they're known for."

Evan ran his finger around the rim of his wineglass, producing a dull, rubbery sound. "A whole civilization's primary intellectual achievement is developing the idea of zero. I don't know if that's impressive or sad."

"It's impressive," Ellen said.

"The Roman Empire collapsed because of not having zero," Bill said. "I read that somewhere."

Zero, none, not there—like the dark matter that dominated the universe. It could be assumed to exist only by its influence on the detectable world. Evan wondered what dark forces were surrounding him at that moment, pulling him in one direction or another.

"Excuse me," Ellen said to Bill, "there's someone I have to talk to." She started back toward the main buffet table.

"Will we be leaving soon?" he whispered.

"No," she said.

"Pretty woman," Bill said, "if you don't mind my saying so."

"I don't." Evan finished his wine in a gulp. "Can I get you something?" he said, pointing to the liquor table.

"Not me. I never drink. It's no good for the liver, and you know what they say, Professor Birch."

"What do they say?"

"You're only as old as your liver."

"I never thought of it that way," Evan said and hoisted his wineglass. "I'll make this my last."

"Birch," Bill said, "sounds familiar. I never forget a name."

"You're probably thinking of the tree. Most people do."

Bill nodded vigorously. "That must be it, because I'm sure I'd remember you."

CHAPTER 24

S o, congratulations," Evan said as Ellen steered the Accord out of the Institute parking lot. "Tyco was the hit of the party. Everybody was talking about her." After he said this he knew he had gone too far. Ellen always zoomed in on hyperbole.

"You heard *everybody* talking about Tyco?"

"Okay, not everybody. I really only had two conversations, one with a guy who rents movies every Friday and Sunday. But the other man, the one talking about zero, he was very interested in Tyco."

"Bill Mathers."

"Right, that's his name. He seemed intrigued by your work, and apparently he has big bucks." Evan didn't see any harm in lying about Mathers's attitude, particularly since Ellen didn't seem very pleased about her performance. She needed cheering up.

"The only way the Institute will get money out of him," she said, "is if he keels over at the cheese table and his wife gives us a big donation out of gratitude." Ellen leaned forward to see past Evan, then pulled out onto the highway.

"That's kind of harsh, isn't it? He seemed harmless."

"Husbands like that aren't harmless."

She shifted quickly through the gears and hit cruising speed. He wondered if he fell in the "husbands like that" category.

"You know, Evan," she said, and he thought she probably started her sentence this way just to annoy him, "you really should have circulated more at the party. You might have heard the other main topic of conversation for the afternoon."

"Which was?"

"You."

The bluntness of her reply seemed crude to him. He looked out the window. In a ball field a father was throwing a small football high in the air to his son.

"You and a sixteen-year-old cheerleader," Ellen said. "That's what everyone was talking about. Your name was apparently all over Channel 4 news this morning."

He had hoped he had scared the television reporter off the story, but obviously not. She had done her piece anyway—without his comments. Why hadn't he taken the opportunity to express his innocence?

"It's bad enough for me," Ellen said, "but think of the impact on the boys at school. This has to be why Zed was acting up."

"Zed's fine now. He understands what's going on. I talked to him about it at the lake."

"Falling in the lake with him was some sort of bonding experience for you two?"

"I think that's exactly what it was."

"Well then, maybe I should take a dunk in the ocean with him because he's still acting cold to me."

"Maybe he's scared to talk to you."

"Scared?"

"Yes, you scared him when you interrogated the boys about the day I picked them up at camp. He was fine until you planted ideas in his head."

"*Interrogated* was his word?"

"If he knew the word, that's the one he would have used."

"I just asked them a couple of questions."

"You could have asked me."

"I did ask you. You keep saying nothing happened."

"Nothing did happen. Don't you believe that?"

"I believe there's something missing from your story."

"I have a *story* now?"

Ellen pulled into the passing lane to go by a tractor trailer full of new cars. "You know, Evan, it's really tiring debating words with you."

"What else is there to debate but the words? That's all we have to communicate with, unless you and Tyco have come up with some better way."

Ellen kept her foot on the pedal, going seventy, seventy-five, eighty.

"She just beats her chest and hoots, and you know what she means, right? It's too bad we got away from hooting a few million years ago. When we started talking, that's when all the confusion came into the world. Somewhere along the way, meaning evaporated. We have to keep asking each other what we really mean."

Ellen hit eighty-five, faster than he'd ever seen her drive. "You're lecturing like you're in the classroom."

"I'm not half this interesting in class, trust me."

"I didn't say you were interesting."

He smiled at her. "Nice comeback. You can go for the jugular when you want to, even when you're speeding."

She eased off the accelerator and turned back into the right lane. Evan looked at the passing trees, a blur of deep reds and burnt oranges. The weathermen had predicted a dull fall because of the drought. But the colors seemed bright as ever.

"Why is it so hard for you to believe in me?" he said.

She reached into her pocketbook under her left arm, fumbling for a while before coming out empty-handed. "That day when you stopped to get the boys, you acted different when you came home. You said hello to me very formally."

"You remember how I said hello to you on August 23rd?"

"I remember because I thought about it that night. You seemed distant."

"What the hell does that mean?"

"It means your mind seemed to be elsewhere. I was looking at you, but it wasn't you. I thought something was wrong."

Evan twisted in the seat belt. "Why are you doing this, Ellen? You're creating a whole story around that afternoon to make yourself believe I had something to do with the girl disappearing. Why do you want me to be involved in this?"

"I don't."

"You act like you do." He held his hands in the air, his fingers slightly apart, as if they were about to grasp something or someone. "Think what that would mean—that my hands, these hands, may have killed someone." He reached out with his left hand, but stopped. He couldn't bear it if she pulled away.

"I think we're all capable of killing someone," she said. "I'm pretty sure I am."

"Maybe in a moment of rage, but afterwards you couldn't just go on with your life. Murder would show in you—and me, too. I couldn't get away with it."

"A lot of people get away with it. There are plenty of unsolved murders."

"You think a lot of ordinary people commit murder and get away with it?"

"I don't know if they're ordinary or not. I don't know what an ordinary person is."

The conversation seemed to him to be disintegrating again, the words losing meaning. He felt helpless to communicate with her.

They didn't talk for a few minutes. The road twisted right, then left, then right. Ellen didn't slow down. Then she reached into her pocketbook again and came out with butter rum Life Savers.

"Here, I'll open it for you," he said. She gave him the package.

"I don't want to feel this way," she said as she sucked on the candy. "It's not a choice. I've hated these last few weeks. I don't know how to act with you."

"I'm sorry," he said. "I wish you could trust me. I wish I were more trustworthy."

It surprised him that it felt so good to say these words.

She drove hunched over the wheel. He had never seen her this tense. He needed to say more.

"I know the circumstances seem incriminating, and part of that is my fault. I haven't been the perfect husband. That's probably why you have trouble believing me. I guess I haven't been so believable before."

Ellen leaned back a little. Her fingers loosened on the steering wheel.

"So I'll admit it, I've been wrong and I apologize."

She glanced over. "For what?"

"Everything. Anything. Whatever you want, I'm sorry."

"Apologizing for everything isn't really apologizing for any particular thing."

"You name the particulars, I'll apologize. You can't get a better offer than that."

"This isn't funny, Evan."

"I'm not joking. I'm apologizing—for letting Carol Sparks get too close to me. No, that's the politician's way of putting it. I apologize for my *self* getting too close to her, there's number one. Number two, I apologize for being investigated for kidnapping Joyce Bonner. You were right, I probably did bring it on myself in some cosmic justice sort of way. I must have willed it to happen by being such a worrier. Number three, let's see . . . there has to be something else. It's the tyranny of three. How about, I apologize for making you suspicious? It has to be my fault that you're so full of doubts about me. You're certainly not a naturally suspicious person, so I must have turned you into a distrustful wife."

"Are you through?"

"I've just begun." He had started seriously, apologizing for every wrong of his life. But she couldn't gracefully accept, perhaps even offer that she could learn to be a bit more trusting herself. She had demanded particulars, chapter and verse, and suddenly he had lapsed into his familiar sarcasm. What else could she expect?

Ellen veered off on the side of the road. The car rolled to a stop on a narrow side shoulder. She put the shift into neutral.

"Feel a little shaking in the wheel?" he said.

Ellen took a deep breath and then blew it out slowly, one of her spur-of-the-moment relaxation techniques. Evan imagined the whole world, all six billion people, simultaneously relaxing at an appointed hour. He wondered if some universal balance would be upset, between anxiety and relaxation, for instance, or the intake of oxygen and exhalation of carbon dioxide. Surely those two things were in a precarious atmospheric harmony. He thought of other universal acts—what if everyone shouted at the same time, or cried, or laughed, or fell absolutely silent. That was the world he would like most to experience for a moment, one absent of all human sound. What would people hear instead?

Ellen folded her hands in her lap. She appeared ready to sit like that for a long time.

Evan watched a minute click off the dashboard clock. "Am I supposed to know what you're doing?"

"I just can't take listening to your sarcasm anymore," she said. "I don't have the energy."

"And I don't want to listen to your suspicions anymore."

Ellen nodded. "Fine, then it's clear we shouldn't be inhabiting the same space right now." She hit the "unlock" button.

"Is that a little hint that I'm supposed to get out?"

"It's a big hint."

"You expect me to get out here on the highway, God knows how many miles from our house?"

She nodded again.

"Well, how about no, I'm not walking home just because you can't stand a little justifiable sarcasm."

Ellen reached over the backseat and grabbed her water bottle. "Then I will." She opened the door and stepped out before he could grab her arm. He looked back, saw a large truck speeding toward her. He opened his mouth to yell, but the truck was coming too fast and loud. She pressed herself against the car. The wind from the passing truck rocked the Accord so hard Evan felt as if they might be whipped over the embankment.

He closed his eyes. He saw her being dragged down the road or tumbling into the ditch. He saw her twisted and broken. He saw blood pouring onto the highway. But when he looked again there she was, still spread out against the car, her arms reaching to either side. She wasn't moving, though, and that scared him—could she be dead but standing? He got out on his side and ran around to her.

Her head was slung back over the roof of the car. Her eyes were clenched. She didn't appear to be breathing.

"Ellen?"

"It missed," she whispered. "I don't know how, but it missed me."

He took her right hand to pull her off the car. It was like peeling a decal from the window. He led her around to the passenger side and opened the door. She stopped there and looked down the road. He was amazed that she might still be considering walking.

"Get in," he said in an authoritative tone that rarely worked with her. "I'm driving us home." She ducked into the seat. He closed the door on her and then pushed down the lock. When he went around to the front of the car he saw the black pocketbook flattened in the road a few feet away. Cars were racing by, a line of them as far up the highway as he could see. He might have to wait minutes for an opening. But he didn't want to give Ellen a chance to get out again and walk. He got down on his knees and leaned into the road just enough to snag the leather handle with one finger.

He jumped into the driver's side of the Accord and handed

her the pocketbook. He felt as if he had done something heroic. She didn't say "thank you."

"You didn't look," he said. "How could you get out of the car without even looking?"

"I was upset. Don't you do stupid things sometimes when you're upset?"

"Not like walking into traffic, no." He took her hand. "You really scared me," he said. "I don't want to lose you."

When she nodded with her head straight ahead, he wondered if he already had.

In the deep of the night he woke and saw her face staring at him from a few feet away, then drop back onto her side of the bed. He raised up on one arm. "What is it?"

"Nothing."

"Why were you staring at me?"

"You were talking in your sleep. You woke me up."

"Sorry." He shifted onto his side, facing her. "Why didn't you just elbow me? Why were you leaning over me?" He thought he knew the reason but wanted her to admit it. Why should he be the only one explaining himself?

"I just was, that's all."

"Was what?"

"I was trying to hear what you were saying—are you satisfied?"

He nodded even though she couldn't see him. "Did I say anything interesting?"

"You were talking to Wittgenstein."

"Really? I haven't dreamed of him in years."

Ellen turned her face toward him. "You've dreamed of Wittgenstein before?"

"Sure, that's not unusual for philosophers. I've dreamed of Kant, too—at least I think it was Kant. He said he was Kant, and why would someone masquerading as Kant appear in my dream? *That*, as the boys say, would be totally weird."

Ellen took in another long breath. Evan counted to twenty-two before she exhaled.

"What did I say to Wittgenstein?"

"You were rambling. Something about silence and words."

"So I make no more sense in my dreams than when I'm awake. At least I'm consistent. But I imagine Wittgenstein knew what I meant."

They lay still for a while, both on their backs. He always felt like a mummy in this position.

"You want to know what I was dreaming about?"

"No."

"I'll tell you anyway, since we're both wide awake. Ludwig and I were talking about not talking—that's the silence part. You were there, too, doing a headstand. Then you turned into a bird."

"What kind of bird?"

It surprised him that she was interested enough to ask a question. Maybe she thought he was making his dream up and wanted to see how far he'd go. "I don't know, a large generic bird. Everybody was turning into something else."

"What did you turn into?"

"I'm not sure. I was growing a very long neck, I remember that." Evan raised up a little on his arm. "So is my subconscious trying to tell me something?"

"You know my opinion—dreams are the brain's way of getting rid of the day's crazy images. They're meaningless."

"Then whatever I say in my dreams is meaningless, too,

right? I could mutter anything in my sleep, and there's no reason for you to believe it's true."

He saw her head move a little on the pillow, what he took as a nod. He was pleased with how he had maneuvered her. He could say in his sleep now whatever terrible thing his subconscious wanted—that he was a kidnapper or killer, for instance—and she would have to agree his words were crazy, the senseless expressions of a brain just taking out the trash.

CHAPTER 25

He had always thought that much of life was sitting around waiting for things to happen. If it was a specific good thing one was waiting for, it was called anticipation. If it was a bad thing, it was called apprehension.

Evan wasn't sure what he was waiting for as he sat at the marble island in his kitchen with the Sunday *New York Times* spread out between him and Ellen. He certainly wasn't expecting to see his name or picture under the headline "Professor Suspected in Cheerleader's Kidnapping." The *Times* had more important stories to cover. On the other hand, he didn't see any way for vindication suddenly to appear in his life, either. It was a stark fact of life that a crime required a guilty party, whether proven or not. He was the assumed guilty man.

She was drinking her third cup of coffee. He hoped it was decaf. She was already so edgy that when he pointed out she was buttering her toast, rather than eating it plain, she said, "I don't comment on everything you eat, do I?" He could think of many times when she had.

Both of them were still wearing their robes. It was almost ten o'clock. The morning sky was bright blue, promising a beautiful fall day. He thought that maybe what they both needed was to get outside, to have a destination.

"You ready to go up and get dressed?" he said.

She drank more coffee. "What for?"

He hadn't thought of a reason. Getting dressed seemed like the first step toward all possibilities.

"What about waking the boys and going to church?" He checked his watch. "We could still make the late sermon."

"Church?"

She said the word as if mystified as to its meaning, or at least confused as to why he would be saying it.

"It's been a couple of months. We should be taking them to Sunday school every week if they're ever going to be confirmed."

Ellen shook her head. "I don't think so."

He didn't know if she was referring to going to church or the boys being confirmed. Perhaps she meant both.

She turned the page, then another. She looked up for a moment, and he thought she might be reconsidering church. "We have to decide about the lawn company," she said. "They sent another notice."

He looked at the section in front of her to see what had prompted this sudden concern for their lawn. It was the movie listings. "The grass was pretty green this summer, considering the drought. What do we need a lawn company for?"

"To do the things you never get around to, like aerating in the fall and spraying for weeds in the spring."

"Spraying *against* weeds, you mean."

The wall phone rang and Ellen leaned off her stool to answer it. "Yes," she said almost immediately and held the receiver toward him. "It's the *Eastfield News.*"

"The *News?* Can't they leave us in peace on Sunday?"

"Ask for yourself."

Evan took the phone.

"Hello, Professor Birch," said a young male voice, "sorry to call so early, but I wanted to make sure to get you today. This is Joe LeFevre from the *News.* I'd like to interview you about—"

"I'm sorry," Evan said reflexively, even though he was not sorry at all, "I'm not doing any interviews."

"You aren't? Well, I already read one story about you, that's why I'm calling."

"If you're referring to the *Pearce Banner,* that story was unauthorized, and if you noticed, I wasn't directly quoted. I'm not talking to reporters about this."

"If you don't mind my saying so, that seems kind of strange."

"It's not strange at all. I happen to value my privacy and that of my family."

There was silence on the line. Evan thought about hanging up, but he didn't want to give the reporter reason to write how rude or angry he was.

"We have almost twenty thousand readers," the young man said. "I'm sure some of them would be interested in buying your book."

"My book?"

"Yes, *Disturbing Minds*—you're the Professor Birch who wrote that, aren't you?"

"I am. So you're calling to do a write-up on my book?"

"Yes, we have an Ideas section on Sunday that deals with different interesting ideas. We thought the article could go in next week."

"Fine," Evan said. "*Ideas* sounds like a good place for *Disturbing Minds*. I'd be happy to talk to you."

"How about tomorrow at three P.M., I'll come to your house?"

Evan suddenly became suspicious. "How about we meet at the Park Cafe over coffee?"

"That's fine."

"And we're just talking about *Disturbing Minds,* is that right?"

"Yes," the reporter said, "what else is there?"

As they got dressed Evan thought of other options for the day. "How about we go apple-picking?" he said. "We haven't been in a couple of years."

Ellen shook her head and sat on the bed to tie the laces of her sneakers. "Not since Adam fell out of the tree and broke his arm, no. I think we should stay away from apple orchards."

"You want to go into the city? We could walk along the harbor."

Ellen stood up. "There are too many people in the city. It's suffocating sometimes."

"Then let's take the boys on a hike somewhere—or we could go canoeing. How about that?"

She didn't say no immediately, which encouraged him. She tossed her nightgown and robe onto the top shelf of her closet. Apparently hanging them up was too much effort today.

"If you want to," she said.

He ignored the listlessness of her response. "Good, then canoeing it is. I'll tell the boys."

Canoeing?" Adam said with the same incredulity Ellen had used in saying "church?"

"Yes, canoeing. We'll have fun." He pulled the covers off Adam and then opened the bathroom door a crack. "Zed," he called in, "turn off the shower and get dressed. We're going canoeing."

"Z. and I could stay here," Adam said. He pulled the covers back over himself. "Mom said we're old enough."

"You're old enough to come with us, too. Throw on sneakers and a sweatshirt. It could be chilly."

Zed stuck his wet head out from the bathroom. "What did you say?"

"We're going canoeing."

"Why are we doing that?"

"Consider it a family outing. Now hurry and put on some warm clothes."

"But—"

"No use arguing," Adam said as he got up and went to his bureau, "Dad's making us."

"Yes, I'm such a terrible father for making you go have fun, aren't I?"

In the back of the Jetta, the twins slunk so far down in the seats that he couldn't see them in his rearview mirror. Ellen was reading a book with a bright yellow cover that made him think of birds. He didn't ask the title.

The drive to the river took no more than fifteen minutes, and he wondered why they hadn't done this before. The twins tumbled out of the car and ran toward the row of overturned boats on the pier. Evan didn't know why they were suddenly so eager.

He paid for a two-hour rental and left the little shop with an armful of oars and life jackets. The teenage clerk walked behind him to the pier and slid the nearest canoe into the water. Adam stepped in first and went to the front. Zed hopped in and went to the rear seat.

"Should we let them paddle?" he asked Ellen as they climbed into the middle.

"Yes, you should!" Zed shouted.

She spread out a towel on the cold metal bench and they sat. "Why not?"

The teenager shoved them away from the dock. "Go upstream first," he said. "Turn around after an hour and the boat will drift back here by itself."

"It's like riding a trail horse," Evan called back to him. "The boat knows its way home."

"I don't know anything about horses," the boy said.

The canoe veered off toward the opposite shore. "Paddle on opposite sides," Ellen told the boys. "That's the only way we'll go straight."

The river was narrow at this point, and the tree limbs bowed over the water. Evan put his arm around her and felt extra clothing under her sweater. She always came prepared for cold.

The twins settled into a rhythm of counting out loud to ten, then switching sides with their paddles. Evan was pleased that they had worked out the system on their own.

Ellen leaned into him. "You know what just came back to me?"

"What?"

"Canoeing in Switzerland."

"When did you do that?"

"*We* did that, Evan. Don't you remember, on Lake Zurich, the summer after we graduated?"

"I remember walking next to a big lake somewhere, but I thought it was in Italy. Did we really go out in a canoe?"

"Yes, it was in Zurich, after we had fondue. We walked along the waterfront and there was the little Italian man renting boats. That's probably why you're remembering Italy. He was pointing and giving us instructions, but we couldn't understand a word."

"Okay."

"Come on, Evan, you have to remember this."

He wished he could. He knew memories were important to her.

"Oh, sure, you mean the Lake *Zurich* canoe trip. We ate at that cute fondue restaurant with the skis hanging on the outside. I kept dropping the meat in the pot."

"All the restaurants had skis on the outside. And it was bread."

"I remember meat."

"You don't actually remember any of it, do you?"

"Yes I do. It was a chilly evening. I put my arm around you, like I'm doing now."

"And then what happened?"

"I kissed you? I mean, I kissed you."

"While you were kissing me, we looked up and saw . . . ?"

"Stars?"

"No, we looked up and there was this huge ship bearing down on us. We barely got out of the way. We could have been crushed by it. How can you forget that?"

"You know I have a notoriously bad memory," he said.

"And this was more than twenty-five years ago—I remember that."

"Hey, Dad, do you hold the paddle this way or this way?"

"Ask your mother, Adam. Apparently she canoed on Lake Zurich."

Adam was twisted around in the front. "Really, Mom?"

"Yes, with a handsome, romantic young man. I wonder what became of him."

"I bet he's still around," Evan said.

"So how do you hold the paddle, Mom?"

"Put your right hand over the top and your left about halfway down. Then let it slide on the handle as you stroke."

"Like this," Zed shouted from the back, but Adam had already turned forward again.

"With your notorious memory," she said, "I could make up anything I want and say you did it."

"Sure, create some memories for me. I've got a lot of vacant space in my brain."

They glided a while past large houses set high up on the riverbank. There were no people in sight. In one yard, a red chair sat facing the water. It looked very lonely to Evan.

"That evening," she said, "you promised me something I've never forgotten."

"What's that?"

"You said you would always tell me the truth."

"Hey, what are you guys whispering for?" Zed said from behind them.

"We're just talking. You concentrate on keeping us going straight."

Ellen touched his leg. "I don't suppose you remember saying that?"

"No, but that was before I started in philosophy, so I might have made that promise."

"You mean you wouldn't promise me that now?"

"Truth is as subjective as opinion. I didn't know that when I was young."

"Maybe you were right when you were young. We don't necessarily get wiser as we get older."

"I don't claim to be getting wiser, but I know enough not to make rash promises anymore."

"Promising to tell the truth is rash?"

"Yes. Promising to *try* to tell the truth—as I interpret it, as I remember it—that much I can say."

"I like your original promise better," she said, "and that's the one I'm holding you to."

They pulled over at a small beach. Ellen laid out towels and handed sandwiches to each of them. She took small bites of carrots and celery. He wondered if she was trying to lose weight.

"We should always eat outside," Adam said. "Food tastes better."

"You didn't have any breakfast," Evan said, "and hunger is the best spice."

"What?"

"It's a saying. When you're hungry, things taste better. If you want to eat outside this winter, we can set up a table for you on the deck."

"You'd freeze your balls off," Zed said.

They both turned toward him.

"What was that?" Evan said.

"Nothing."

"You said something."

"I said he'd freeze his hands off."

"No he didn't," Adam said, "he—"

"Hey, look."

They followed Zed's finger to the upper branches of a large willow tree.

"There's a mess of crows up there."

"It's a murder of crows," Ellen said. "That's what a group of them is called."

"That's cool. Do crows really murder?"

She nudged Evan in the side. "This is your question."

Why would she say that? He could only see one side of her face, not enough to read her expression.

"No, Zed, crows don't murder like people do. But they do get in fights and can hurt each other. And sometimes you'll hear them flocking in the woods to pick the meat off something dead, like a deer. They get into a feeding frenzy. It sounds like they're committing murder."

The boys finished their sandwiches and hurried back to the canoe. "Come on," Adam said, "we're wasting time."

Ellen unzipped her pocketbook and plunged her hand in, rooting around on the bottom.

"Are pocketbooks standard equipment on canoes in Lake Zurich?"

"If you want Life Savers, yes."

He stood up and folded one towel. Her hand dipped back into her large black satchel, came out with something that she looked at briefly, then dipped in again.

"Your pocketbook is like the ocean floor," he said. "Only a very small part of it has ever been mapped."

She laughed and pulled out a package of Life Savers. "Butter rum, anyone?"

They all said yes.

Evan took the longer road home to prolong the outing. He pointed out bright red sugar maples and yellow beeches. The boys grunted at each tree, their way of acknowledging they had heard while not losing concentration on their video games. Ellen didn't look up from her book. She didn't even grunt.

"Anything interesting?" he asked.

She glanced out the window and then realized that he was referring to her reading. "Archbishop Usher calculated that God finished creating the world on Friday, October 28th, 3438 B.C. Apparently he didn't specify a time of day."

Adam leaned through the opening in the backseat. "Is that true, Dad?"

"That would make the world only five and a half thousand years old. Does that sound right to you?"

"It's like billions of years old," Zed said. "That Usher guy was stupid."

"Not stupid so much as lacking information."

"If the world was only five and a half thousand years old, when did the dinosaurs live?"

"Good question, Zed. Ask your science teacher."

Evan saw the sign for Eastfield State Park ahead and turned left.

"Are we going to the lake, Dad?"

"No, not today."

"Why not? Come on, Mom, you want to go, don't you?"

"That's not a good idea."

Evan wished she could have just said no or that they had to get home instead of referring, even obliquely, to the kidnapping. He didn't want the park to be forever tainted for them.

"We'll be all right," Zed said. "We won't go out of your sight."

"We could buddy up," Adam said. "I'll buddy with Mom, and Z. can buddy with Dad."

"What if I want Mom?" Z. said.

"Do you?"

"I don't care. I'll take Dad, I guess."

"Then if somebody tries to grab us, we yell and kick him and then all four of us jump him. We could catch the kidnapper, Dad."

Ellen turned the page to her book. Evan kept driving, right past the entrance to Eastfield State Park.

CHAPTER 26

E van walked down the long corridor of the Arts Building with his bulging briefcase weighing down his right arm. He was sure he looked lopsided. He thought it would be smarter to carry two briefcases, each sharing the load. But then neither hand would swing and he would seem robotic. There was always a trade-off.

He did not look up as he passed people in the hall. A philosophy professor could not be faulted for being lost in thought, so that was the demeanor he affected. He had started out the day as normal, ready with a nod or hello to everyone he passed. But he noticed students giving him long stares and fellow professors avoiding his glance altogether. No one said,

"What a crazy story in the *Banner,* Birch. You must be ready to sue them."

He was left with the conclusion that a sizable number of people were ready to believe he was leading a double life—devoted father, husband, and teacher on the one hand, and cunning adulterer, kidnapper, and killer on the other. If it had been some other double life—as a spy, for example—he might have felt flattered. But to be generally conceived of as a murderer was unsettling.

Before he reached the end of the hallway he heard voices coming from his classroom. He wondered for a moment if he had gotten the day or time wrong and was walking into a more popular class. When he turned in the doorway he was stunned. At least thirty students were spread out over the room. Some were leaning against the windows. A few were sitting on the steps of the risers. He checked the door—P3—and his watch—2:30. This was his Monday edition of "Introduction to Philosophy."

He had always run an open class, which any Pearce student could attend, no questions asked. But in the five years of advertising this policy in the course catalog, he couldn't remember more than three or four students auditing even for a day. Mostly who came was the visiting boyfriend of a girl, and neither paid much attention.

Today he recognized only a half-dozen faces. The other students were there, he supposed, to see him squirm.

He set his briefcase on the floor. He took off his jacket and draped it over his chair. He loosened his tie. He was giving himself time to think. To proceed as usual would be ridiculous. And yet to confront head-on the reason they were there would open himself up in a way that he couldn't imagine. He certainly didn't want to answer questions about his encounters with a missing girl.

He thought he might remark in some whimsical way about his sudden popularity, but another idea came to him.

"Well," he said, "it seems my little trick to fill up the classroom worked. The hint of scandal always brings out an audience."

The students looked from one to the other.

Evan erased the blackboard of its unfathomable physics equations. When he turned back to the class he said, "I see that you're confused. You don't know whether I planted the story in the *Banner* or not. Perhaps I was conducting an experiment. It's difficult discerning truth, isn't it, Mr. Winokur? You've learned that in this class, haven't you?"

"Yes, Professor Birch. Truth is pretty slippery."

"That's an apt way of putting it. Truth is pretty slippery." Evan folded his arms. "I should warn all of you newcomers, I intend to talk for an hour about Kant's categorical imperative, as translated into R. M. Hare's prescriptive approach to ethics. So you might want to reconsider your choice to be here. Once I shut this door, I lock it and nobody gets out till the end of the lecture, isn't that so, Ms. Grinaldi?" It wasn't, of course, but he thought she was timid enough that she would play along.

"The only way out's the window," she said, and he smiled at her embellishment of his story.

Evan tapped his fingers on the desk. Then he looked at his fingernails and noticed a speck of black under the middle finger of his right hand. After forty years, some gravel was still there from his fall in the driveway. His father had said it would poison him and tried to gouge it out with a needle. As usual, the old man had been proven wrong. Evan wished he were still alive to show him.

No one was leaving the room. The threat to bore them with Kant and Hare hadn't worked. Evan reached into his pocket for his car key and walked toward the door. He would have to appear, at least, to lock them in.

"Hold it," a boy in the back said as he stood up. "I think I'm in the wrong class."

As he passed down the tiers, a girl got up to follow him. By the time they reached the door, students were lining up to leave. They were unusually quiet and orderly, Evan noted, perhaps feeling a bit chastised. He smiled at each one, as if the greeter after a church ceremony. "Come back another day," he said.

When he closed the door and turned around, there were only four students left in his class, two fewer than usual. Ms. Grinaldi was gone.

"Okay," he said as he walked behind his desk, "let's talk about morality."

Carla was on the phone when he passed the receptionist's area, but she hung up quickly.

"Professor, wait, I have to tell you something."

Evan motioned toward his office. "Come on in."

She hurried by him and sat in the visitor's chair.

"What's on your mind?"

"I talked to the police."

She blurted out the words as if they had been waiting on her tongue for hours.

"There's nothing wrong with that, Carla. I thought they might interview you at some point. I should have told you."

"I didn't want to talk, but they said they could subpoena me."

He wondered whether Malloy had delivered this threat with a smile or not.

"I hope the police didn't scare you."

"I *was* a little scared. I never talked to the police before."

"I hadn't either before all of this." Evan sat in his chair and moved some papers around his desk. He didn't want to put her on the spot by looking at her directly. "So, what did they want to talk about?"

"That day, when the girl disappeared."

"What about that day?"

"They asked when you left the office."

Evan flipped on his computer. "That was over a month ago, Carla. I'm sure you couldn't remember that far back."

"No, I didn't."

Evan nodded.

"I had to look it up."

"Look it up where?"

"I keep a notebook with the professors in it. When somebody leaves for the day I put down the time. That way when I get a call I can say how long you've been gone. A lot of people ask that."

"I see. When does your notebook say I left that day?"

"It was early, about two P.M. You got a call, then you left."

"And do you note down whom phone calls are from?"

"They asked me that, too. No, I don't keep track of calls. But they said that was okay because they can check the phone records."

"Of course. But they'll only see who called the general number, won't they, not whom the call was for?"

"That's right. I didn't think of that."

"Well, most likely it was my wife calling," Evan said, "reminding me to get the boys. She always thinks I'll forget."

"That's probably it," Carla said. She tugged her brown skirt down over her knees. He had often thought she had pretty legs, and he wondered if she knew he thought that. It was not a compliment that he could say aloud.

The phone rang at the receptionist's desk, and she jumped up from the chair. "I hope I didn't get you in trouble. I didn't want to do that."

"No, don't worry," he said, and he was charmed by her concern not to harm him.

He reached the Park Cafe at two minutes past three o'clock. The place was almost empty. The waitress pointed him toward a small table, but he asked for a window booth.

"We don't put singles in booths, sir."

Evan looked around the restaurant. "Even when no one else is here?"

"It's a policy, that's all. I didn't make it."

"Well, I'll be two anyway. I'm meeting someone."

He ordered a cranberry muffin and coffee. From his window spot he could look across the street to the border of the park. The leaves were still so thick on the trees that he couldn't see far in. He thought that a straight line would take him past the information booth and on to the lake. He wondered if Mr. Bonner stopped in here to refresh himself after his search. Perhaps he was out there at this moment poking through leaves for the remnants of his daughter's blouse or pants. It was a depressing thought.

"You're the professor?"

Evan looked up. The waitress was standing over him. Her name tag said "Dawn." He thought she seemed more like a "Dolores" or "Betty."

"Which professor do you mean?"

"The one I got a call for out back."

Evan rose half out of his seat. "Oh, yes, I suppose I am. Should I go back there to take it?"

She looked at him as if he were crazy. "Nobody goes in the kitchen, Bernie's law."

"Bernie?"

"The cook."

"Then how do I get my call?"

"I took the message. It was a funny name. Joe something. He said he can't meet you. He said you'd know what that means."

"Okay, did he say anything else?"

Dawn thought for a minute. "He might have said he was sorry."

She returned to the counter, and Evan wondered what had prevented Joe Something from making his appointment. The most likely possibility was that he was called to cover a breaking story. But of course, he might also have found out by reading his own newspaper that his interview subject for the day was considered a prime suspect in a crime. The *Eastfield News* would certainly not want to feature the author of *Disturbing Minds* in its Ideas section.

Evan looked over to the counter and caught Dawn's attention, then made a little writing motion in the air. She leaned through the swinging back door and a large man in a green apron, apparently Bernie, came out. They spoke for a minute, she nodded toward Evan, and the man came over with the check.

Evan took out a five-dollar bill.

"It's $9.95, Professor."

The title didn't sound too flattering coming from this man's lips. "Are you sure?" Evan said. "I just had a muffin and coffee."

"There's a booth charge for singles. Five dollars."

Evan pulled out another five from his pocket and handed it over. He slid out of the booth, and Bernie stepped back a little.

"You want your nickel?"

"Keep the change," Evan said. On the way out he smiled at Dawn and strangely enough, she smiled back, as he supposed she had been trained to do. He wished he had left a proper tip for her.

He came through the garage door into the hallway and stopped, turning his head from side to side. Ellen was standing at the kitchen sink. She twisted her head around and said hello.

"You don't smell something?" he said.

"What?"

"There's a rotting odor in here." He picked up the wooden fish leaning against the wall but saw nothing on the floor behind it. He opened the pantry closet and stuck his head in for a moment. "Are you cooking anything?"

"No," Ellen said, "I'm not cooking anything rotten."

He looked around the corner up the rear steps, and the back door opened behind him. The boys came in, and with them, a rush of cool air that blew away the odd smell.

"Hey, Dad, what are you doing?"

"Sniffing for foul odors," he said.

"Oh. When's dinner, Mom?"

"Not for a while. We're eating late."

Adam grabbed a banana from the bowl on the center island. Zed opened the shelf over the stove and went up on his tiptoes to reach the bag of York peppermint patties. He took two and put the rest back.

"They're supposed to be out of your reach," Ellen said.

"Nothing's out of my reach now."

"I'll remember that."

The boys left the kitchen and Evan started after them.

"Ray Warren asked us if we wanted to go to the symphony in two weeks," Ellen said. "I told him yes. They're good seats, and free."

"Is he going, too?"

"Of course, and Joanne."

"I'll go if you two sit between him and me. I don't want to talk to him."

Ellen leaned against the counter. "You have some little objection to all my friends, don't you?"

"No, it's just a few of them I don't feel comfortable with."

"And what exactly is the annoying imperfection you've found in Ray?"

Evan thought he would ignore the mockery in her question. Then he decided to embrace it. "His *imperfection* is that he makes a career out of being interesting."

"What does that mean?"

"It means he tries too hard. He has his hair in a ponytail and wears a beret, for God's sake."

"He lived in Paris for three years."

"I lived in Austin for five years and you don't see me wearing a ten-gallon hat."

Ellen opened the dishwasher and started unloading the glasses from the top shelf. "Well, he likes you, and your appearance in the news doesn't seem to bother him."

His *appearance*—she made it sound like he had sought out the notoriety for himself. "So now I'm a social pariah who should be grateful for anyone willing to be seen on the street with him?"

She turned back toward the sink. "I've had a long day, Evan. Just show up in two weeks and be nice to Ray. Is that too much to ask?"

"Of course I'll be nice. When am I not nice?"

She didn't answer. She was staring into the dishwasher. He thought there must be something odd in there—a dead mouse, for instance.

"Come here."

He walked over and looked down to where she was pointing. "What?"

"You see the tea bag holder?"

"Yes."

"I told you not to put it in the dishwasher."

"Why can't it go in the washer?"

"Because it's small and drops through the rungs, for one thing. It's been broken twice and I've had to glue it back together, so I don't want it subjected to hot water."

He leaned over closer. "It looks okay to me. It didn't get broken."

"I don't care that it didn't get broken this time, I just don't want it in the fucking dishwasher! Can you understand that?"

Evan turned around and nudged shut the kitchen door. He waited a moment for her to calm down. "Do you need to curse at me like that?"

"Yes, apparently I do because you haven't gotten the message before."

She moved in front of him and started pulling soup bowls from the bottom of the dishwasher. She stacked them on the counter so carelessly he thought they would break, and would she blame him for that, too?

"Would you mind telling me what you're really angry about?"

She turned half around with knives in her hand, the blades up. "I'm angry that the tea bag holder is sitting in this dishwasher after I've told you at least three times not to put it there. That's what I'm angry about." Her voice was unnaturally calm now, and he wondered how she could switch volume so quickly.

He took the knives from her and put them in the utensil drawer. "It's not possible that you're angry about me being in the news? Did that come up again today with Ray or someone?"

Ellen pulled the little blue ceramic dish from the washer. "No, it's this, Evan, this, this." She shook the tea bag holder in the air. "Don't put this in the fucking fucking dishwasher!"

He nodded to her and left the kitchen. All the way down the hall he could hear dishes banging into dishes.

He thought it best to stay out of her way until dinner. He went to his study and closed the door emphatically behind him. He hoped that she heard. It was silly to slam a door, of course. Powerless people slammed doors. He *did* feel powerless in the face of her sudden outbursts. Her anger scared him. He didn't know what she might do if provoked—throw a knife at him? That seemed like a possibility, especially if he didn't play the submissive husband.

Evan picked up the closest book at hand, his own, and began reading the introduction: "The unexamined life isn't worth living, Plato said. It was a self-serving opinion that endorsed his chosen pursuit in life—philosophy. Philosophers examine life, sometimes their own, but more often the common existence of all people. In *Disturbing Minds,* I—"

I, I, I . . . The smallest of words in the English language stood for one of the largest concepts—the human ego. Sometimes that ego turned on itself. He thought of Tolstoy . . ."I am always with myself, and it is I who am my tormentor." Evan agreed with the first assertion: He *was* always with himself, in body and mind. But was he his own tormentor? He didn't think so. Wittgenstein had an inner compulsion to self-contempt that drove him to atone for his sins, both imaginary and real. Evan didn't feel any such internal conflict. He was as he was, a fly in the bottle trying to find its way out. He didn't think he should have to apologize for that.

Ellen had said they would be eating late, so he waited till seven to go to the kitchen to see about dinner. She wasn't there. On the center island sat two large pizza boxes. He opened the top one. It was empty. He opened the bottom one and saw almost a full pizza left. He pulled out a large slice.

He hadn't heard her leave and hadn't heard anyone come, so how had these pizzas appeared? He couldn't figure that out. He ate his piece over the box. It was made the way he liked it—less cheese, more sauce—so he assumed she had given these instructions to the restaurant on his behalf. The pizza tasted good even though barely warm. He could have heated it in the microwave, but he didn't want to spend sixty seconds in the kitchen watching his pizza heat up. He didn't always look at the small efforts of his life like this, but when he did he usually found them pointless.

He presumed Ellen was still at home, probably upstairs in

the guest room. She liked sitting in the old wooden rocker reading. He tried to sense her presence in the house, to feel her in the same general space that he inhabited, but he couldn't be sure.

He finished his slice and closed up the pizza box. There was a lot left. The boys would ask to have it in the morning. He had heard somewhere that cooked tomatoes were particularly healthy. That seemed like a good enough reason to say yes to pizza at breakfast. Perhaps he would have some himself.

He worked in his study until a little past nine and then went upstairs to check on the boys. They were sitting next to each other on the bottom bunk, Adam letting a Slinky fall from one hand to the other, Zed stuffing pennies into a paper holder. It seemed like the innocent poses they might have just jumped into when they heard him coming. He figured they had hurriedly switched off the computer, and he resisted the temptation to see if the monitor was still warm.

"Hey, guys, what are you up to?"

"Nothing much. It's pretty boring," Adam said.

"Totally," Zed said.

"Well, life's boring a lot of the time. You might as well get used to it."

He wished he hadn't said that. A nicer father would have suggested they sneak downstairs and get ice cream, even though it was past their usual snack time on a school night. A more spontaneous father would have suggested they play a game—maybe Anti-Monopoly, even though it would take an hour.

He moved around the room, picking up T-shirts and socks and shorts lying on the floor. He dropped the pile on the bed between the boys.

"Were you and Mom fighting again?" Adam asked.

The question surprised him.

"Fighting when?"

"Before dinner."

"Your mother was just explaining something to me in a loud voice. She wanted to make sure I heard her."

"*We* heard her."

"You did?"

"Yeah, she used the F-word."

"Well, I'm sorry you heard that. She's been pretty upset about things lately, and she kind of lost it for a minute. She's fine now." Evan turned toward the door.

"Are you getting divorced, Dad?"

He whirled on them. "Divorced? No, why would you ask that?"

"When parents fight all the time they get divorced."

"We're not fighting all the time. We've just had a couple of loud discussions about the thing with the police." Evan watched the Slinky dropping from hand to hand and the pennies going into the paper container. It seemed like the boys were doing these things in slow, repetitive motions, as if to hypnotize him.

"Any more questions?"

"No."

"Okay, it's almost time for lights out now, so put your things away."

The boys grabbed at the clothes on the bed, and he wondered how they could tell which were their own. Maybe they just divvied up everything half and half, or maybe they wore each other's clothes. He didn't know.

Zed took his armful to his bureau and folded each thing before putting in the drawers. Adam carried his clothes to his closet and dropped them on the floor. Then he turned around. Evan expected "Good night" or "Love you." Adam said, "A kid at school's telling everybody you did it."

Did *it*. As a euphemism, *it* certainly had to be the most all-encompassing. He tried to seem unfazed. "What's *it*? I do a lot of things. Everybody does."

"You know what, Dad."

"I suppose. But I wonder if *he* even knows what he means."

Evan realized that he had probably just done it again, twisted up words in an irritating way, yet neither of the twins seemed bothered this time.

"He's like the stupidest kid in our class," Adam said.

"In the whole school," Zed said. "Nobody listens to him."

"I'm glad to hear that. But if it gets hard on you what kids say, you'll tell me, right?"

Zed stood up straight in the middle of the room and punched into the air. "I'm going to hit him in the face if he says it again. Pow, pow, pow."

"I'll hold him and you hit him," Adam said, "right in the mouth."

Evan felt the odd inclination to say, *Yes, good idea, go get him.* It would be irresponsible, of course. And he figured the boys only felt confident in making their threats because they knew he would tell them they couldn't carry it out.

"You want us to beat him up, Dad?"

Evan saw a red spot on the carpet near the bathroom. Dried blood, no doubt—Zed's blood. It was a trace of his son that he would leave there forever.

"I appreciate your wanting to defend me, guys, but you can't stop stupid people by hitting them. So if I hear of either of you starting a fight, I'll ground you forever and a day."

"*Forever?*" they said in unison.

"And a day."

"There's nothing longer than forever," Zed said.

"A really long time then."

"You're weird," Zed said.

"Good weird," Adam added.

"Thanks," Evan said. "I haven't gotten many compliments lately."

When he went into the bedroom Ellen was already in bed, with a book propped on her chest.

"Oh, good, just in time," she said. "Close the window for me, will you? It's getting chilly in here."

He didn't hear any remnant of anger in her voice, nor any hint of apology, either. She was apparently proceeding in her recent pattern, as if their argument hadn't occurred. He liked this new way of getting over fights.

He closed the window and then sat at the end of the bed, next to her legs. "I heard the window theory of change the other day."

She looked up quickly from her book, more responsive than usual. "What's that?"

"People don't change until they absolutely have to, and the perfect example is with an open window. We won't get out of bed to close it until we're so cold we have to. We never get up when we're just a little cold."

"This theory of yours applies to more than windows, I presume."

"It's not my theory, and it applies to all life—government, business, relationships, everything."

"An all-encompassing theory of behavior—that's what you're always looking for in philosophy, isn't it?"

"I'm not saying the window analogy explains all behavior, just one aspect of it." He kicked off his shoes. "What are you reading tonight?"

"*Being Dead.*"

"What's that, reports from the afterlife?"

"No, it's a novel."

"Is this novel as cheery as the title suggests?"

"It's depressing, especially the first chapter. But it's powerful, too."

Depressing and *powerful*—the combination of the words intrigued him. He figured he was back on solid enough ground with Ellen that he could needle her a bit, as he normally would. "Do you ever think what else you could be doing besides reading powerfully depressing books?"

"Such as?"

"Well . . ." He couldn't think of a thing. She worked at the Institute three days a week, took care of the kids, bought groceries, made dinners, ran the house. He certainly couldn't ask any more of her. "You could just do nothing once in a while."

"Thanks for the suggestion, but I'm not fond of doing nothing. Besides, I'd disappoint myself if I stopped now. I said I would read a book a day for a year."

"I'm sorry I challenged you."

"I'm not doing this because of you. Reading keeps me focused. Every day I learn something new. It's aerobics for my mind."

She looked down at her book, and he stared at her for a minute. He thought she had never looked more beautiful. Her lips were dark, her cheeks slightly flushed, her eyelashes perfectly curled. He wondered if the earlier eruption of anger had set off some beneficial hormones inside her.

He lay across her legs. "What do you remember when you're done?"

"What?"

"When you finish a book, how much do you remember? Take *Anna Karenina*—Anna cheats on her husband with Count Vronsky, and when he jilts her she throws herself under a train. That's all there is in my memory about that book. Or *A Tale of Two Cities*—'It was the best of times, it was the worst of times, it was the age of wisdom, it was the age of foolishness . . . ' The opening is all anyone remembers."

"Madame Defarge knitting her death list of people doing injustices—I remember that."

"You're way ahead of most people then. How about an easy one, *Jane Eyre*—you read that a couple of months ago."

"Jane Eyre was an orphan girl who came to live at Thornfield Manor and fell in love with Rochester. Or he fell in love with her, I'm not sure. They probably fell in love with each other. And he hid his crazy wife in the tower."

"Sounds like Cliff Notes," he said. "They could boil down *Disturbing Minds* to a sentence—'Philosophers think too much and act badly.' That would sum it up."

Ellen closed *Being Dead* and put it on her nightstand. He noted the bookmark about two-thirds of the way through.

"Going to sleep without finishing?"

"I finished earlier. I was just rereading a few passages."

He undressed in the full light of the room, tossing his clothes on the chair. He turned toward her for a minute, naked, and then switched off the light. When he got in bed he moved toward the center where she was, and the bed boards squeaked under their weight.

"We can't do anything," she said. "The boys are still awake."

He kissed her on the neck. Then he rose up and kissed her on the lips. "Tomorrow we fix the squeak, okay?"

She ran her hand down his chest. "First thing in the morning."

They lay together for a while, with his leg on top of her thigh. After a minute it got too warm and he drew back from her.

"Can I ask you something?" he said.

"Yes."

"This afternoon, were you really just angry about the tea bag holder?"

"Yes, Evan, that's what I was angry about. Don't ever fucking put it in the dishwasher again."

"Okay," he said. "I won't ever fucking do that again."

They kissed again, and when he pulled away he licked his lips to savor the taste of her.

CHAPTER 27

Two days passed. Evan rarely thought in such small periods. He preferred to measure life in seasons, or semesters, where a sweep of time could blur the ups and downs of everyday life.

There was much he wished to blur—Dean Santos grilling him again about "when will this all end?" Paul Curry leaving cryptic messages through Carla, then not being in the office to take the return calls. The strange looks he received on campus, even from Fred the janitor, who had now become formal with him, calling him Professor Birch instead of Evan. Even worse, perhaps, was the sudden feeling in his mouth that his teeth weren't aligned anymore. He found himself tapping his jaw several times a day. What would people think he was doing?

It was the first Wednesday of the month, his usual date for holding evening office hours. Forty-five minutes had already passed, and no one had showed up, which gave him the chance to grade papers. He was pleased with the performance of his "Necessity of Time" seminar. In particular he liked Anna Shepard's statement that time didn't exist—not past, present, or future—that we all lived in "time-passing." Evan thought this concept had merit, even when extended, as Anna had done, to the unborn and the dead. It might be a comfort to Mr. Bonner to think of Joyce existing in the same state of time-passing as himself.

Evan put the blue books in his briefcase and then ducked his head into the reception area in case a student happened to be lingering out there, too timid to come into his office. From the sociology end of the corridor he heard laughter, and it occurred to him that whenever there was laughter in this part of the building, it always came from sociology.

He went back into his office and called up his e-mail account. There was one new message with the subject header "READ this." He clicked on it and three lines appeared:

Admititadmititadmititadmititadmititadmititadmititadmitit
admititadmititadmititadmititadmititadmititadmititadmitit
admititadmititadmititadmitityoucan'tgetawaywithit.

He counted twenty "admit its." The exact number, he supposed, might be considered a clue to the sender's identity. He assumed that the college's systems department could trace the message back through its server, if it was an on-campus mailbox. Electronic threats would not be tolerated, a recent memorandum had advised. The guilty party would be dealt with swiftly and harshly.

Evan reconsidered the message. "Admit it" was actually more of an imperative than a threat, and "You can't get away with it" a simple declarative statement. It wouldn't be wise, he thought, to make too much of this. The sender was no doubt attempting to unsettle him, and Evan did not wish to give the perpetrator that satisfaction.

He hit the "delete" button. The message disappeared, and right away he felt better.

When he came into the kitchen, the small counter TV was on. He called out, "Hello, I'm home." No one answered.

He reached to the TV to turn it off but saw the banner at the bottom: "Breaking News . . . Suspect Cornered Inside McDonald's Restaurant." Evan turned up the volume.

"These are our first shots, our first aerial shots, from Chopper 11 in the air over the scene. It's a waiting game now, Diane."

"I'd say so, Bill. There are no less than two dozen police cars sealing off that neighborhood. We aren't showing you live pictures of the police positions because we don't want to give the suspect any helpful information. But the hope here, obviously, is that he will take the sensible course and give up and not compound the tragedy that we're already going through."

"An interesting point, Diane, is that this is considered to be one of the safest sections in the city."

"That's certainly true. I lived there for several years, and I can tell you that it *is* one of the safest sections in the city."

"Evan?"

He spun around. Ellen was standing in the doorway.

"There you are. I called when I came in."

"They found her."

"Found her?" He turned back toward the TV. "This is about Joyce Bonner?"

She shook her head. "No, that's a shooting in California. Detective Malloy just called to say they found the girl."

Evan flipped off the TV. "They're sure it's her?"

She looked at him curiously, then stepped into the kitchen and shut the door behind her. He supposed she didn't want the boys to walk in on them.

"You didn't hear the report on the radio?"

"No, I was listening to music on the way home."

"Then . . ."

"Then what?"

"You just assume she's dead?"

"What do you mean?"

"I said, 'They found Joyce Bonner,' and you asked if they were sure it's her. You assumed they found her dead."

He stared at her. Why was she twisting up his words like this? What was she trying to prove?

He tried to remain calm. "Ellen, every time I say something, you analyze it like I'm on the witness stand. Of course I assumed she was dead. How many missing cheerleaders show up alive after a month?"

"Missing people do come back sometimes," she said.

"Then you'd have a big smile on your face and be shouting, 'Evan, darling, they found Joyce Bonner—she's alive and everything's all right now!' "

Ellen leaned on the island. "Evan, sweetheart . . ."

"You don't sound like you mean it."

". . . they found her dead this afternoon."

Dead. The word, one syllable, was too short to carry the weight of the single most important event in life. Of course, to

Wittgenstein, death wasn't part of life at all. Dying was a life experience, death itself wasn't. Evan considered that quibbling with the words, because surely all of life was on an unbroken continuum toward death, not dying. It was all time-passing, anyway.

Ellen was staring at him now. He supposed he had gone a long time without responding.

"Where was she found?"

"On the rocks below the Ledges at the park."

He nodded. "That's a dangerous place to walk. Remember when we took the boys on the path up there a couple years ago? We said they should put up a barrier."

"I said that."

"Huh?"

"I said they should put up a barrier. You said that we can't eliminate every risk in life. People have to take responsibility for walking down a path."

"Right. You don't see signs and barriers all over Europe. They assume people are smart enough to stay away from danger."

Ellen took an apple from the fruit bowl. The grapefruit were gone.

"So when did all of this happen?" he asked.

"The detective called about fifteen minutes ago," she said. "He missed you at the office, so he's coming out here to talk to you."

"Here? I don't want Malloy here. Why didn't you tell him I'd go to the station?"

"He didn't ask my permission. He just announced he was coming over."

"Are the boys upstairs?"

"Yes."

"Then keep them there. Okay?" he added to soften his command.

"Are you telling me to stay upstairs, too?"

"Yes," Evan said, "that's probably best."

Nice home, Professor."

"Thank you," Evan said as he closed the front door behind Malloy. "Of course, I didn't build it or even design it. All we did was pay for it."

Malloy looked up at the high ceilings as if unaccustomed to so much space above his head. "Still, it's a nice house."

Evan led him into the small sitting room off the front hall. He couldn't remember the last time he had brought somebody there. He thought it might have been Paul Curry coming to make out their wills.

Malloy walked past the green leather chair that Ellen had declared the most comfortable one she had ever sat in and stood by the wall, his arm leaning on the thin wood molding. "You heard the news, I suppose."

"My wife told me when I came home. It's quite a shock."

"I imagine it is for the Bonners. They had hopes she would come back alive."

"How are they taking it?"

"Not good. The girl was in pretty bad shape when Mr. Bonner found her."

"*He* found her?"

Malloy looked puzzled. "That surprises you?"

"Yes, my wife didn't say. I thought it was the police."

"Well, Ralph Bonner says he met a man at the park two weeks ago who told him where to look for his daughter. Had your first name and fit your description. Was that you?"

"Sure it was me, but I didn't tell him where to look. I just saw him poking around in the bushes near the lake and we got to talking. I said the police had probably gone over every inch of ground around the information booth—that's right, isn't it?"

Malloy nodded.

"So I suggested there were other places he could look."

"Like the Ledges?"

"Yes, it's a remote spot. I think I said the Ledges and the ball fields and a couple of other places, too. It's not like I said, 'Go to the Ledges, you'll find your daughter.'"

"He remembers you being very precise."

"Come on, Detective. If I had anything to do with this, why would I send him to the exact spot he could find her?"

Malloy didn't answer. Evan assumed it was a police tactic—shut up and let the nervous suspect talk, which he did indeed find himself doing. "A person would have to be crazy to do that. I'll admit to a lot of faults, but I'm not crazy. Ask anybody who knows me."

"I'm sure you're not. But a person can seem one way to everybody on the outside and be completely different on the inside—like your Mr. Wittgenstein, for instance."

Evan couldn't recall ever hearing Wittgenstein referred to as a "mister." He was always just "Wittgenstein." Certainly he wasn't "your Mr. Wittgenstein."

"Actually, Detective, I'd say Wittgenstein isn't so unusual. Most people aren't what they appear. We think we know our colleagues or friends and especially our spouses. Then they do something that astounds us. It's as if they've turned into a different person." Evan thought of Dickens's observation—"Every human being is a mystery to every other."

"That's my point. They have secret lives you never know about."

"By definition you aren't likely to know about a secret life. The only cases of deception you find out about are the bad deceivers."

"I bet an educated man would be a good deceiver—like Wittgenstein, or yourself."

Evan didn't grasp the connection between education and deception, nor himself and Wittgenstein. Was Malloy implying some secret sexual double life?

"Your faith in my ability to deceive is heartwarming, Detective, but I don't think I'm any better at it than the next guy." Evan sat in the green chair. He could feel the cold leather through his shirt. "What do you think happened to the girl?"

"We're still making that determination."

"She could have just been walking up there alone and slipped, right? That's happened before."

"Has it?"

Evan figured the detective must know about the woman sliding over the side of the Ledges on a rainy day some ten years before. Why was he playing dumb?

"It was soon after we moved to town," Evan said. "I remember reading the story in the paper and thinking that the park must be dangerous. I'm surprised you haven't heard of that accident."

"I've heard of it," Malloy said.

"Then you know that falling's a possibility."

"Everything's a possibility," he said, "until we determine the one thing that actually happened."

When Evan went upstairs he saw Ellen sitting in the rocking chair again in the spare room. She wasn't reading. She wasn't rocking. She looked up, obviously expecting him to report on his talk with Malloy.

"There's nothing much new," Evan said. "The detective just wanted to check on a few things."

"He stayed a while."

"He goes on sometimes."

"He was curious about your telling Mr. Bonner where to look for his daughter?"

Evan tried to think how she would know Malloy had done that. There was only one way. "You were listening?"

"No, I was *hearing* when I went to shut the door to the boys' room. Sound travels in this house."

"If you heard, then why are you asking me what he said?"

Ellen started rocking. "You met the girl's father at the lake?"

"Yes. A couple weeks ago."

"You didn't tell me that."

"I didn't want to upset you. I've tried not to worry you with every little thing that's happened."

"Meeting Mr. Bonner is a big thing, Evan. You told him where to look for his daughter's body."

"No, Ellen," he said, since she had used his first name, "I didn't do that. I thought you were listening—or hearing?"

"I didn't hear everything."

He turned toward the door. "Then why don't you call up Malloy and get him to fill you in? I'm sure he'll be happy to know my wife is as suspicious of me as he is."

Evan left the room without giving her a chance to answer. He stopped outside the door, just beyond her sight, and waited for her to call after him. His face felt flushed. His hands were shaking a little. She would hate that he was sarcastic but even more that he had walked out on her. He liked getting in the last word for a change. But how would she take it?

He heard nothing, not even her breathing.

He tiptoed along the wall, down the hallway. He tried to pass by the boys' room unnoticed but Zed shouted to him, "Hey, Dad, what's a fly . . ."

He put his hands in his pockets and went in their room. The twins were sitting at their desks. He hoped they hadn't heard the latest argument.

"What did you say, Zed?"

"What's a fly called that's lost his wings?"

"I don't know, what?"

"This isn't a joke. I'm really asking."

"Oh, well, let's see—what's a banana called after you eat it?"

"I asked you first," Zed said.

"I suppose he's a used-to-be fly." Evan knew he wasn't really answering the question. Describing something in terms of what it once was hardly described it now. He didn't think Zed would notice, though.

"I'd call it *dead*," Adam said. "A fly has to fly to find food or he'll die." He slammed shut his book. "Done!"

"You finished your homework, too, Zed?"

"I only have extra credit problems left for math. But they're impossible. I bet even you couldn't do them."

Evan knew this dare was Zed's way of asking for help, and so he looked over his son's shoulder at the assignment: "Without converting to numbers, do the following arithmetical processes in Roman numerals. XXVII plus XIV. XLVI minus XXII. For additional credit, multiply VI by XXII. Show your work or no credit will be issued."

"See," Zed said, "nobody can do this, right?"

"The Romans must have, at least adding and subtracting, when they were trading goods with each other. But I don't know about multiplying. Maybe that wasn't necessary for their lives."

"It's not necessary for *my* life," Zed said and stuffed his math sheet into his book.

"Your teacher is just trying to get you to stretch your mind. That's why you're in advanced math. Not everything you learn has to be useful."

Adam put his books into his bookbag. "Can we go on the computer for like fifteen minutes, Dad?"

He looked at the small oval alarm clock on their nightstand. It said 9:05.

"Sorry, it's time for you to get into bed and read."

"It's Wednesday. You're supposed to read to us, remember?"

"I know. But I have to talk to you about something first."

"What?" Zed said as he sat on the bottom bunk to pull off his sneakers.

"You know the cheerleader that was missing, and the police were asking me questions."

"Yeah."

"Well, the detective I've been talking to just came by the house. He said they found the girl today in the park."

"Really?" Adam said. "She's been living there the whole time?"

Zed hurled his sneaker across the room, and it bounced against the wall over Adam's head. "No, stupid, she's dead."

"Don't call me stupid."

"Then don't *be* stupid."

"I'll kick you in the teeth again."

"No you won't. I'll kick—"

"Shut up!" The words came out just as Evan intended them, loud enough to stop the twins in their tracks. He had always asked them "to be quiet" before. He rarely had to yell. "I'm telling you that a girl was found dead. That's not your cue to start fighting."

Evan heard steps in the hall, Ellen running toward the room. "What's going on?" she said. He didn't like her tone.

"I told the boys to shut up, that's what's going on."

"Did you have to yell at them like that?"

"Yes, I did. Once in a while I get to yell around here, and this was one of those times." He turned back to the boys. "Okay, guys," he said in a softer voice, "now what do you want me to read to you?"

CHAPTER 28

Evan wasn't sure he should make this call. In fact, he was pretty sure he shouldn't. Still, the following morning he shut the door to his office and told Carla he didn't want to be disturbed. Then he picked up the phone and dialed Mr. R. E. Bonner, as the listing read in the white-pages directory. Besides offering sympathy, Evan thought he could dispel the idea that he had known where the girl would be found.

A woman answered. Evan figured it to be Mrs. Bonner.

"Hello," he said softly, "is your husband there?"

"What? What do you want?"

"May I speak to your husband?" he said more loudly.

"He's not home."

"Will he be back soon?"

"Who is this?"

"You don't know me, but I met your husband, and I just want to speak to him for a minute."

"He's not talking to reporters, if that's what you are."

"No, I'm not. I don't speak to them either."

"I don't know where he is. We've had bad news, and he's gone out."

"I'm sorry."

"He . . . well, he's not . . ."

"You don't have to explain. I'll try him another time."

"Another time?" she said in a wondering voice. "How long would that be?"

"However long you say. I don't want to bother him."

"I don't believe he can be bothered at this point."

"I see," Evan said.

"He lost the most precious thing in his life, his daughter."

"It's a terrible loss."

There was silence for a moment. Evan waited.

"He won't recover," Mrs. Bonner said.

"I'm sure in time—"

"No, he won't recover. Joyce meant everything to him, *every thing*. He had no room in his life for anyone else."

Again there was silence. Again Evan waited.

"Me included."

"Excuse me?"

"He had no room in his life for anyone else, me included. That's the fact of it."

"I'm sorry."

Evan heard a little rustling sound, perhaps a hand pulling a tissue from a pocketbook. "I never admitted that to anyone, isn't that odd? You call up and I start talking."

"You just needed someone to listen, I guess. You have a lot bottled up."

"Sometimes I think I'll explode. I lost a daughter in this, too. He takes the grief all for himself."

"It's just a stage everyone goes through. He'll shake it off in a few days," Evan said. He did not know on what basis he was making such pronouncements. He had little experience with grief of this magnitude.

"He said some terrible things to me. I don't know if I can forget."

"Forgetting is difficult," Evan said, "perhaps the most difficult thing we're asked to do in life."

"Yes, I suppose you're right," she said. "By the way, what's your name?"

"Evan."

"Well, Evan, I'm Irene, but you can call me Mrs. Bonner. I never use my first name. It's an ugly name. Joyce is beautiful. I named her myself."

"It is beautiful."

"You go ahead and call another time, Evan, whenever you want."

"I will," he said, just as he was thinking that he wouldn't.

As he headed out of the Humanities Faculty Building, a large black Labrador came galloping up the steps. Evan scanned the Arts Quad and didn't see anyone looking his way, so he quickly shut the door. The dog skidded to a stop, then stretched up to the handle and pawed. "You're out of luck," Evan said, keeping his hands close to his body. "Now run along somewhere else." The Lab sat at the door and barked.

"Sorry, pup," he said and started down a step. He heard the door open up behind him, and the dog barreled in. Out came Professor Raines.

"Hello, Birch."

"Oh, hello," Evan said.

"Better watch yourself," Raines said with a little laugh.

"What?"

"You can get yourself in hot water around here not accommodating the canines. You don't want to go against the wishes of our dead founder. People have been fired for less."

"Yes, I know. I'll be careful."

The two split off, Raines taking the center path through the Quad as Evan veered left, as usual, around the perimeter. They were both heading to the Arts Building, but neither had ever changed his path to walk with the other. Evan wouldn't have minded the anthropologist's company. He had always thought Raines a sensible man.

Evan was late getting to his "Necessity of Time" class, and he didn't care. He walked his usual stride, without any hurry to his step. It was quite possible that the small seminar room would be filled with students, and how would he rid himself of the gawkers this time? He doubted the "I see my little trick worked" ploy would clear them out again.

When he made it to the room, there was just a single student—Anna Shepard—sitting in the front row. She looked at him with a quizzical expression.

"Ms. Shepard, has the plague decimated our ranks today?"

She pointed to the blackboard behind him. He turned and saw the message: Time Canceled Today—Wittgenstein.

"Who wrote this?"

Anna shrugged. "It was there when I came in."

"Is it supposed to be a joke? *Time* canceled?"

"I thought it meant the class was canceled."

He leaned into the hallway to see if anyone was lurking there to observe the effect of his joke. There was no one. He turned back to Ms. Shepard. She was bent over a rubber tube. He smelled glue.

"Did anyone else in the class see this?"

"All of them, that's why they're not here."

"Then why did you stay?"

"I've got stuff to do," she said, "and it's quiet here."

"Then I won't disturb you by giving my lecture."

"I don't mind, Professor, I can fix my tire and listen, too."

She did not look up when she said this. She seemed to be in the midst of some particularly delicate maneuver. He thought there must be some professors' motto—"Even if only one shows up, I will teach."

So he set himself up at his desk. "Okay then," he said, "I'll begin."

After twenty minutes of dissecting Kant's view of time as conscious experience and then moving on to his conclusion that humans don't actually perceive time, but rather, events taking place *in time,* Evan perceived something himself—a hissing sound coming from Anna Shepard's inner tube. He couldn't bear lecturing any longer to a single student intent on repairing a flat bicycle tire. "That's enough for today," he said.

"It was very interesting," Anna said.

"Thank you." Evan slid his seminar notes back into his briefcase and left the classroom. He headed out into the afternoon feeling a little lightheaded. He supposed he should have eaten lunch, but he hadn't wanted to appear in the cafeteria or the faculty lounge. He couldn't guarantee how he would react to the next rude stare or dismissive glance. It was quite possible that he might hit someone.

As he approached the faculty parking lot he heard a car door shut and sensed someone coming up behind him. He thought of the intimidating e-mails and wondered if he should feel scared. He wasn't scared, though, which he figured was the answer to his question. He was only a few steps from the Jetta anyway.

"Birch?"

Evan turned to see a small man dressed in a dark suit that appeared slightly too big for him.

"It's Professor Birch, actually. Can I help you?"

"What happened with my daughter?"

Evan had suffered through surprise visits before where one parent or the other—often the father—sought him out, demanding to know why his son or daughter was failing a class. Usually it was later in the term, after academic warnings had been sent out.

He set his briefcase on the hood of the Jetta and pulled out his grade book. "What's your daughter's name?"

"Joyce Bonner."

Evan gripped the book tightly so that it wouldn't slip to the ground. He was surprised that he hadn't recognized Mr. Bonner. The tie and jacket made him appear a different man than the one poking in the woods around the lake.

Evan started to extend his hand, then felt that might not be the right thing to do. He tried to read the emotion on Mr. Bonner's face, but he was never good at doing that. There were too many emotional states and too few facial expressions. Inevitably he misjudged.

"I'm glad you came to campus, Mr. Bonner," Evan said. "I tried to call you earlier, but I reached your wife. We talked for a little bit," he added and then worried that he shouldn't have admitted that if the two of them were arguing. "Shall we go up to my office where it's more comfortable?"

"I didn't come here to be comfortable. I want to know what happened with Joy."

Evan nodded. "I'm sorry, I don't know what happened. I told the police that. I spoke to Detective Malloy on Wednesday, as a matter of fact. I've been talking to him for weeks to try to help out the investigation, but I don't know much of anything."

Mr. Bonner stepped a little closer. Evan had his back to the car. There was no place to go.

"You told me where to look for her body."

"No," he said with a little laughter in his voice. He always disliked that awkward laugh that crept into words when clearly there was nothing funny. "I can see how it might seem that I did. But I was telling you generally some places to search. I think I mentioned every section of the park."

Mr. Bonner stared. Evan looked away and saw a few students talking loudly as they walked toward the Arts Quad. He didn't think their comments had anything to do with him. He was glad, though, that there were people about.

"I don't believe you."

Evan couldn't remember anyone ever saying such a thing to him so simply and clearly. He had almost always been believed in his life, at least until this episode.

"I know you'd like some answers, I just don't have any." Evan gripped the handles of his briefcase. He thought he could use it as a shield, if necessary. "I admit there's been a series of . . . *coincidences*." This was no time for subtlely. He would use the word as everybody understood it—two events happening simultaneously as if by mere chance. "And these coincidences put your daughter and me in the same place at the same time. But there was no intent on my part to be with her. In fact, I never knew I was in her presence until after she disappeared and the police started questioning me."

Mr. Bonner lifted his palms to his face, covering his eyes, and rubbed. When he took his hands away, there were two red marks.

"All coincidences?" he repeated.

"Yes, everything."

He stroked his chin as if he once had a beard. Then he reached across the space between them with his right hand. Evan smiled and extended his own. Mr. Bonner shook it for a moment, staring into Evan's eyes, and said, "I still don't believe you." Before the sentence was fully out of his mouth he flipped over Evan's arm and pressed his thumb into a spot just below the wrist.

"That hurts," Evan said and then thought how stupid he sounded. Of course it hurt.

"Tell me what happened to my daughter."

The pain felt like . . . why was he trying to put it into words? "I can't talk like this."

The thumb on his wrist eased up a little.

"Tell me."

"She came out to the college for Arts Camp this summer, and apparently she was in my car one day with some other kids and dropped her lipstick in the backseat. That's all I know."

He knew more, of course—the lighter, the library book, the face filling his rearview mirror.

Mr. Bonner looked into the backseat of the Jetta where a dozen copies of *Disturbing Minds* were lying spine up in a box. *Disturbing Minds, Disturbing Minds, Disturbing Minds* . . . Why couldn't he have chosen an innocuous title? He had considered other possibilities—*The Lives of the Philosophers*, for instance, but that recalled Plutarch. Or *The Philosophic Mind*. Either one of them seemed better at this point.

Mr. Bonner let go of Evan's hand. "You have two boys?"

"Yes. Twins."

"I have one girl. One beautiful girl."

Still the present tense? When would this man accept the reality of his daughter's death?

"I'm sorry, I really am."

Mr. Bonner turned and rubbed his hands together as if massaging out the stiffness. "Your sympathy means nothing to me."

Evan nodded but didn't know what he was assenting to. That his sympathy was worthless? And was all sympathy worthless or just his own in this particular situation? He was inclined to believe the former. In a binary world, there were only two states: existence and nonexistence. Joyce Bonner had slipped from one to the other, a fact that no amount of his sympathy could change.

When Evan ducked into his car, his neck suddenly ached, and he wondered if he had wrenched it twisting in Mr. Bonner's grip. He sat for a moment, letting the adrenaline settle in his veins. It was quiet inside the car. He felt as if he were sealed in.

He watched Mr. Bonner's retreat up the slope of the street away from campus. He didn't begrudge the man's violent reaction. He was sure he wouldn't be in a believing mood two days after finding a child of his dead.

He pulled slowly out of the parking lot and let the car coast down the hill away from campus. A few students looked over at him as he passed. His old Jetta was well known on campus. No one waved.

As he turned onto the main road, the low afternoon sun bleached his dirty windshield white. He didn't bother trying to spray wiper fluid. He knew there wouldn't be any. He squinted to see better and noticed a single crack of the glass running diagonally across his line of vision. Where had that come from? He accelerated down the road as he considered the possibilities. The crack was too long to have been made by a stone thrown up by a car or truck, and besides, it hadn't been there when he parked that morning. The thin groove seemed as if it were made by a sharp object, like a box cutter. He assumed he was the object of vandalism.

A light flashed red in front of him—the new light at the outskirts of Eastfield. He hit his brakes too hard and felt the car skid. He couldn't remember whether he should steer into the skid or out of it, so did nothing, just held the wheel as the car slid sideways down the road. Four or five seconds later, the car stopped. He hadn't hit anything, and nothing had hit him. He was a little disappointed. The world had spun out of his control for a few moments, and he had ended up just a few yards farther than where he'd begun.

A large man dressed in a red flannel shirt tapped at the car window. Evan opened the door to a burst of cool air.

"You okay?"

"I'm fine. Thanks for checking."

"No problem," the stranger said. "You must have hit some gravel back there. Lucky you stopped when you did." He pointed to the side of the road. Evan leaned out of his car and looked over the hood. A foot from his right front tire, the earth dropped away into a gulley. He couldn't see how far he might have fallen.

"Facilis descensus Averno," Evan said.

"What's that?"

"It's easy to fall into hell."

The stranger smiled broadly. "Latin right? I took that in school—*Omnia Gallia in partes tres divisa est.*"

"You remember well," Evan said as he wondered, what well-worn phrase would his years of teaching be reduced to? "I am, therefore I think too much"—that would be appropriate.

"Try to keep yourself on the road now, will you?" the man said and started walking away.

"Wait," Evan called. The man turned. He was wearing a small flag on the lapel of his jacket, three rectangles of color. Evan didn't recognize the country. "It really matters to you that I don't fall off the side of the road?"

"Sure."

"Tell me, why does it?"

The man shifted his weight, one leg to the other. He shrugged a little, a delicate gesture. "I don't know. It just does. What are you, some kind of minister or something?"

"No, I was just wondering."

"Well, I don't like seeing anything get hurt. I've always been like that, even as a boy. If a spider gets in our house, I put my hand down till he crawls on it and I can take him outside. That's the way I am."

"And everybody knows that about you, right?"

"Sure, I mean, my family and all. I teach my boys that, too."

"They'd never in a million years believe you'd hurt a living thing." Evan said it as a statement, not a question.

"No, that wouldn't be me."

Evan reached his arm through the car window. "Glad to have met you," he said.

The man grinned. "Yeah, me too. Maybe we'll run into

each other again sometime—I don't mean like with our cars or anything."

"It's possible," Evan said.

"Okay then." The man turned away.

Evan couldn't really foresee their paths crossing again. It would take some similar unlikely act of chance. "Hold on." He reached into his shirt pocket. "Here's my card. I teach at the college. If you're ever up that way, stop in. I'll give you a tour." He didn't know what was possessing him. Ellen would be amazed.

"Professor E. Birch," the man read off the card. He smiled broadly. "My wife says I'm not sociable, but here I am talking to a professor. She won't believe it."

"My wife says the same thing," Evan said. "Wives don't always know what we're capable of, do they?"

The garage was blocked by a small white Toyota, left with its door open and motor running. He didn't recognize the car. He assumed someone was making a delivery. Perhaps Ellen had ordered in dinner. He waited for a minute. No one came out, and he suddenly worried that there might be something wrong inside. He parked the Jetta at the end of the driveway.

He reached the basement door as Margaret Hope came out carrying a long narrow box. It was big enough to hold a dozen roses, or perhaps a rifle. It was an odd thought—Margaret as a sniper, wearing camouflage, shooting from the roadside at passing cars. What would Ellen have to do with this? His imagination failed him.

She followed Margaret out of the house. "Oh, Evan, you remember Margaret Hope."

"Yes, certainly," he said. "Nice to see you again." He

thought he might add, "I was sorry to hear about your lips," but she was past him in a second. He didn't hear her greet him at all.

He stood next to Ellen as Margaret put the box in the trunk and then backed out of the driveway. As they both waved he said, "Was I friendly enough?"

"You were fine," Ellen said.

"Don't you think she should have said something to me, a quick 'Hi,' for instance?"

"She said hello."

"No, she really didn't."

"I'm sure she meant to. Margaret has a lot on her mind lately."

They went inside and heard the phone ringing. Evan ran upstairs and grabbed the kitchen phone.

"Professor, it's Robert Malloy."

"Yes, Detective."

"I have Mr. Bonner in my office."

"Oh?"

"He said he just went to see you on campus."

"Yes, we talked in the parking lot for a few minutes."

"He came to turn himself in."

"Turn himself in for what?"

"He said he assaulted you."

"Assaulted me?"

"Touched you with the intent to cause harm—that's one definition of assault. He thought you'd be calling to press charges."

"It was no big deal, Detective. The man just lost his daughter."

"You won't be filing charges?"

"Of course not. The thought never entered my mind."

"I'll tell him that," the detective said. "He'll be relieved, I'm sure."

Evan hadn't left the kitchen when the phone rang again. It was Paul Curry, and he sounded anxious. At least that's how Evan interpreted his tone over the crackly cell phone connection.

"Glad I caught you," the lawyer said, as if Evan was the difficult one to reach. "I spoke to the DA's office and they're not saying much. We'll know more on Monday after the autopsy results come in. Then we'll see if there's anything we have to worry about."

"Like what?" Evan asked. "What would we worry about?"

"Signs of struggle, foreign blood on the girl's body, sexual assault, DNA under her fingernails—that kind of thing."

"Paul, you seem to be forgetting that I told you I didn't have anything to do with Joyce Bonner. There couldn't be any evidence like that to worry about."

"I hear what you're saying, but let's cross that bridge on Monday, okay? I'm heading into court right now. I got to run. Have a nice weekend."

"Sure, go," Evan said as Curry hung up. "Go, go, go!" he shouted into the receiver.

Ellen touched his back. "What's going on?"

Evan clicked off the phone. "That was our friend Paul, the lawyer, who's worried my blood and DNA are smeared all over the body of a dead girl. But we'll cross that bridge when we come to it on Monday. In the meantime, I'm to have a nice weekend."

CHAPTER 29

Evan heard nothing on Monday. He called three times to
Curry and left three messages. There was no call back.
He considered trying to reach Detective Malloy but de-
cided against that, not wanting to appear too anxious.

Two more e-mails appeared in his inbox. He decided that
they were meant to be *intimidating,* one notch below *threat-
ening,* which would trigger his informing the police. At this
point he wasn't planning on telling anyone. He preferred to be
intimidated in private.

The first message invited him to take a walk at night by
himself on the path above the Ledges. The second message
said "Admitit" seven times, a number whose significance
eluded Evan. He hit "reply" to both e-mails and advised the

anonymous sender to cease, but as he expected, his messages came back marked "Delivery Failure." The intimidator had covered his tracks.

When he pulled into the school pick-up area that afternoon, the twins were standing on either side of a small dark-haired boy. Evan unlocked the back door, and all three got in.

"This is Zach," Adam said, "he's new."

The boy stuck his hand out. "I'm Zach."

Evan shook the little hand. "Nice to meet you. Do you need a ride home?"

"Not right now."

"We kind of asked Zach over," Zed said.

"That's nice, but you're supposed to check with Mom or me first."

"We couldn't, Dad, 'cause the phone's broken outside the school. If you'd give us a cell phone we could call you."

"You guys get a cell phone when you drive, and that's years away. You sure it's okay with your mother for you to come over, Zach?"

"He doesn't really have parents, Dad."

"I have a temporary mom," Zach said.

"A foster mother?"

"Yes, and she said I can stay out after school as long as I'm home for dinner."

"All right then, buckle up."

He pulled out of the school parking lot as the three of them rooted in the cushion for their seat belts. Several times Zach said, "Thanks." It was one thing to be polite with an adult, but this boy was polite to other ten-year-olds. Evan found that strange.

He drove slowly, trying to overhear the whispering in the backseat, but he could only catch a few words.

After a while Zed said, "Zach hears things, Dad."

"He does? Like what?"

"Like music. He hears it even when it's not playing."

"Is that right, Zach?"

"Yes, sir."

"Are you hearing anything now?"

"I hear all the time."

"What kind of music?"

"I don't know the name, but it's classical."

"You hear this in your head?"

"No, in my ears."

"Like ringing in your ears?"

"Yes, sir, but it's not ringing, it's music."

"You don't have to call him 'sir,'" Adam said, "does he, Dad?"

"He doesn't have to, no, but he can if he likes."

Zach sat forward. "What *should* I call you?"

Evan, Mr. Birch, Professor, sir—he didn't know which would be appropriate. He never knew how to have his sons' friends address him.

"I could just call you 'Dad' like they do."

Evan turned half around. "What?"

"I mean, if you want me to," Zach said. He didn't look away, which Evan found remarkable.

The twins squeezed the boy from either side. "Yeah, Dad, let him call you that."

"Okay, 'Dad' it is."

Evan turned back to the road as the three of them dissolved into fits of laughter saying "Dad, Dad, Dad."

In the evening he sat with Ellen in the living room. She was reading. He was preparing notes for the week's lectures, but his mind kept drifting back to Paul Curry's comments.

What if the police found unexplainable blood or DNA on Joyce Bonner? They might seek to match it against his, and it would look suspicious for him not to cooperate. Yet DNA was passed between dozens of people every day, wasn't it? That afternoon at the Arts Camp when he gave her a ride, for instance. Perhaps their hands had brushed against each other as she got in or out of the Jetta. At the very least he had touched some part of the car—a door handle, for example— that she had touched.

"Listen," Ellen said. " 'The Moving Finger writes; and, having writ, Moves on: nor all your Piety nor Wit Shall lure it back to cancel half a Line, Nor all your Tears wash out a Word of it.' "

Of all the quotable quotes from Omar Khayyám, why would she read him this one? Did she think his piety or wit or tears were trying to wash out some recent blot in his life? He agreed that would be impossible.

"Depressing but true," Evan said, "or maybe it's true but depressing. We can't erase a thing we've done. I wouldn't try," he added.

"Here's another one," Ellen said, " 'That inverted Bowl we call The Sky, Whereunder crawling coop'd we live and die.' "

Evan didn't respond this time beyond a nod.

"If you're ever on a game show," she said, "and they ask you who wrote something, you can always guess Omar Khayyám or Shakespeare and you'd probably be right."

"And Wittgenstein."

"No, nobody quotes philosophers. Maybe Oscar Wilde."

"Okay, Omar Khayyám, Shakespeare, and Oscar Wilde. I'll remember those three for the next game show I'm on."

"You're being sarcastic again?" she said.

"Not again. More like *still.*"

Ellen raised *The Rubáiyát of Omar Khayyám* in front of her face. Every once in a while he could hear her reading something to herself just barely aloud.

Sometime later, while Evan was dozing on the sofa, the twins thumped past the living room and into the kitchen. He heard the refrigerator and various cabinets being opened.

"Don't make a mess," he yelled in to them.

"We won't."

Ellen had turned the television on low, so as not to wake him. He kissed her arm. "Anything interesting?"

"Not really. We get what—seventy channels? And there's nothing worth watching." She picked up the remote and clicked off the TV.

Evan sat up on the sofa. "Did you find the new friend the boys brought home today a little odd?"

"I only saw him for a few minutes. He seemed quiet and polite—I guess that makes him different than most ten-year-olds."

"He asked if he could call me 'Dad.'"

Ellen leaned under the coffee table to get her shoes and then slipped them on. "When did that happen?"

"He was calling me 'sir' in the car when I was driving them home and the boys said he didn't have to do that. Then he said, 'I could call you Dad like they do.' The boys wanted me to, so I said yes."

"That might not have been a good idea."

"No?"

"You're not his father."

"I know that."

"You may confuse him. Or he could get fixated on actually having you for a father."

"I thought I was just doing something nice for a kid who doesn't have parents. And the boys didn't seem to mind sharing me."

"I know your heart was in the right place," Ellen said, "but I think you better keep your distance. You never know what can happen."

"The kid just wanted to pretend he had a father for a little while. I don't see any great harm in that."

The twins came out of the kitchen carrying sandwiches, chips, and drinks. Evan checked his watch. "You guys are pushing the time with your snacks. You should be in bed reading soon."

"We will be," Adam said. "Can Zach come over again tomorrow?"

Evan felt Ellen's leg stiffen next to his, a signal, he assumed. "Not tomorrow," he said.

"The next day?" Zed asked.

"We'll think about it for this weekend."

"Cool, then he can sleep over, right? He doesn't make any trouble. He's like the quietest kid we know."

"I noticed that. It seems like you've become friends very fast."

"Best friends," Zed said.

"How did that happen? He's not like the other boys you hang out with."

The twins looked at each other and shrugged. "We hang out with Zach now," Adam said.

Zed nodded. "And he hangs with us."

On Tuesday, a day Evan typically came in late, he opened the door to the Humanities Faculty Building and there was Carla.

"Professor," she said and grabbed his arm, "come here."

She pulled him down the hall and under the stairwell. He couldn't imagine what was going on.

"There's a man upstairs. I think he's from the police. He's waiting right outside your office."

"A short man, blinks kind of oddly?"

"That's him. He's spooky."

"It's Detective Malloy. He's been dropping in for weeks now to talk to me."

Carla let go of his arm. "Oh, I thought he was going to arrest you or something and maybe you shouldn't go up there."

"Thanks for the warning, but there isn't any reason for him to arrest me."

"Are you sure? Sometimes police don't need a reason."

"You're right, Carla, but still I have to see him."

Good morning, Professor."

"Detective," Evan said and put out his hand, "come in my office."

"I thought I might catch you here between classes. You spoke to your lawyer, I guess."

"Curry? No, why, what happened?"

"I left a message with him last night."

"Why didn't you just call me?"

"Sometimes it's good to follow protocol."

"I've been breaking protocol talking to you for weeks."

"That's true."

"Well, what's the news?"

"Based on the autopsy results the DA finds no reason to proceed with the investigation of you into the death of Joyce Bonner."

Evan blew out air—relief. "You've come up with another suspect?"

"No, there's insufficient evidence at this point to establish that any crime was committed."

"So it was an accident, like I said?"

"That's the coroner's opinion."

Opinion. The word seemed insufficient to Evan. He wanted the coroner to declare the unalterable fact that Joyce Bonner had died by accident. He realized that was impossible. An *accident* was merely what was left when no other purposeful act could be proven. It was the default state.

"You don't sound like you agree with your coroner, Detective. You still think a crime was committed and I had something to do with it?"

"Yes."

"Is that yes to both questions?"

"Yes."

Evan took off his jacket and draped it over the back of his chair. "Despite what the autopsy shows, your official police instinct tells you there was some foul play with the girl's death, and I'm involved?"

Malloy nodded. "It's my instinct, based on the evidence."

"I think if there was evidence you would have arrested me weeks ago instead of continuing these little chats of ours every few days."

"I'll call them coincidences, if you prefer. There are a lot of them in this case, and I've learned over the years that coincidences happen for a reason."

Evan smiled at the contorted logic, or was it straightforward . . . *illogic?* "If you check the dictionary, you'll find that coincidences happen by chance, not reason."

Malloy shrugged. "I'm just telling you what I think."

"What exactly do you think?"

Was there ever a broader question asked of a man? Evan doubted it. Wittgenstein would have considered the question unanswerable. But the detective was going to have a go at it.

"What I *know*," he said, "is that a girl was found dead by her father at the bottom of a ledge, where you suggested he look."

"Among other places."

"Yes, among other places. I know she wasn't in the habit of going off on walks by herself, particularly in the rain."

"Habits have to start somewhere," Evan said. "Maybe this would have been the first day of the rest of her life taking walks alone on rainy afternoons."

Malloy nodded and then switched to a shake of his head. "I don't think that's likely. I also know you came in contact with this girl during the camp at the college in August—the records show that. She was in your car, which we confirmed with the other students you gave a ride to. And I know you were spotted in the parking lot at the park the day she disappeared, a fact you neglected to tell us."

"I neglected to tell you I was spotted?"

"You neglected to tell us you were at the park."

Evan reached into his pocket, found a peppermint candy, and offered it to the detective, who shook his head. Evan unwrapped it for himself. "That makes what you would call an open-and-shut case?" he said as he sucked on the candy.

"It makes a highly suggestive case."

"In other words, the apparent coincidences suggest to you that I lured Joyce Bonner onto the path and shoved her over?"

"I believe it's likely you were with the girl on the path when she went over. That's the only scenario that fits all the facts. But the coroner reports no signs of struggle, no unexplained marks on her body, nothing inconsistent with her simply falling down the side of the ledge. Officially the investigation into this case is suspended, pending new evidence."

Suspended, not *terminated.* It could be reopened at any time. That was not a comforting thought to Evan.

"Well, I'm sorry if my apparent innocence disturbs you. If there's anything I can do . . ."

Malloy walked a step or two, reached the opening to the reception area, and turned around. "Maybe there is something."

"Okay, shoot," Evan said with a carefreeness to his voice that he thought perfect. He felt ready for anything.

"It's kind of an unusual request."

"I'm a philosopher, remember? The odder the better."

"Well, you could admit to me that you did it."

The peppermint flavor suddenly overwhelmed Evan's taste. He reached into his pants pocket for a Kleenex and spit the candy into it. He set the wad of tissue on his desk. "What?"

Malloy came back toward the desk. "You must want to inside. People who are involved in crimes always want to tell someone."

Evan scraped his tongue against his teeth to get rid of the residue of peppermint. "That's an interesting observation, but your basis for believing it can only be that some criminals have apparently confessed to you. You have no way of knowing how many other guilty people have declined the opportunity."

"So you're declining?"

Declining, like other guilty people? Evan was impressed at the cleverness of the detective's question.

"I have to say I don't feel any overwhelming urge to confess to you, given my professed innocence and the potential consequences."

"There wouldn't be any consequences. Like I said, there's no physical evidence. And the coroner states the death was accidental." Malloy brushed his hand down his pants. "It would just be between you and I."

"Between you and—" Evan hesitated correcting the detective's grammar. That would be condescending. "And I," he said, "like a secret confession?"

Malloy nodded and then pointed at the ball of tissue sitting on the desk. "Have any more of those candies?"

Evan leaned back over his desk, opened the top drawer, and found one. He tossed it across the short space between them. "Of course, you could be wearing a microphone and recording all of this."

The detective put the candy in his mouth and then raised his arms. "Pat me down if you'd like. I don't go in for tricks like that. Besides, a verbal confession probably wouldn't hold up in court, even if I was recording it."

"You're serious. You're actually suggesting that I confess to you that I killed Joyce Bonner."

Malloy lowered his arms. "I didn't say you killed her. You could have just met her on that path up there and she fell. Maybe you had an argument. You broke things off, for instance. She could have gotten hysterical and fallen over."

The idea intrigued Evan. He had apologized to Ellen when he had no reason to and felt surprisingly good about it, even if he had ended up more sarcastic than serious. Why not confess now, too? Wittgenstein thought it the means of cleansing his soul of all its sins, even the imaginary ones. Some of his friends didn't even remember the supposed insult or injury. Still, he confessed to them and apologized. He cleansed his conscience. Admitting to murder, Evan figured, would be the ultimate confession one could make. But would there be the same redemptive value to confessing as claiming innocence?

"I could say anything, of course. You wouldn't know whether I'm telling you the truth or not."

"Go ahead," Malloy said, "say anything, whatever you want."

"Okay, Detective, if it will make you feel better, I will confess."

Malloy's eyes started blinking their odd rhythm, what Evan took to indicate excitement.

"I confess that I've thought about sleeping with every pretty girl who has ever taken a class with me. I confess that I've asked some of them to come to my office just because I wanted to smell their hair. I confess I've touched some of them casually, my leg to theirs, as we went over a paper. I confess that I've wanted to kill a few people in my life—and I even went so far one time as to make notes about how I might do in a fellow professor. I'm afraid I burned the evidence, though, so I can't offer any proof. I confess that I'm so in love with my own existence that I can't imagine the world continuing when I die. I kind of think life itself must cease when my self of selves expires—pretty solipsistic of me, wouldn't you say? I confess that I've wished to be married to a different woman several times, but that was early on, before the boys were born, and now I can't imagine being married to anyone else. I confess that I'm not as confident in myself as I seem and I'm surely not as competent in my profession as I would like."

Evan stood up, and it surprised him how much taller he was than the detective. He couldn't remember looking over another man's head like this and felt awkward about it. He sat down again. "This feels like one of the Twelve Steps in AA—which one is it?"

"Nine, I think."

"Yes, nine. Call up everyone you think you might have hurt in your life, confess your transgressions against them, and apologize, right? The list would be pretty long in my case."

"It would be for anyone. We hurt people every day in ways we don't even know."

Malloy's sentiment impressed Evan, and the sad thought crossed his mind that the detective might have gone through the Twelve Steps himself.

"I'm really cheating, though—I'm confessing everything to you rather than to those I hurt."

"This isn't AA. You don't have to follow any rules."

"No rules. I like the sound of that. How about no laws, too?"

"For the next few minutes, no laws, either."

"You have that power, Detective?"

Malloy nodded.

"Okay then, I'll keep going. I confess that I've enjoyed this little game of ours over the last month. It's made me feel . . . important, I think that's the word, in a notorious sort of way. And sinful, too. I've behaved far too well in my life. I've almost bored myself at times. So being accused of having a salacious double life was exciting. That's rather perverse, isn't it?"

Malloy's eyes widened, what Evan took to be agreement.

"Let's see, what else. I confess that I stole five dollars from the collection plate at church when I was a boy. The pastor saw me and didn't say anything. I always wondered why he didn't tell my parents. But maybe that's going back too far for you. In high school I plagiarized a speech that won a contest. I've never admitted that to anyone before. *I plagiarized*—you don't know how liberating it is for a professor to say that out loud. In college I smoked enough marijuana to keep me high as a kite, but only on weekends. I set very strict limits on myself. After I graduated I fudged my résumé to get my first teaching job. I said I'd been a teacher's assistant while I was doing my master's. Actually I only made it to the classroom once, but that wasn't really my fault. I have a rather unexplainable fascination with lips—it would take a psychologist to figure that one out. A few years ago I even put on lipstick to see how I'd look. I wonder if other men do that."

Malloy flipped the peppermint from one side of his mouth to the other, and Evan could hear it roll over his teeth. The candy pressed out against his cheek, a perfect little ball. "I wouldn't know," he said.

"You never had the urge to do something a little odd, Detective? Never tried on your wife's stockings just to see how nylon feels against your skin?"

Malloy shook his head so automatically that Evan figured it was useless to prod some sort of oddity out of this man's intentional behaviors. Besides, with his blinking and twitching, the detective already had enough strangeness in his unconscious life.

"Where was I? I could go on confessing like this all night. I confess that I like confessing—Wittgenstein was right."

"Wittgenstein again?"

"Yes, Wittgenstein, again and again. My wife said he's my favorite philosopher, and maybe he is. He had a distorted self-awareness. He didn't think he was a good person. That's why he enlisted in the Austrian Army in World War One. He said it was his chance to stand eye-to-eye with death and become a decent human being."

"War changes people, I'll vouch for that."

"I'm not sure war transformed Wittgenstein in the way he wanted."

Malloy pointed at the cover of the book on Evan's desk, *Ludwig Wittgenstein: The Duty of Genius.* "That why he looks so sad there?"

"Yes, transitively and intransitively speaking, Wittgenstein looks sad in this picture. Actually, I don't recall many stories of happy events in his life. I wonder if he ever laughed."

"Everybody laughs at something."

What would have made Wittgenstein laugh? Evan remembered the joke about decapitation. He could conceive of that story making God laugh, but Wittgenstein would have been a harder conquest. He would not have gone in for situational humor. The joke would be the words.

Evan looked up, and it surprised him to realize that he had been discussing Wittgenstein with a policeman. What were the odds of that happening a month ago?

Malloy swallowed hard, and Evan figured he was ridding his mouth of the peppermint candy. He had a sour expression on his face.

"I guess my confessions aren't quite what you were hoping for."

The detective shrugged a little, and Evan felt a tremendous urge to please this man, to bring some sort of completion to their brief relationship. There was a way. He would do what Malloy asked.

"Okay, here it is, Detective: I confess that I caused Joyce Bonner's death."

Evan said these words with more sincerity than he had

expected. There wasn't the trace of a put-on. He had acted well—so well, in fact, that he began to feel guilt. It was warm and full and overwhelming. Guilt filled him up and was spilling over. It was hard to understand, but the guilt felt good. Evan almost wanted more of it. Maybe this is what Wittgenstein had succumbed to, the addictive quality of guilt.

Malloy swallowed. "How did you cause her death?"

Evan was glad for the question. He needed to focus. "We argued, like you said, on the Ledges, and she fell." He imagined the scene—the girl clawing at him, then punching him with her small fists—her father had said she was a fighter.

Now for the reason they had fought. "She wanted to be seen with me—in public, I mean, as if we were a couple, not just teacher-student, and I told her that couldn't happen. She became enraged and scratched me with her long red fingernails on my neck and arms. Luckily I was able to cover the marks with my shirt, that's why you didn't see them. She punched me, too—pretty hard, actually." Evan liked this little added description. He even punched the air a few times, like the twins did.

"Punched you," the detective repeated.

"Yes."

"And did she hurt you?"

Could a teenage girl hurt a grown man in a fight? Certainly one odd punch could have caught his nose or stomach, perhaps even knocked the breath from him for a moment.

"A little, yes, she wouldn't stop. I tried to grab her hands, but I couldn't. That's when I shoved her away, and she slipped." Evan pictured Joyce tumbling backward, her arms windmilling to try to keep her balance, then the ground giving out under her feet. *Facilis descensus . . .* but surely not into hell for this young girl. *Facilis ascensus caelo*—was that the way to say it? Heaven would be her fate, he was sure.

"Well, Professor, you've given me what I asked."

Evan smiled. "You were right about confessing. I do feel better."

"That's why it's so popular at church."

"Not my church. I don't think I've ever confessed before in my life."

Malloy checked his watch. "Well, I'll be going now."

Evan was surprised. "Going? I thought you'd want to know how we came to meet, how many times we saw each other, that kind of thing." His mind was racing with the possibilities—the notes passed back and forth on matchbox covers, the rendezvous at the hotel and the park, the embraces, the groping, the sheer illicitness of it.

"That won't be necessary. I'm sure now you had nothing to do with Joyce Bonner's disappearance."

Evan replayed the sentence in his head to confirm the negative . . . "I'm sure you had *nothing* to do with Joyce Bonner."

"What do you mean? I just confessed."

"Yes, for my benefit, you confessed. I got you talking about the girl, and it seems that you know very little about her. She had the habit of biting her nails since kindergarten, so it's not likely she scratched you. And she broke her right wrist cheerleading a couple of weeks before she disappeared. Her arm was in a sling. So obviously she couldn't have hit you with both hands, like you said."

Evan felt his mind processing the information more slowly than usual . . . biting her fingernails, arm in a sling, she couldn't have hit you. What it all added up to was that the detective considered him innocent.

He felt a little let down at the news. Gone was the single thing that connected them—suspicion.

Malloy wiped his lips with the back of his hand. "Maybe

she had an infatuation with you, I don't know. But I'm guessing you never realized it and probably never met her, except for those few minutes in your car."

"That *is* what I've been telling you all along."

"I had my doubts. It's the nature of the job. I look for the truth, and often it comes out in strange ways."

Again, the truth. Evan couldn't think of any other time in his life when the truth had appeared so often. "What if Mr. Bonner had mentioned the sling to me at the park and I'd incorporated that into my story? You wouldn't have cleared me just because she bit her fingernails?"

"I might have. It only takes one detail that doesn't fit to overthrow a theory. You probably know that from philosophy."

Evan did not know this at all. Philosophy was much more art than science, so it could allow for a few errant details in the interest of preserving the larger truth. It impressed him that police work would hold so dearly to the small facts of life.

"So that's what it takes to prove one's innocence in a case like this, an accidental mention of a girl scratching?"

"It wasn't so accidental. I prodded you into talking about her. It's often revealing what people say once they get going. Truth is in the details."

It was a convenient adage, but Evan didn't believe that truth was always in the details. More often than not, the details obscured truth.

"It's curious," he said. "I told you the truth before, and you didn't believe me. I tell you lies today, and you do believe me. I don't quite know how to explain that. I'm not sure even Wittgenstein could explain it."

"There's no need to trouble him about this, Professor. Explain what you can and leave the rest alone. That's the way to get along in this world."

CHAPTER 30

A s Evan came into the house from the garage, he threw off his jacket and let it fall wherever it wanted. He liked thinking that his jacket might have some intent, perhaps a latent desire to float free for a moment before falling to the floor. He threw his keys into the air, too, and they clanked into the tile.

After his initial, curious disappointment at being called innocent, he now felt enormously relieved. The possibility of a trial no longer hung over him. His reputation was cleared. He wondered if the *Banner* and the *Eastfield News* and Channel 4 would run headline stories about his innocence as quickly as they had the suspicion of his guilt. He assumed not.

"Ellen?"

She didn't answer, but he heard her footsteps coming down the stairs and he hurried into the hallway to meet her. She appeared with the mobile phone pressed to her ear. She stuck a finger in the air to say that she would be a minute. He followed her back into the kitchen.

"No, I never had this problem with the boys," she said, "but I read about it, and you could try a rice sock. Just fill a cotton sock with rice, I don't think it makes a difference, white or brown. It'll hold heat or cold and mold to your chest."

Ellen listened for a moment. Evan sliced his hand across his neck to tell her to cut the call short.

"Or cabbage leaves. Everybody says they work, but nobody can explain it. Just make sure to bruise the leaves before putting them on you. Okay, I better go, Carole. Evan's in desperate need of my attention."

Ellen hung up and then sat on a stool. "What's going on?"

"I've been officially declared innocent."

He saw a vague confusion in her face, not the expression he was expecting. "What do you mean?"

"Detective Malloy came by again today and after we talked for a while, he said that he's dropping the investigation. He's convinced I'm innocent."

"How does he know you're innocent?"

"It was an absurd conversation, actually. I'm not sure I can explain it. He got me talking about Joyce Bonner as if I really had done something to her in the park, and I guess I described a lot of things wrong. I said—"

"Wait a second. You described doing something to her?"

"I know it sounds strange. It was like a what-if scenario he wanted me to try. I guess he does this with a lot of suspects. And I said that Joyce scratched me when actually she had a habit of biting her nails down to the skin. She couldn't have scratched me."

"That's why he decided you're innocent?"

"Not just that, no. I said she hit me, too. With both hands." Evan rapped his fists in the air in demonstration, just as he had done with Malloy. "It seems Joyce had her right arm in a sling from a fall cheerleading, probably one of those pyramid things they do. She couldn't have thrown punches like that."

"She wasn't wearing a sling in the paper."

"That was a picture from earlier this year."

Ellen glanced at her pocketbook sitting on the counter.

"What?" Evan said.

"Nothing."

"You don't seem too thrilled about this."

"It's just a sudden turn of events. That detective has been after you for weeks."

"Well, he's after me no more."

Evan picked up an apple from the fruit bowl and took a bite. He didn't even wash it first. He wondered why he ever bothered to worry about such a small risk.

"Maybe he's just saying he's dropping the investigation so you'll let your guard down. That's possible, isn't it?"

"I never had my guard up, Ellen. It's not like I had anything to hide." He took another bite of the apple and set it on the table.

She went to her pocketbook and took out a white envelope. She held it up for him to see, and he understood by how close she kept it to her body that he wasn't supposed to take it, just like the matchbook weeks ago. Across the front, in red ink, was his name—Professor Birch, Pearce College. In the return address space there were just initials—JB. "I found this in your jacket last week," she said.

"My green jacket again?"

"No, your tan one."

"What did you do, go through my whole closet?"

"Yes."

The answer startled him. He would have expected some story about the understandable circumstances that led her to go through his clothes, perhaps in search of where a button she had found on the floor might need to be sewn. "What about my drawers and desk, did you go through them, too?"

"Your desk, yes."

"You went through my papers, my letters, my grade book, everything?"

"Yes."

"This is unbelievable. You ransacked my personal things looking for clues." He looked at his hands—they were fists—and he lifted them both and pounded them on the counter. "It never ends. There's just one suspicion after another thrown at me." He rubbed his hands together, trying to soften the sting. "But you know what I find more offensive?"

He waited for her to ask what. He thought he deserved that much from her. But she just stared at him.

"It's that you don't have the decency to lie about what you did."

"What *I* did?"

"Searching through my clothes. You . . . did . . . that."

"You want me to lie about it?"

"Yes, then I could hold onto the illusion that you think I'm a decent human being."

"I can't lie."

She said it as if her honesty were an unquestioned attribute of herself, and something undeniably admirable as well. He had never held honesty in such unquestioned esteem. In fact, he found her pride in her honesty distinctly annoying.

"Why can't you lie?" he said.

"I can't, that's all, and I don't want to."

"We act like we're immortal—that's a lie. We act like we're unselfish—that's a lie. We act like we trust people—that's obviously a big lie. We all lie every day in our words, our thoughts, our acts."

"Well, I'm not lying about this. I went through your closet because I wasn't satisfied with your answers."

"Do you realize what you're saying? You think you might be married to an adulterer, a pedophile, a kidnapper, not to mention quite possibly a murderer."

She shook her head, but not as vehemently as Evan might have wished. "I'm just not sure you weren't involved with that girl somehow, and then something happened. I don't know what."

"Somehow, somewhere, at some time you think something might have happened—that's not a very specific charge against me."

"I'm not making charges, Evan. I'm trying to make sense of things. This isn't easy for me, you know."

"Easy for you? You're second in line of suffering here. I'm the one suspected of being a terrible human being. I'm the accused." He picked up the apple and took another bite. The tartness of the taste surprised him, and he dropped the remaining part back in the bowl. "So what does this letter say—how much she's in love with me and I'm madly in love with her or some other wild fantasy?"

Ellen shrugged. "I don't know what it says. I didn't open it."

Her restraint amazed him. "You've been carrying around an unopened letter to me, possibly sent by Joyce Bonner?"

Ellen nodded.

"What were you waiting for?"

"I don't know. I was just waiting."

"So you thought this was the perfect time to bring it out? I came home excited that Malloy won't be nipping at my heels anymore, and you decide to toss another suspicion at me."

She lifted the remains of the apple from the fruit bowl and tossed it in the trash.

Evan felt like taking a bite out of another apple and another and another and dropping them all in the fruit bowl. He couldn't believe how petty his thoughts were. "What do you want me to do, Ellen, explain how this letter got into my pocket and how it's not what it seems? Would that make it easy for you? Or would you file my explanation away as another one of my stories that seems just a little too pat?"

Ellen bit on her lip, which Evan took to mean she was considering his question. He thought of what his explanation might be. He routinely left his jackets hanging unattended in his office, particularly in warm weather, as it had been lately. Carla took several breaks each day, which would have given Joyce Bonner the opportunity to sneak the note into his inside pocket, assuming he would find it when he put on his jacket to go home. It was the kind of thing a teenage girl might do to her secret lover. It would be thrilling for her, and romantic. She wouldn't know that he rarely checked these pockets, since he never put anything in there.

He thought this story highly believable, especially since it wouldn't make any sense that he would have purposely left a sealed letter from Joyce in his jacket. He was about to offer this account when Ellen started picking at some small spot on her pantleg, and he changed his mind.

"You know," he said, and when he heard himself say these

words he promised himself not to be so hard on the boys when they started sentences this way, "no matter how good my reason is, I don't think it would be enough. So I'm not going to make this easier for you. I've convinced Malloy, I've convinced Carla, I've convinced Zed—I shouldn't have to convince you. As a matter of fact, I'm done offering explanations. You decide on your own whether you have faith in me or not."

"Faith is irrational, look at the facts. Don't you teach your students that about God?"

"I don't try to undercut their religion, if that's what you're implying. I just make them think about the nature of their faith in anything that can't be based on facts. But with faith in me you have nineteen years of facts to rely on."

Not all the facts during that time would argue in his favor, he knew. There was his behavior with Carol Sparks to consider, and the flirtatious former neighbor who liked to drop over when he was in and Ellen was out. She hadn't mentioned that yet, but Evan was certain she hadn't forgotten. Still, he felt sure that the vast evidence of his married life demonstrated that he was a trustworthy person, that his word should be believed.

Ellen turned the letter around in her hands.

"You could open it," he said. "Maybe it's from someone in the college with the initials J.B. . . . a Jack somebody."

"It's not from a man," she said. "Look at the handwriting."

His name was swirled on the envelope in red ink. The tail of the final "h" in Birch was looped back over his last name. Ellen was right—no man would write this way.

"So maybe it is from Joyce Bonner and she's asking for her lipstick back. There are plenty of innocent possibilities."

"And one suspicious possibility."

"Yes, in a sea of innocence, there's one suspicion bob-bing about."

Ellen saw Evan's keys on the floor, looked perplexed for a moment, and then picked them up. "Despite what you think, I really want to believe you."

"That's a start. All belief starts with wanting to believe. But even if you believe me, what will you do with the letter?"

"I don't know."

Evan nodded at her pocketbook, and it surprised him that this was the same one that had been flattened by the truck. Didn't she have any others to replace it? "You sure you weren't carrying around the letter to take it to Detective Mal-loy, turn me in?"

"Don't say that."

"That's what we're talking about, isn't it? You can't decide whether you should hand over potentially incriminating evi-dence to the police."

Ellen shook the keys in her hand, then did something that puzzled him—reached out and dropped the keys back on the floor, just where they had been. He didn't know what to make of it.

"You said you can't lie," he said, "but you're withholding the truth, aren't you?"

"I don't know what the truth is."

"What's in that letter might give a glimpse of the truth, and you fear that it might send me to prison for the rest of my life. That's what's holding you back. But if I caused a girl's death, I *should* go to prison, even if I am your husband. That's your dilemma—choosing what's right for justice could be terrible for me, you, and the boys."

"Spoken like a true philosophy professor, just the facts, no emotion allowed."

"I *am* a philosophy professor—at least for the moment. Dean Santos doesn't seem thrilled to have an accused person on his faculty."

Ellen kicked at the keys and sent them sliding across the tile. "Just stop all of this, Evan, and tell me what to do. I'm asking you."

He shook his head. "Like Socrates, I think it would be unseemly for me to beg for my life. Open the letter if you think you should. I'm not worried about the consequences."

"Just tell me there can't possibly be anything in here that hurts you."

"I can't promise that, Ellen. Lies can hurt me. The truth shouldn't be able to—that much I know."

He had no idea how this scene would end. Would she open the letter or not? And which outcome did he want? Would opening it show her faith in his innocence or her belief that he should suffer the consequences of his actions, whatever they might be? If she chose not to open the letter, would she be demonstrating her fear of his guilt or faith in his innocence?

Ellen held the letter in her two hands. She turned it over once and looked at the address again. She shrugged. Then she ripped.

Evan felt relieved. Apparently that was what he had been wanting her to do. "I wonder what Paul Curry would say about this—destroying possible evidence."

"I imagine he wouldn't advise it. Of course, Paul's been married three times." She tore the two pieces into four and the four into eight and the eight into sixteen. Then she held the bits of paper out to him. He opened his hand and she dropped them in. "Burn them," she said, "don't leave a trace."

He nodded. "So that's it, it's over, no lingering doubts that will come back to haunt us in ten years?"

"Promise again you'll always tell me the truth, then I won't have any doubts."

He smiled a little. "I'll always tell you the truth, as far as I know it. That's the best I can do."

She came close to him, her chest to his, and slipped her hands in his jacket pocket, as she often did. "Let's forget this whole thing then, never mention it again."

"That's fine with me. But other people might not give up their suspicions so easily. Malloy could go on TV to explain how he knows I'm innocent and some people would still say, 'I bet there was *something* going on.'"

"Let's not worry about some people right now, Evan." She pulled her right hand from his pocket, and with it a cigarette lighter. "You sure you haven't started smoking?"

He took the lighter from her a little more quickly than he intended. "A colleague left this in my office. I keep forgetting to give it back." It surprised him how naturally the lie flowed from his brain to his tongue so soon after he had vowed to tell her the truth. But the lie was justifiable—there was no need to test her in the first minute of her newly professed faith in him.

"I was only kidding," she said. "You could never hide smoking from me."

"I wouldn't even try," he said.

They walked out of the kitchen into the living room holding hands, which they had not done in a long time. Her hand felt as big as his, which he had never noticed before.

On the top of the bookshelf, the beatific smile of the Dalai Lama stared up as they passed by. Good karma was flowing through the house again.

CHAPTER 31

That night, in his study, an hour after Ellen had gone up to bed, Evan laid out the pieces of the letter on his desk. He could make out fragments of a few sentences . . . "when I saw," "if I can't," "waiting is like . . ." He wished to know how that phrase ended. He wouldn't expect anything profound in a metaphor from a sixteen-year-old. But perhaps love or infatuation or whatever state she had aroused in herself had led her to some novel form of expression.

He liked the idea of her wanting him. It flattered him. But was that a sick thought? The girl *was* dead. Her passion was dead. Her wanting was dead. To take any pleasure, even flattery, from her now, was perverse. He should stop thinking of her.

He picked up the word "live" and tried it at the beginning and end of the dozens of fragments. Perhaps Joyce had been thinking of throwing herself off the ledge. "If I can't *live*"—the torn piece didn't fit there, either. The word didn't fit anywhere.

He wondered if he should burn the letter, as Ellen had said, or file it away in his cabinet. He might want to see it again as a reminder of the dangers of getting too close to a student.

But there were risks keeping the letter, if not now then later. He imagined decades after he died, someone sorting through his papers. The letter would be a hint of a scandal, something any biographer would love to chance upon. Of course, no one would write his biography. He was an obscure philosophy teacher with one major credit to his name, a book called *Disturbing Minds*. He wasn't famous.

Still, if someone did, he might conclude that Evan was disturbed himself, like Wittgenstein and so many other philosophers. The records would show that the Jetta had been impounded. The headlines would announce that he was suspected. The letter from Joyce Bonner would confirm some sort of love affair, even if one-sided. The biographer would hunt through original sources and might overlook, even purposely, the final determination of Evan's innocence. Looking back from fifty years, one could assume that the charges against him merely couldn't be proven.

"Dad?"

One of the twins stood in the doorway wearing an oversized black T-shirt that fell almost to his knees. The front listed Aristotle's categories—Quantity, Quality, Relation, Position, Place, State, Action, Affection, and Time.

"Isn't that my shirt?"

The boy shook his head. "You gave it to me, remember?"

"No, I don't. What are you doing up, anyway?"

"I couldn't sleep. My evil twin keeps talking."

"Your what?"

"I decided I got an evil twin for a brother. He talks in his sleep now."

"I see. Maybe it's time we moved one of you to the spare room."

"No, it's okay. I kind of like hearing him." The boy walked around the desk and leaned against Evan. "What's this?"

"It's just a letter that happened to get torn. I was putting it back together."

"Want me to do it? You know I'm great at puzzles."

"That's okay. I've seen all I need to. I'm putting it away now, and you have to get to sleep."

The boy squeezed between the chair and the desk and sat on his father's leg. He put his arm around his father's shoulder. Evan remembered the years when both boys would climb onto his lap and curl up there like large cats. He turned a little and smelled his son's neck—Dial soap.

"It would have been cool if you had an evil twin, too, Dad. I was hoping you did."

"An evil twin does evil—that's not something to wish for."

"I know." The boy pointed at the word in the middle of the letter—"Love." He leaned forward and pointed at other places—"love," "love," "love."

"Somebody love you, Dad?"

"I hope a few people love me. You do, don't you, Zed?"

The boy sat back and hugged his father hard. "Adam," he whispered in Evan's ear, "I'm Adam."